LUCHA OF THE NIGHT FOREST

ALSO BY TEHLOR KAY MEJIA

We Set the Dark on Fire
We Unleash the Merciless Storm
Miss Meteor

LUCHA
OF THE
NIGHT
FOREST

Tehlor Kay Mejia

MAKE ME A WORLD
NEW YORK

MAKE ME A WORLD is an imprint dedicated to exploring the vast possibilities of contemporary childhood. We strive to imagine a universe in which no young person is invisible, in which no kid's story is erased, in which no glass ceiling presses down on the dreams of a child. Then we publish books for that world, where kids ask hard questions and we struggle with them together, where dreams stretch from eons ago into the future and we do our best to provide road maps to where these young folks want to be. We make books where the children of today can see themselves and each other. When presented with fences, with borders, with limits, with all the kinds of chains that hobble imaginations and hearts, we proudly say—no.

All rights reserved. Published in the United States by Make Me a World, an imprint of Random House Children's Books, a division of Penguin Random House LLC, New York.

Make Me a World and the colophon are registered trademarks of Penguin Random House LLC.

Visit us on the Web! GetUnderlined.com

Educators and librarians, for a variety of teaching tools, visit us at RHTeachersLibrarians.com

Library of Congress Cataloging-in-Publication Data is available upon request.
ISBN 978-0-593-37836-6 (trade) — ISBN 978-0-593-37837-3 (lib. bdg.) — ISBN 978-0-593-37838-0 (ebook)

The text of this book is set in 12-point Adobe Jenson Pro.
Interior design by Jen Valero

Printed in the United States of America
10 9 8 7 6 5 4 3 2 1
First Edition

For the forests that raised me,
in the hopes that we might still save them

LUCHA OF THE NIGHT FOREST

1

Robado was a night place, and tonight Lucha Moya was glad of it. In night places, no one looked twice at a girl like her. Even one with a long knife strapped to her belt.

In the south ward, at the very tip of the city, the streets were already filling with workers ready to celebrate the end of a grueling day.

Revelry wasn't Lucha's purpose tonight, but the crowd served her needs nonetheless. She slipped in among the bodies, moving north, trusting that her expression would deter conversation if her knife didn't. She had no friends to worry about offending. None in the south ward, and none in this entire cursed city.

But no one came to the Scar—named for its utterly barren land—to make friends. In fact, no one *came* here at all. You were born here, you died here, and you lamented your rotten luck every day in between.

Lucha lamented her own as she fought her way out of the neighborhood she called home. The long, windowless manufacturing buildings with dilapidated worker housing crowded

1

in alongside them. The narrow tail of land pushing right up to the bank of the blighted salt river.

Too many bodies, Lucha thought. *Not enough space to breathe.* But that was how it had always been. If you wanted air, you had to pay for it. And the price was too high for most.

She stayed to the center of the road despite the crush, avoiding the river. She'd always been repelled by its expanse of murky nothingness. The salt that leached into the soil and killed everything living for a mile in any direction. The tang of it tainted the air, too. It warped the pressed wood-pulp walls of every structure, making gaps for the dark humors of the forest to steal in . . .

Enough, Lucha chastised herself. *Plenty of monsters you can see in this world, no sense worrying about the ones you have to imagine.*

Lucha knew the monsters of Robado as well as anyone— she'd lived here as far back as her memory stretched. In a larger unit with windows until she was nine. That hadn't been quite as bad. But then her father had died, and everything had changed: their household income cut by half, her mother growing less and less reliable in her grief. They climbed down the housing ladder one rung at a time. Ever closer to the river. Beginning again, and again, and again . . .

But none of the units or sectors of the south ward Lucha had lived in had been remarkable. There was only one remarkable thing about Robado, and it came into view as Lucha turned onto the stone-paved road heading north.

The Bosque de la Noche was nothing but a massive, dark shape on any map she'd ever seen. The southern border was always defined by the curve of the river penning it in. But the forest itself extended to the northern edge of the page, staining it with solid ink, giving the impression the mapmaker's brush had simply gone on until it could go no farther.

No one knew what was on the other side—or if there even was one.

Lucha's steps slowed without her permission, her eyes drawn as always to the trees. Everyone else in this place seemed to avoid looking at the forest. Its seemingly sentient presence. But Lucha had never grown out of her childhood fixation with the wall of greenery that was their constant companion.

The forest was said to be uninhabitable. The governors of the Elegidan continent—skittish as squirrels and twice as greedy—refused to recognize any territory north of the river. They took their shares of Robado's ill-gotten profits readily enough, but they claimed no authority in the city. Or any of the responsibility that would go with it.

The mapmakers, for their part, blotted the wood into their landscapes without sparing a stroke for this wound of a place clinging to its edge.

Like we don't even exist, Lucha thought, still loitering in the middle of the road.

"Watch it!" snarled a man heading south. Lucha staggered backward, reminded of the dangers of standing idle. The little cart the man pulled turned sharply and splattered her shoes with mud.

She was about to shout something rude when she saw the cart's tiny passenger. A girl of no more than four. She dangled her bare feet over the edge as her father rolled her along.

Lucha smiled, remembering her younger sister, Lis, at that age. Her huge brown eyes and shining curls . . .

"Better watch out!" the girl called in her lisping baby voice. "El Sediento will get you if you look too long!" Sticking her fingers into the corners of her mouth, the girl stretched her smile too wide and rolled her eyes back so only the whites showed.

The cart rolled on. From the direction of the night greenhouses drifted a song in a language she did not know. Lucha turned her boots north again. Along with the crowd of greenhouse workers, she moved into the city's center as twilight gathered above the treetops.

It was here that the bodies around her became an impediment. The stream pooled at the Plaza de Centro like the huge marketplace was dammed. Greasy animal-fat lanterns flared to life as Lucha fought against the workers already queueing up to buy. Her pulse picked up speed.

The stall counters were lined with food and drink. Jars of cloudy cider made from a berry that was poisonous until fermented, carved wooden boats filled with chunks of meat in the same oil that made the lamps burn.

Other stalls sold handmade wares to tempt the superstitious. Stone talismans for protection, bundles of herbs for luck or love or money, tiny candles in every color said to ward off this or attract that. At one booth, an old woman sat silent in a black veil. In front of her were tiny painted portraits, their eyes drawing Lucha's gaze.

The pale, angular face of a man, eyes black as the night itself. In his hands, a clay cup of blood. *El Sediento*, Lucha thought with a thrill. They'd all been warned as children not to linger too long in the trees for fear that he'd steal their souls—and even skeptical Lucha, so consumed with the practical details of her family's survival, had seen him in her nightmares more than once.

She averted her gaze out of instinct. It landed on the next portrait instead, a woman this time. A goddess. Her face was round and shining. Her hair streamed all around her. Her eyes were somehow penetrating, even in this diminutive size.

The contrast was clear. Good and evil. Shadow and light.

Lucha turned away from this one, too. The old woman behind the counter was tempting fate even displaying it. Talk of this goddess, or any other, was forbidden in Robado.

The crowd grew livelier as Lucha reentered it, and she more desperate to be free of it. Not a single proprietor named their *true* product. They didn't have to. The legitimate goods were just for show. It was what was under the counters that sold—passed from closed fist to shaking fingers. Paid for with teetering stacks of rusty coins, or else desperate promises that they'd pay tomorrow. *Tomorrow . . .*

Olvida. The forgetting drug.

In the Bosque de la Noche, and nowhere else on the continent, grew a short, scrubby bush, with silvery leaves that seemed to catch even the dimmest light. The Pensa plant. So named by the roaming witches and wise men who had once chewed it, it had been part of religious rituals before Robado had even existed. The leaves produced a mild, sleepy euphoria. They enhanced the voices of the spirits with whom the users communed.

If only people had left well enough alone, Lucha often thought. If only no one had ever discovered that, smashed to a pulp, its potent juice wrung out and heavily processed, the Pensa plant became infinitely more powerful. No longer used to gently open the mind to greater currents of inspiration. Instead, to obliterate it.

And so the greenhouses of Robado had been built to grow a domesticated version of the Pensa plant, and the manufacturing buildings to process it. The purified result was a powdered substance called Olvida—which produced a powerful forgetting effect. For a time, it would steal your cares, your worries, your memories. An effect in high demand in a city like this, where every day was a long, dangerous trudge toward sleep.

Olvida was the lifeblood of Robado—and the rotting death creeping through it.

"Forget for a night?" asked a hooded man at a stall without a line as Lucha passed. "All your worries gone, little sister. Your dreams at your fingertips."

Lucha knew she should keep her eyes forward, but there was something about the way he said it. *Little sister.* It snapped in her like a dry twig begging for a flame. As if Lucha weren't out here tonight because of her own little sister, left hungry by the drug in the man's pockets.

She stepped up to the stall, anger kindling in her chest.

The acid emptiness in her stomach only fed it. "You're lucky I have somewhere to be," she said, pulling her knife before she could think better of it. "If I didn't, I'd slit your throat."

Instead of cowering, the man only smiled. The row of teeth he exposed was rotten. "You'll be back, little sister," he said. "They always come back."

"I won't," Lucha spat. "Not ever."

"She's holding up the line!" said a high, thin voice from behind her. "Out of the way!"

Several more voices joined in, a queue building behind Lucha as she stood with her knife exposed. Her cheeks flushed with a fury that died when she turned to look at them.

Lucha wanted to kill this man. To kill every bastard who sold Olvida in this marketplace. In Robado. In all of Elegido. Instead, she sheathed the knife and pushed through the crowd of faces with their haunted eyes, trying not to look for her mother's.

The north ward was deserted by the time Lucha reached it.

All the rest of Robado was built on the salted ground, safe from the forest's rampant growth. But Los Ricos, the self-appointed rulers of this lawless city, had grown greedy, and thus the north ward had come to be the kings' seat of power. Carved into the center of what had once been an ancient woodland.

As far as anyone in this place knew, there had never been Robado without Los Ricos. They had built it, they controlled it, and Olvida funded it. For most people, that was plenty of knowledge. What did it matter where the city had come from when your whole life was built around surviving another day in it?

Lucha remembered the smell the day the kings burned the clear-cut trees to make room for the metal buildings that formed their compound. Like a snuffed mourning candle. Her family's own mourning candles had still been burning then, her father barely a month in the ground.

Lis had suffered from nightmares as the bonfire raged, Lucha remembered. She'd cried out in her sleep.

The forest hadn't taken the invasion passively, either. The morning after the burning, the former copse had been filled with white mushrooms, each one taller than a man. Silent sentinels. A warning, unheeded.

When they'd tried to cut the mushrooms back, two more had grown in the place of every one. Eventually they'd stopped cutting, and the mushrooms had become a permanent fixture. A graveyard. A place of endless superstition and speculation.

"What's your business here?"

Internally, Lucha swore. She'd been counting on making it to the gate uninterrupted.

"Miss? Your business?"

The soldado seemed sober now, but the haunt of past forgettings hung around his eyes and bracketed his mouth. His expression betrayed his impatience. The taut line leading to his next fix seemed a second from snapping.

Lucha knew this look well enough from home. She would need to tread carefully.

"I have an appointment," she said, betraying none of the fear tunneling into her bones.

The soldado stepped closer. "Girls are supposed to report to the west entrance."

She bristled at the way his voice lingered on the word *girls*, his tone somewhere between shaming and lechery. "I have an appointment with Señor Marquez." Lucha didn't drop her gaze, though the soldado's posture demanded deference. "He's expecting me."

As she'd predicted, the man's eyes dilated slightly, the sour perfume of his fear on the air. She should have known better than to be relieved. Fear was a knife's edge, and there were two sides you could fall on.

"Señor Marquez can pick you up at La Casa del Pecado like he does all his other putas," he said at last, confirming Lucha's worst suspicions with the narrowing of his bloodshot eyes. "This isn't the salt swamp. In the north ward we don't let trash spread its stink unattended."

The soldado grabbed for her before Lucha could come up with a contingency plan. Instinctively, she stepped out of reach. Her heart pounded wildly. La Casa del Pecado was the exclusive club of Los Ricos—kings of the Olvida trade and the closest thing Robado had to a government. Girls disappeared into the west entrance every day.

Lucha had known a good many people who'd gone in— some willingly, some not—but not a single soul who'd come back out again.

The soldado charged at Lucha now, enraged by her escape attempt. He had both her arms in his grip before she could retaliate, dragging her past the mushrooms toward the compound's fence.

"You can't take me there," she said through gritted teeth. "I told you, I have an appointment with Señor Marquez. Take me to him. He'll tell you." Lucha bit her tongue before she could say *please*.

She'd stab him before she begged him. If only she could get a hand free . . .

The north fence stretched across the road from edge to edge. As they passed through the gates, the soldado wrenched Lucha's arms back, forcing her to look up at it. It was all metal. Twelve feet tall and topped with vicious spikes.

The soldados never bothered to wash off the blood. Every desperate olvidado who tried to climb it—tempted by storehouses full of fix—left a piece of themselves as a warning.

In Lucha's chest, fear curled like a leaf at first frost. "Just take me to Señor Marquez," she repeated, thinking of her sister, alone and hungry. Her mother, who had been doing so well . . .

Her captor was indifferent. Even if Lucha screamed, no one would come. She wouldn't be the first or last victim of soldado cruelty in the north ward tonight.

But you're not a victim, said a voice inside her. *Would you really have made it to sixteen in a place like this if you were?*

She didn't think, didn't plan. Just let her body go limp, forcing him to bear the full weight of her. He was too disciplined to let go, but he grunted with the extra effort, loosening his grip on her arms just enough.

This was madness, and Lucha knew it. She'd never make it out alone. A fight with a soldado inside the compound was suicide. But a quick death fighting for her freedom was better than a slow one at the hands of the vicious, greedy men awaiting her.

And if she was very lucky (or very good) she might just avoid both.

She wrenched herself free and drew her knife, sweeping the man's legs with a low kick. She pressed the sharp edge of the bone blade she carried to the thick vein in his neck.

"You'll pay for that, puta." His eyes were murderous, a sheen of sweat on his brow. He lunged before she could act, ignoring the knife, his hand grasping her throat.

Lucha gasped; the knife clattered uselessly to the ground. The soldado's grip was iron, and his pitiless eyes told her that Pecado would have been a mercy. That she'd be cocooned by the worm-white roots of the forest before the sun rose.

Beneath her, the roots themselves seemed to agree. The soil swelled, tossing like a wave. Her breath, trapped in her chest, caught fire. Lucha's body, as it scratched and pulled and writhed, felt far away now. No more than a dream. Her gaze, going hazy and strange, sought the tree line like a last glimpse of home.

What she saw was much stranger.

A tall, slim outline of a man, face pale and sharp as her blade. Long dark hair. Too long for a man's in Robado.

Lucha remembered the painting, the little girl on the cart lisping and chanting. Had Lucha looked too long? Was he here to collect her soul?

She would be ashamed to admit it later, but it was the fear of this that made her fight. Push back against the still-swelling ground. Dig her fingernails into the back of her captor's hand until she drew blood.

You won't take me today, she thought. Even as her lungs promised to burst in her chest. Even as her vision went dark, the soil revolting against the soles of her boots.

It was the end, no matter how she fought, or feared.

And then, just as surely, it wasn't.

The hand released her, and Lucha took great gulps of precious air. Her fingers fisted into the soil, which had gone still the moment she drew breath.

She looked up when she was able, squinting through her tears. She searched for the soldado who had let her go. But all she saw was a mushroom.

Tall as a man. Pale, with bleeding red spots.

The warning, Lucha thought, backing away. The same message the forest sent when a tree was felled.

The guard was still standing, but the mushroom's flesh had grown around him—*through* him—until his rage-twisted countenance was all that remained. Set into the stipe of the mushroom like a horrible, twisted clock face.

He was deathly still, and Lucha was alone.

2

In the stories, the forest goddess had once walked the earth alongside humankind.

She'd bestowed the gift of magic on her most devoted—magos or brujas who could wield the forest's power as their own. Even the stories agreed the goddess had abandoned her people—fled back to the celestial plane and left the world to its wickedness.

In whispered stories, the hopeful said that humanity was living through a period of tribulation. That one day the goddess would return them to an age of abundance not seen since she'd last walked here herself. This deliverance, said the whisperers, would come in the form of a savior. The goddess's chosen champion . . .

If that was true, Lucha thought, the savior would probably skip over Robado altogether. Leave them in the murk and the mud while the rest of the world ascended into divine light . . .

Or however the story went.

Before she'd grown so cynical, when she'd still been a child, Lucha had watched the trees, waiting for the leaves to part.

She'd pictured a being of shining divinity, stepping through to return life to the Scar.

She'd never spoken of this hope. Tales of the savior were forbidden, along with talk of the goddess who would send them. Punishable by imprisonment if you were lucky—the unceremonious removal of your tongue if you weren't. The stories were passed in whispers, couched in tales where the players had different names. Perhaps they were all the more powerful for that.

But Los Ricos knew the power of hope. And little by little, Lucha lost hers, just as they intended. She had taken up the knife. She had stopped waiting for the leaves to part.

Now she looked again at the sickening sight of the soldado. She was frozen by it—even though this hadn't been her doing. Lucha was just a girl. A south ward dreg with an olvidado for a mother and a restless, wandering sister. Even if she'd wanted to (and maybe she had), there was no way she could have done this.

But if the kings would take a tongue for a story—what would they do if they believed the evidence pointing right at her? Believed Lucha had somehow stolen a little of the forest's power for her own?

It was time to run, she told herself. Before it was too late.

But she didn't. And then it was.

"You're a long way from the south ward, Lucha Moya."

There was no forgetting, past or present, in Alán Marquez's face. His eyes were too round—pale and fishy above the swell of his cheeks. Lucha waited as he took in the scene.

She knew he wouldn't miss a single detail: The mushrooms. The unfortunate state of the man they had subsumed. Even the marks Lucha's boots had made in the dirt as she fought.

"I suppose you have a good explanation for all this."

"I was hoping you had one," she returned, without missing a beat. "That's what Los Ricos hired you for, isn't it? To uncover the forest's mysteries? I'm sure you'll have it sorted out in no time."

Alán had once been the boy next door, but that didn't mean she could tell him the truth.

That the mushroom had come into being when *she'd* been on the verge of death. Hallucinating a fairy-tale monster . . .

Alán's eyes were on her, searching for exactly what she wasn't saying. Lucha felt a fearful chill trace her spine. He was as little like the boy she'd known as she was like the girl she'd been—and he had the might of the kings behind him now. Lucha had nothing but her own shadow.

"If I recall, I'm not the only one who once felt the pull of the forest's mythology," he said. His voice was still light—the sharp edges carefully concealed.

"It's been a long time since then," Lucha replied. "Different things pull me now. Speaking of which, do you have a job for me?"

Another long pause, during which Alán seemed to look inward instead of out at the horror before them. Lucha counted every heartbeat as she waited, wishing she had something to pray to.

"My purse is always open to you," Alán said at last. Behind

his eyes, something seemed to snap shut. "Good cazadoras are hard to find—even annoyingly irreverent ones."

Lucha winced, but followed as he set off toward his office. She'd never liked to be called *hunter*. It made her sound ruthless. All she'd ever wanted was to survive.

"I'll confess I was surprised to get your note," Alán said as they fell into step. The husk of the soldado was finally behind them. "I seem to remember you telling me rather forcefully that you wouldn't be back."

She remembered too, though she had hoped he wouldn't mention it. The bloody knife between them on the desk. Her mother at home—clear-eyed and sober, full of promises.

Lucha had been a fool, and not for the first time. It didn't change the facts.

"I'm here, aren't I?" she said simply, and left it at that.

A patrolling guard passed them then, heading toward the mess in the road. Lucha's heart began to race, but Alán just waved a lazy hand. "Clean that up," he said, pointing toward the mess. "First thing tomorrow, we're clear-cutting the western tract of forest. It's time to start construction on the new outbuildings. See that the cutters are ready."

"You think that's wise?" Lucha asked, unable to stop herself from seeing him with fungus where his eyes should be.

"If we don't fight back, we'll all have mycelium hearts by summer."

Lucha, the fear of Pecado still pounding alongside her pulse, didn't dare tell him what she really thought: that if they didn't stop cutting back the forest, they'd have something much worse.

Alán's office had metal walls and furnishings—a symbol of his status. Most traders wouldn't cross the cursed river, so anything you couldn't make from the forest itself was rare. Valuable. A symbol of power stolen or bargained for.

Lucha had always found it distasteful. As if power or money had ever made a better man.

Inside, Alán removed his jacket and took his place behind the massive desk. Lucha's eyes wandered. This was the most curious room in the Scar. Perhaps even the world.

Mushrooms under glass, faintly glowing; cuttings of plants foreign to the area; bones—some familiar, some unfathomably strange. There were drawings in frames and laid flat on tables, each showing some grotesque or mysterious thing.

Then there were the books. Ancient, most of them leather-bound. Some in languages Lucha couldn't read. Books that might have been banned or burned if they were discovered in a worker's unit.

But Alán hadn't lived in one of those for years. He alone among Robadans was permitted this fascination with the forest's more occult potential—and only because the kings needed him to exploit it for their own gain.

This was what it meant to own a scrap of power in a place like this: to be used, or to be destroyed.

One of the books drew Lucha's eye now, as Alán removed his rings with his back to her. It lay open on the surface of his usually spotless desk like it had been hastily abandoned. Lucha leaned forward to take a closer look.

The illustrated page showed a dense thicket of trees— a man standing among them. On the opposite page was a human-shaped figure, vines trailing from their fingertips, a look of agony clearly captured even in the rudimentary drawing.

Alán turned, and Lucha pretended she hadn't been looking. He slid the book off the table and out of sight in one fluid motion.

"So, you have a job for me?" she asked. "I'd like to be home before sunrise. You know how it gets over there."

"I do, and you will be," Alán said. "This one's close. Just a mile or so to the west."

The west, Lucha thought. The tract of trees he'd just ordered the guard to clear. He was going to use her to help him destroy it. "You know our deal," she said with forced lightness. "I work out of town. At least four miles, no more than ten."

"Demanding," Alán said. "I like that in a woman."

"Don't," she said, shrugging off the advance. Her skin crawled. He'd never been this way before he moved behind the fence.

Alán raised his hands. A surrender that wouldn't last. "Someday you'll learn to appreciate my charm."

"I appreciated it more before you started saying things like that."

He appraised her again, a different light dancing in his

18

features now. "You amuse me, old friend," he said. "But don't forget your place." He pulled out a wooden box as Lucha swallowed bile, wanting to walk out, knowing she couldn't. Not with her mother gone, and facing a long recovery when she returned. Not with her sister hungry.

"What's the bounty?" she asked at last. She hoped he heard her grind her teeth.

"Fourteen pagos," he said. "Fifteen degrees north, forty east." He tossed her a metal tag with a number engraved on it. Proof of her acceptance. "And, Lucha?"

She stared him down, this stranger.

"Don't turn your back on this one."

"I never show my back to an enemy," she said, and backed out of the room without letting him out of her sight.

It wasn't until she reached the quiet of the road west that Lucha let herself feel the weight of all that had befallen her today.

The empty house. The streak of good days broken; the cycle reset again. How many times had Lucha relaxed? Let the burden of care fall from her shoulders? Thought of the future in a tenuous, hopeful way?

It didn't matter how many times. The result was the same. One night, the end of the workday would arrive, and her mother would not. Lis would grow restless and irritable as the time between meals stretched.

That was when Lucha would take the road north. To earn

the bounty that would keep them fed until their mother returned from the forgetting that had tempted her.

Yet despite the resentment that dogged her steps, Lucha found them taking a comfortable rhythm down the dark path. Out here, it was easy to believe nothing existed beyond the dense, tangled mass of life surrounding her.

Inside the city, the forest's presence felt ominous. But out here, when Lucha was alone, it gentled. Curious, rather than punishing. The leaves glinted, welcoming in the moonlight. The paths opened wide to her steps.

Without evidence of the kings and their edicts around her, it had always been easy to believe there was something more benevolent in these woods than monsters.

A breeze kicked up, whistling in the trees. The dead underbrush whispered; the living vines chattered. There was an energy here Lucha had always been drawn to. Something bigger than her small life and all the fetters that kept it that way.

She checked her bearings once more. Half a mile to the coordinates Alán had given her—from there, it would be up to her to find the nest. Luckily, this wasn't her first hunt.

Lucha examined each tree: the tall álamo temblóns, with slender white trunks and spade-shaped leaves that shook when the wind blew; the massive circumferences of the montezuma, bark folded in on itself again and again. It created secret hollows and lines like an old fortune-teller's face. Then there was the llorón, whose feathered branches hung to the ground. The leaves were black as night. They danced in the slightest breeze.

These were usually the first to show the white.

"Got you," Lucha said, grabbing the offending branch when she spotted it at last. It was thin and supple, and it pulled back against the intrusion. Pale among the richness surrounding it, its leaves were furled and leached of all color.

Lucha followed it until she found another, and another. The dying spread. A tangled web, leading her deeper. It wasn't long before she found another offender—a pale vine hanging from a massive espino. Big as her thumb, it was covered in thorns that would break off in your skin if you weren't careful.

Next was a jacara. Stripes of its deep purple blossoms pale as death in the moonlight. She didn't have to look hard to follow the path now. She left the road. The white was everywhere—the smell of lye and rotting thick in her nose, warning her away . . .

The glade, when she found it, had been devastated. Trees ripped from the ground. Enormous claw marks across the earth. Everything lifeless and pale. On the back of Lucha's neck, her skin prickled. The quarry she'd come seeking was near.

Eyes forward, she told herself. *This is no time to lose your nerve.*

Behind a bone-white stump she crouched, waiting. Moonlight was the only illumination, but with her eyes held wide it was enough. It wasn't conscious, exactly, the way she prepared. More an agreement she came to with the glade. She closed her eyes despite the danger, acknowledging the power here, feeling it acknowledge her. Did this ritual help her stay hidden from the beasts? Her skeptic's mind said no, but one didn't abandon superstition at a time like this.

"Where are you?" she asked the night, settled at last. And the night responded.

The creature entered the glade from behind. Branches fell from their trees; the earth beneath her trembled. Lucha barely whirled around in time. In the stories, they were called sombralados, and to see one was to be marked for death. If that were true, Lucha thought, she'd be dead fifty times over.

It stood at least three times taller than her, its wings unfolding into a massive black banner against the ghostly pale of the grove. A crow, shadows cloaking its bones in place of feathers. Its red eyes burned demonic in its skeletal face.

This close, Lucha could see the dark mist clinging to its bones. It paced the rotten-smelling grove, digging its shining, vicious talons into moss and vines. Earth flew up in clumps behind it.

Enough of your tantrum, she thought. *I want to go home.*

As if it had heard her, the monster pointed its beak to the sky and opened it wide. The shriek it loosed rattled Lucha's teeth in her skull. It was a sound no living creature could make. She found herself clinging to the stump that hid her, clinging to any good memory she could muster.

Root candy, she thought desperately. The feel of the sun on her shoulders. Her sister's smile when it broke through her scowl. Soon, even those comforts were gone. The dissonance took everything but her last desperate thought. *It'll end.* But when it did, it was almost worse. The sonic wave retreating; Lucha, weak-limbed and wobbling. She drew the feeling of the grove around her once more, fastening it like a cloak.

The sombralado paced, restless. Shadows scattered as it moved, then re-formed. It was now or never. Lucha's heart pounded a deafening rhythm in her chest. Determined to be heard in all its glory in case it was silenced forever tonight.

Around them, the trees bucked and reared in the wind. In the center all was still. *The eye of the storm*, Lucha thought, her head clearing. It was what she called the times when her mother had come home prematurely. When the next disappearance loomed too close.

The memory reminded Lucha of her purpose. It melted her fear away. But the bird would not slow—just paced in its restless circles, frustratingly out of reach.

"*I'm right here*," she whispered, tightening her grip on the knife. The monster did not turn.

At the sombralado's feet were the bones of hunted creatures. Lucha couldn't prove any of them were human, but she suspected she wasn't the first cazadora to try her luck with this beast. The rest would have been burly men. They hunted in groups, most often, and split the bounty.

Lucha, by contrast, was slim as a sword in the moonlight. Two braids streamed down her back, her lightly freckled face turned upward. She might as well have been a sapling for all the attention the monsters paid her. Their indifference gave her a deadly advantage.

She remembered when she'd first discovered it. This ability to walk before them without attracting their ire. Lucha had only been thirteen, wandering too deep in the trees. The red eyes had passed over her then, as now, and when the call for cazadoras had gone up she'd tried her luck. Hoping it would hold.

It had. And it had again. Lucha had built a shaky life on this invisibility, but every time it was tested she quaked to her core.

Every muscle in Lucha's body tensed as tonight's sombralado turned. Its gaze tracked the forest around it. Lucha's instincts, as always, screamed at her to hide. She held her ground. The burning red eyes passed the place where she stood.

One heartbeat.

Two.

The eyes didn't find her. Talons continued to ravage the ground.

Frustrated, the sombralado squawked, blowing the leaves back all around it. Lucha had always considered her invisibility a blessing. A way to feed her family. But tonight, she couldn't help comparing the monster's indifference to the blank face her soldado captor had worn as he choked the life from her.

South ward trash, said his voice in her head. *A waste of air.*

"I'm not a waste," Lucha said aloud, as if daring the creature to hear her. To turn. Under her feet, the ground began to tremble.

The sombralado stretched its flightless wings, scanning for the threat it could sense but not see. The trees. The pile of bones. It looked anywhere but at Lucha with her knife, coiled to spring.

There were more ghosts than the soldado crowding into the space between Lucha and this creature now. Alán came next, eyes trailing up and down Lucha's body without permission. He didn't see her, only wanted her for his own gain . . .

"Look at me!" Lucha cried. She forgot Lis, forgot her own empty belly. Forgot the ticking clock and the barren cupboards as the monster—like all the monsters before it—took the face of Lucha's mother, and said she was nothing.

That it would never see her.

Never choose her.

"LOOK AT ME, DAMN YOU!"

In the fracture caused by her hurt Lucha felt the separation of herself from the forest. But she didn't care.

Rejected by the forest. Rejected by the city. By her family. The tears made her half blind, but the bone of the knife knew its kin. Lucha followed it across the quaking ground toward the sombralado just as it turned to face her at last.

It was the shock of locking eyes with the monster that stopped her tears. There was no denying it. Her reckless, terrible pleas had been answered. The ground shook, and the ghosts abandoned her. Her mother, too. All that was left was this horrible bird, who had seen her at last. And Lucha with her knife—weak, and breakable both.

The forest revolted around her, the creature screamed again. The message was clear: She would die here. Die for her recklessness. For her pride.

"Not today," Lucha said. The knife tip would not stay still. It was the only thing between her and her fate, and she lunged with it. With everything she had left.

Strange things happened in the Bosque de la Noche every day, that much was known in all of Elegido. Monsters were born and died without a human ever laying eyes on them. Witches and spirits and (some said) even deities walked in its shadows.

But even those things couldn't explain why vines tangled around the skeletal ankles of the beast as Lucha flew toward it. Why its wings froze in the air, exposing its chest. Why the shadows that cloaked it parted to reveal the place where its heart should have been. Inviting Lucha to end its reign of terror.

All that remained, once this was done, was to strike.

It was over in a single heartbeat. The shadows retreated, skittering off into the darkness of the underbrush around them. The bones, an indifferent host, collapsed.

The glade was deadly still, which was why (Lucha would later tell herself) she saw the man so clearly this time. It was only a moment. A flash, and then he was gone.

A curtain of black hair. Eyes, obsidian coins in a face like a mask. An expression that said he would stalk the places that promised her death until one of them kept its vow.

3

The creature's beak weighed at least ten pounds, but Alán wouldn't pay without confirmation of the kill. Lucha hung the sharp, terrible thing alongside her knife and filled the pouch at her waist with talons to sell or trade.

So burdened, she walked the long road back into town.

Her body, robbed of its adrenaline, was sore in a hundred places. The north ward loomed.

Crossing back into the mushroom grove, Lucha cast one last glance over her shoulder. The wind-tossed branches bade her farewell, casting a web of tangled shadows. Was he still with her? Stalking her steps? Biding his time?

A nursery rhyme sprang to mind, ominous as the night:

El Sediento, the thirsty man calls,
He creeps through the ground, or right through the walls.
If he comes close, look away! Look away!
Elsewise with the light of your soul you shall pay.

Lucha pushed away the rhyme with a shudder. The lights of the north road were just ahead. She would leave this skittish, child's fear in the darkness with him. She would forget his face.

But the back of her neck prickled all the way to the fence.

Lucha reached Alán's office without further delay, easing the metal doors open quietly. She dropped the beak on his desk beside the ticket. "I'm in a hurry."

"Are you all right?" Alán hastily covered an open volume in front of him. The same book from before, Lucha noted. This page showed a glowing sphere deep in the trees, golden against the writhing green.

Lucha lacked the energy to even be curious. "Fine," she said. "My payment, please."

"That looks deep." He reached across the desk like she hadn't spoken. His fingers were short and stubby, bare of their rings.

Lucha slapped his hand away before it could reach her face. "This is the part where you pay me, so we can go our separate ways. At least until I have no choice in the matter."

Eyebrows nearly meeting his hairline, Alán opened the lacquered wooden box at his elbow and counted out fourteen copper coins. He hesitated, then added three more. "The extra are for your charming company."

Lucha took the fourteen, left the other three. "I only want what I've earned."

"From what I've heard, you're more than a little in need of a friend right now," Alán said. He reached for her again, her wrist between his clammy fingers. His thumb stroking her skin. "There's no reason it can't be me. You liked me once, don't you remember?"

There was something slimy in his voice as he said *friend*. Lucha recoiled from that as much as the touch of his hand.

"That was then," she said, unable to conceal her anger. She remembered the monster with his leering eyes. A warning. "Now you're just the man who doles out the bounties. Nothing more." Her head pounded as she turned away. This night had taken more from her than she'd had to give.

"You should be thanking me." His tone oozed condescension until anger flashed. "You're not even worthy of my charity."

Lucha didn't reply. She would mourn the boy she'd known in her own time.

"If you're not going to play nice . . . ," he snarled, as if her silence had further enraged him. "You'd better watch out."

Shaking her head, Lucha eased the door open and left without a word.

The road back to the south ward stretched endlessly. Olvidados clustered in the marketplace, leering. Some called out to her. Lucha ignored them. At this time of night they would be too far gone to give chase.

Every stall was now closed—save for one. The veiled woman with her tiny portraits peered out at Lucha. Her eyes said she'd seen a hundred nights like this one.

"Girl, you've got the stink of the woods on you."

"I'll be sure to bathe," Lucha said without stopping.

"He's looking for you." Her eyes were so dark they seemed to swallow the torchlight. "Best sleep with salt under your bed tonight."

Some impulse led Lucha to pull one of the sombralado's talons from the pouch on her belt. She approached the stall, setting it down before the old woman.

"It's he who will need protection from me."

"Take him," the woman replied after a moment of appraisal. She pushed the tiny portrait of El Sediento toward Lucha. "He belongs to you."

She'd intended to refuse. Instead, Lucha watched her hand—pale in the moonlight, but steady—take the picture and slip it into her pocket.

On the road south she had no company but her thoughts, and they treated this rare moment of peace like a battleground.

The red eyes of the sombralado haunted her. The feeling of being vulnerable. Had she lost her protection against the monsters for good in one rash moment? And if she was truly at risk in the wood, how would she support her family?

Questions ate the tails of answers until Lucha's mind was a pit of writhing snakes. It was only the singing that broke her free. Her feet had led her back by instinct to the place she'd first heard it.

A low, smoky voice painted circles and curves on the night

30

air. Lucha, alone in the street, closed her eyes. The music washed over her. And then, abruptly, it stopped.

"Sing us another one, pretty girl."

"Perhaps a dance. Look at the hips on her."

From relaxed, Lucha was immediately on alert again. She knew these voices, even if she didn't know their owners. Voices of those attracted to even the smallest display of power. They would destroy the singer for daring to create something beautiful here. Lucha should have known better than to enjoy it.

"No, thank you," came a voice in answer. Polite but firm.

"She thinks we're asking," said one, with an unhinged giggle.

"We're not asking." The sound of a knife unsheathing accompanied this.

Lucha knew she should keep walking. Robado was not a city of neighborly concern. To care in a place like this made you a fool, or a mark. Nothing more noble.

"I've got work to do," said the singing girl now. Despite the obvious threat, her voice was steady. "Show's over, I'm afraid. Have a nice night."

"You think you can turn your back on us, puta?" Another weapon. Lucha could hear its metal edge meeting the air. "We'll tell you when the show's over."

The voice in Lucha's head told her more insistently to move on. This girl had known what she was inviting when she dared to sing. Nothing pure in this place ever went unsullied. Getting involved wouldn't change that.

But Lucha drew her knife anyway, following some impulse into the doorway of the greenhouse.

They had the singing girl cornered. Her honey-brown skin glowed in the light of the tiny phosphorescent plants lining the raised beds. She should have been afraid. Instead, the expression on her face held some unfathomable heartbreak. As if each of these repellent men were somehow precious to her and she were being forced to watch them waste away.

Lucha shook herself. Whatever story this girl's face told, these men were strangers to her. And if Lucha didn't step in, they'd kill her or worse.

"Why don't you leave her alone?" she asked.

Both men turned to face her, but the girl remained transfixed. "Oho, two for the price of one," said the man on the left. His hair hung oily into his face. His small eyes narrowed. "Get her over here."

"I wouldn't," Lucha advised the other man. The adrenaline returning to her veins felt good after the long, lonely walk. When there was danger, there was no time for worry.

"Stupid girl," said the other man thickly. He was taller. Hair thinning and prematurely white. Clothes filthy and fraying. He lunged.

Lucha had fought much worse than him in the past few hours alone. She didn't bother with the knife. A quick jab to the throat with her fist had him doubled up and wheezing. She kicked him over, turning to face the other.

"Get up!" the second man called to his prone comrade. His

feet were too active, dancing from side to side. They did nothing but betray his nervousness. Behind him, his captive stood still, her eyes on Lucha. "Get up, will you?"

Another wheeze, and a groan. The prone man stirred, but did not rise.

"What's it going to be?" Lucha asked, aware of the effect of the streaming moonlight on the pale of her knife's blade. "Retreat? Or die?"

The man's eyes darted between his friend, the singing girl, and Lucha's weapon. He held his own knife too tightly, his knuckles white on the hilt.

"Don't hurt them." The girl's voice held desperation. Genuine concern for these men who would have killed her—or worse. "They're not in their right minds! Please, you can't."

A little of the fury coiled in Lucha's muscles dissipated, but she couldn't show weakness. If she did, they'd be back the next night, and the next.

She stepped forward, knife outstretched. The standing man flinched. Lucha laughed. "Take him and go, before you have more to regret than your cowardice."

"Filthy puta," he said, though he didn't take his eyes off her knife as he roused his friend. "You're not worth the trouble."

"Whatever helps you sleep at night," Lucha said, watching them retreat. In a moment, the greenhouse was silent again. Lucha felt suddenly awkward. The singing girl's eyes were on her now. The desperation in them lingered.

"Thank you," she said. "I didn't expect anyone to come."

"Normally no one would," Lucha said, sheathing her knife. "I'd think twice before drawing attention to yourself at this hour again."

The girl furrowed her brow, and Lucha thought this would be the moment she showed some reasonable emotion. She didn't appear to be armed, and if she had any skill in combat she would have defended herself . . .

But when she spoke it was not to express fear, or relief: "It's them I'm worried about," she said. "It's not safe out there."

"Let me get this straight," Lucha said before she could stop herself. "You're an unarmed girl, alone in the night garden, and you're worried about the *safety* of the two men who just threatened you at knifepoint?"

When the girl met Lucha's gaze, there was something steely in her features. "That's right," she said. "There are plenty of people to worry about me. Who's going to worry about them?"

Shaking her head in disbelief, Lucha prepared a counter-argument. About all the violent acts she'd seen committed by people under the influence of the forgetting drug. About things that could have happened *tonight* to this girl if Lucha hadn't come along.

But before she could utter a word, a sudden spell of dizziness overtook her. The ground lurched beneath her feet, rearing up to meet her knees.

"Are you all right?" The girl was beside her now, face swimming too close.

"I'm fine," Lucha said thickly. "Long night. I'll just . . ." She

34

trailed off, the pounding in her head so loud she couldn't hear her own words.

"This looks deep," the other girl said, almost to herself. As she did, Lucha could feel the sting along her cheekbone for the first time. The place where Alán had attempted to touch her. "I can fix it, if you'll let me."

There was something in the way she said it: *I can fix it.* They were words Lucha had seldom heard. It was the child within her who answered, before reason could take over.

"If you're sure it's not too much trouble."

The girl guided Lucha to a low bench before turning to a watering station against the wall. The pain from the wound had begun to radiate. Infection would be a death sentence, and they didn't have the luxury of first aid at home. She told herself that this—and not the mysterious air about the girl— was the reason she stayed.

As Lucha waited, she took in the details of the night garden she'd missed during the rescue. The air was gently humid, the light low but effusive. In the raised beds grew silvery sage stalks with glowing blue blossoms like clusters of bells. Translucent, barely-there stems held ephemeral blooms like butterfly wings.

Lucha's mother had never been entrusted with work like this. Delicate, and intentional. With her track record, she was shunted to the larger, windowless buildings where the hefty Pensa stalks were stripped of their leaves. It was brutal work. Exhausting and dangerous.

Her mother was out there tonight, too, Lucha thought. Prowling the same streets as those lecherous men.

Who's going to worry about them?

Lucha had spent her life worrying. It had never made anyone any safer—least of all her mother.

The singing girl returned with a bowl of clean water and a small basket. "The cut I can stitch in a few minutes," she said. She settled down beside Lucha on the bench, examining her face again. "Unfortunately, time will have to take care of the withdrawal."

At this, Lucha was suddenly all too aware of how she must look. Walking out of the darkness in the witching hour. Disoriented and weak. A deep cut across her face . . .

Olvida entered the body through an open wound. Tolerance spread in the blood like rot, making each dose less effective than the one before. Olvidados who began with near-invisible wounds progressed quickly to opening long gashes in their skin and packing them with deadly amounts of the powder. Chasing oblivion.

With a cut this size on her face, Lucha knew she must look seasoned. Like someone who had long since moved past the stage of pinpricks.

"It's not what you think," she said quietly.

"I didn't mean to imply—"

"No," Lucha said, aware of the hundred times she'd heard denials like the one she was about to make. Hers just happened to be true. "It was a reasonable assumption. But I *don't* take Olvida."

"It doesn't matter to me either way. I only want to help."

It was there again, that look she'd given the men before. That sadness. The desperation to save someone. But Lucha Moya had never needed saving.

"Really," she pressed. "I'm a cazadora. I've been hunting tonight. Got on the wrong side of a sabuesa and here we are."

Sabuesas were common fodder for cazadoras in the city. Feral, doglike creatures with insatiable appetites and bites that festered.

In other words, a cazadora hunting one successfully on her own wouldn't require an explanation.

Lucha waited, a little shamefully, for the awe or intimidation her profession usually inspired. It didn't come. Instead, the sadness in the girl's expression evaporated in an instant.

"And what was the sabuesa's crime?" she asked coolly.

Lucha bristled. "Violent criminals *and* feral monsters, is there anyone you won't defend?"

"No," said the girl, clearly unmoved by Lucha's criticism. "Is it all right if I touch your cheek?"

Lucha gritted her teeth, aware of the pain again. "Whatever you need to do."

Her head swam as the girl pressed a soaked rag to her face. Next, though, she applied some herbal-smelling salve that left a delightful coolness in its wake. When she touched the wound again, Lucha barely felt the pressure.

The girl stitched with slow, precise movements, inching her fingertips along Lucha's cheekbone. In a moment, Lucha had forgotten the argument. When was the last time someone had touched her face like this? Gently. With the intention of healing, not hurting . . .

"Hold your head still." The music was back in the girl's voice. She moved one hand down to Lucha's jaw and cupped it softly, guiding her gaze to the front again. Lucha's breath caught in her throat, a small hiccup she devoutly hoped the girl hadn't heard.

Intent on her stitching, the girl leaned forward, and from the corner of her eye Lucha saw the neck of her shirt gape. Suddenly, Lucha's throat was dry. This room was too small for inching fingertips and the pounding of her heart.

She promised herself she wouldn't look. She couldn't.

When she did, she wished she'd kept her promise. Instead of an expanse of sepia skin, Lucha saw something that made her jerk backward, the thread pulling tight in her face until it stung.

It was the top of a deep green tattoo, which Lucha knew would extend down past the girl's navel. It wasn't just any tattoo. It was the mark of the forest goddess, and it was forbidden in Robado—along with any mention of her existence.

Everything clicked into place, then, as Lucha sat silently reeling. The savior complex. The empathy even for the lowest of Robado's scum. The reverence for the life of a half-mad dog. This girl didn't have a death wish. She had faith. And in a place like this, that was a hundred times more dangerous.

"I should really get going," Lucha said.

"Not with a half-stitched wound, you shouldn't," the girl replied.

But how could Lucha stay after what she had just seen?

She'd been only ten the one other time she'd seen this mark. She'd had Lis in tow, scanning the faces in the plaza as the light faded. Two soldados had dragged a woman into the crowd before Lucha could find their mother. Everyone had gone silent. But they hadn't looked away as the men tore the woman's shirt open.

The look on the woman's face would be forever burned into Lucha's memory: the fierce pride in her eyes that the men hadn't been able to erase with all the violence at their disposal. They'd shouted to the gathered crowd that the woman was a bruja. In league with the forest's dark spirits: the skeletal birds that terrorized the town. The feral beasts that roamed the streets unchecked.

Even El Sediento himself.

Lucha had gotten the message, loud and clear: Anything from the forest was evil. Dangerous. But most importantly, it put you at odds with Los Ricos. Drew their attention. Which was the last thing you wanted in a place like the Scar.

Beaten and bleeding, the woman had been dragged off to Encadenar—Robado's only prison. Lucha would have bet her entire bounty that the woman was still there.

If she was alive.

And yet, here was this girl, humming as she stitched, wearing that mark as if it weren't a target on her chest.

"There," she said now, tying off the thread and snipping it. "Does it hurt?"

"No," Lucha replied, reaching up to touch it herself. The

neat line of stitches extended along her cheekbone farther than she'd expected. "Thank you for your help." She didn't meet the girl's eyes as she gathered herself, getting to her feet. She needed to get out of here as quickly as possible. Association was as bad as guilt, or worse. She wouldn't accept a life sentence for someone else's zealotry.

"The thread is made of a special root fiber," the girl was saying, oblivious to Lucha's discomfort. "The stitches will dissolve on their own in a week or so. Just keep it clean and it should heal up fine."

"Thank you," Lucha repeated, already heading for the door.

"Wait," the girl said, and Lucha should have kept walking. Right out into the night.

But the memory of that hand gently cupping her cheek made her turn.

"I never got your name," the girl said.

There were stories about the power of names. Too many to count. "Lucha Moya," she said anyway.

"Paz León," said the girl. "Maybe I'll see you again sometime."

The branches of her tattoo were still just barely visible above the neck of her shirt.

"Don't count on it."

4

Lucha told herself she'd forget Paz. She lied.

All the way back to the south ward housing unit, she tried not to think of the monsters the girl had lured with her singing. The tattoo that branded her an enemy of Los Ricos, barely hidden.

What must it be like, Lucha wondered, to believe in something so much that nothing scared you?

Her own hours were plagued by fear. It had haunted her steps all night. The soldado's hands around her neck. The demon-red eyes of the sombralado locking on hers. The pale man who lurked in the darkness, ready to collect something she had never meant to promise. And those were only tonight's horrors . . .

As Lucha drew closer to the housing units, lost in thought, she heard laughter floating out of the gloom. Her wandering thoughts stalled as she puzzled over the sound. Most olvidados were sleeping through the first hours of remembering now. Blissfully ignorant of the hell that was to come.

The source became clear soon enough: a knot of kids no

older than herself, lurking on the path that led to worker housing. A few of them leaned against the maintenance building, passing something between them. Lucha could smell the bitter leaf on the air. Their limbs hung loose and lazy.

She was going to walk past without looking. The casual intimacy among them was more than she could take tonight. A reminder of the road not traveled.

For her, there had always been more important things than friends.

She reached up reflexively to touch the place where Paz had cupped her cheek.

"*Oh no, quick, hide me!*"

This panicky voice would have been easier to ignore were it not so horribly familiar. Lis wore a short skirt and their mother's favorite scarf tied into a top that left her shoulders bare. Her hair was loose, eyes lined with something dark. The older boy beside her looked down with a clumsy young predator's eyes.

"What's wrong with you?" asked another girl, leaning into the boy. Her hair was short, sticking up at all angles.

"That's my sister!" Lis whispered, her voice still carrying easily. "She'll go all self-righteous if she sees me. Damn, damn damn." She held out a hand to the boy now. "Give me another puff before my burial."

It had been stupid, Lucha knew, to believe she had earned some peace after all she'd been through tonight. "I'll take that," she said, holding out her hand for the cigarette as she approached. She was careful to keep her face in shadow. She didn't need any questions about where she'd been. Not from these vermin.

Lis dropped the end of the grubby, smoking thing on the ground rather than hand it over. She rolled her eyes as she stepped on it.

"Let's go," Lucha said.

"You can't make me go anywhere." Lis narrowed her eyes, hitching up the scarf. "You're not my mother."

"You're embarrassing yourself," Lucha said. She stepped on the burning ember again for good measure. The whole Bosque de la Noche could go up in flames and this girl would never notice. "You look like a child playing dress-up."

"Looks pretty good to me," mumbled the older boy under his breath.

Some of the fight still lingering in her, Lucha slapped him across the face. He staggered back, cursing.

"Watch yourself, puta." He spat on the ground at her feet.

Lucha couldn't help it. She laughed out loud. His face was so boyish and round, his fingers pudgy as they massaged his jaw. "On the list of monsters I've faced tonight, you don't even rank," she said. Then, to Lis: "Come on."

"Lucha!" Lis hissed. "I'm with my friends!"

They were near the same height now. It surprised her. But she still grabbed her sister's upper arm hard enough to pinch and dragged her from the scene. "Your *friends* are a bunch of dregs headed for the spikes on the north ward fence." She didn't bother to lower her voice. "Forgive me if I'd rather not visit you there."

"I can't believe you would humiliate me like that!" Lis dropped her aloof act the moment the crowd was out of earshot. "They're probably laughing at me right now! Why can't you just get a life and leave me alone?"

Lucha laughed again as their unit came into view. The sound was hollow, even to her own ears.

The windows were dark, of course; no one was home.

"I'm just trying to be myself." Lis was still ranting. She whined like the child Lucha had never been allowed to be.

The unit doors didn't lock. One more way Los Ricos reminded the workers who was in control. Dwellings were provided to keep the laborers close to their stations—but they didn't belong to the people who lived in them. Nothing did.

Inside, Lucha lit the table lamp and tried to calm down while Lis continued to huff and storm.

Rise above, she told herself.

"Hello?" Lis screeched. "Do you even understand what you just did to me? Do you even care that you're *ruining my life?*"

This, Lucha couldn't ignore. She was no saint, after all. Just a worn-out girl who'd had a very, very long night. "You're unbelievable." The room was dark and musty around them. Something had gone rotten in the sink. When was the last time someone had cleaned in here?

"You just want me to be like you!" Lis stalked over to the tiny dining table, throwing herself into a chair and crossing her arms.

"I want you to be better!" Lucha turned away from the

murky sink water to glare at her sister. "I want you to stop hanging out with dregs who don't care about you. I want you to stop mistaking *that* for a life and get a real one. That way maybe the fact that I can't will actually mean something."

There was an awful pause.

"That's what this is all about, isn't it?" Lis said. "You. It's always about you. You just use me as an excuse not to have your own friends. That way you can keep pretending you're a martyr and not a coward."

Lucha could feel it in the air between them. They were approaching a line that couldn't be uncrossed. She did nothing to stop it. Here would be her excuse at last. To leave the dishes and the empty money pouch and this scowling, ungrateful girl and never come back.

"I didn't ask for your sacrifice," Lis said, getting up. She took a step toward Lucha like she meant to hit her. "I don't want it."

Lucha moved with intention. Precision. Turning to the sink, she reached in and found the slimy thing stopping the drain. It came loose with a sickening sound. The fetid water drained slowly.

"You don't want my sacrifice," she repeated. "Fine." She faced her sister, stepping into the lamp's light, aware of the effect her stitched cheekbone would have.

"What happened to you?" Lis was still angry, but she was wavering. This was the moment. Lucha could cross the room. Embrace her sister. They would apologize, and a shaky cease-fire would carry them to the next fight.

"My face got sliced in half while I was trying to get you

45

these," Lucha said, holding out the fourteen copper coins. She hardened the edges of her words, making weapons of them. If there was to be peace tonight, Lucha would not be the one to broker it. "You're so independent? You don't need me? Here." She threw the precious coins onto the floor. They scattered and rolled in every direction.

Lis watched them with her chin jutting out. Every inch the stubborn child.

"Our mother should be back in three days," Lucha said, the anger taking over her tongue. "Or a month. Or never. I'm going to bed, and I'll be gone before you wake up. Good luck."

"Perfect!" Lis said. "Don't come back!"

Lucha scoffed. "Come back here?" She looked around, taking in the filthy dishes. The empty table. "Why would I do something like that?"

The flimsy pulp door to their mother's bedroom barely made a sound when Lucha slammed it. It was tidy in here. A guest room, at best. Had her mother known this morning that she wasn't coming home? Lucha couldn't help but wonder. Or had it been an impulse decision: an offer by a fellow worker she didn't have the strength to refuse. A siren call from a man in the marketplace . . .

Pulse still racing, Lucha paced the room. An animal in a cage she'd long outgrown. Her argument with her sister played on repeat, drowning out the rest. "*Get a life,*" she said in Lis's high-pitched voice, pretending the words didn't cut deep. *I would have,* she told herself as anger teetered on the edge of despair. *If I'd had any other choice.*

Lucha lay down on her mother's bed. The endless night and all its terrors pulled at her, river mud at the heel of a boot. She would sleep—just for a little while. Then she'd be gone for good.

The sky was the deep blue of pre-morning when Lucha awoke. Her dreams were still close to the surface. Paz, in the center of the plaza, her chest bared to jeering onlookers. El Sediento, across the crowd, his gaze boring into Lucha . . .

At first she thought he had followed her into waking. That the creaking door would reveal him and he'd take her at last. But then she heard sniffling. The bed sank down on one side. The blanket lifted.

"Mama?" Lucha asked, disoriented.

"Don't leave." Lis pressed herself into Lucha's back like a stray cat. "I'm sorry. Please don't leave me alone."

Lucha reached behind her, finding her sister's fingers and squeezing once. Twice. Dawn was still an hour off. Nothing felt real. Her words from earlier, the scattered pagos on the floor. What did any of it mean, really? It would always come back to this.

They were two scared girls, keeping a bed warm for no one.

They were together.

They were alone.

"I'll never leave you," Lucha said. Tears closed her throat. "Never."

Lis sighed. Relief. Lucha could almost picture the skin smoothing between her brows. She was snoring before the sky changed hues again, trading its deep blue for the promise of another morning.

But there would be no more rest. Not when Lucha had just made a vow she wasn't at all sure she could keep.

The knock came sometime later, when Lucha's thoughts had been spiraling too long. She met it bolt upright, her heart speeding up to a gallop. There were no friends to come knocking. No family.

It could only be bad news, then. As if there were any other kind in Robado.

Lucha eased her way out of bed, hoping not to wake her sister. Her mother had been gone for two days. Not her longest absence, but troublesome. Was this it? Lucha wondered. The knock she'd been dreading since childhood? The one that told her she and her sister were orphans?

Maybe they're here for me, she told herself by way of comfort. The soldado with a mushroom for a heart swam to the surface of her memory. The sombralado's demon eyes locking, at last, on hers. The specter of a man, marking her.

Then there were the quiet moments with Paz in the greenhouse—the branches of her tattoo brushing her collarbones in warning.

The knock came again, louder, and this time it woke Lis.

"Come on," Lucha said when her sister's eyes went wide. "Together."

Lucha's hand was steady, opening the door to reveal Alán Marquez.

"What are you doing here?" Lis asked, wedged between Lucha and the door. "I thought you moved to the north ward."

"Good morning, Moyas," Alán said, ignoring Lis. His gaze homed in on Lucha. "You expressed a desire to end our friendship last night. I'm here to honor that."

"What is he talking about?" Lis mumbled. "I thought he was with *them* now."

Lucha shushed her—hand extended, fingers spread. This would be delicate enough without Lis in the crossfire.

"I said what I meant." She kept her tone calm. Light. "I've never been one to claim what I haven't earned. We haven't been friends in a long time, Alán. Why pretend otherwise?"

"Why, indeed?" Alán asked. "Which brings me to the reason for my visit."

"Just tell us what you want," Lis said. "We're busy."

"Fierce as your sister, aren't you?" Alán shifted his attention to Lis. "And, if you'll permit me to say so, even lovelier. You've grown out of that scrawny colt phase nicely."

"As much as we all love compliments," Lucha said, gritting her teeth, "I know you're very busy today, what with your excavating plans. We wouldn't want to keep you."

His smirk disappeared. "I'm going to enjoy this more than you know."

Lucha's fingers found her sister's outstretched hand. They waited together.

"It's about your mother," Alán said. Lucha's heart plummeted.

"She hasn't shown up for work in two days. We need to contact her."

"We haven't seen her since yesterday morning," Lis said. "Sorry, can't help you."

"No idea at all where she might be, then?" Alán asked.

Lis shook her head. Lucha thought of the countless disappearances before this one. The shadowed corners of the marketplace. The filthy house at the river's edge where their mother had stayed for a week once, until Lucha tracked her down.

She banished the images. *Eyes forward.* "We don't know where she is," Lucha said. "As you know, this isn't the first time she's gone missing. Mostly she comes home on her own when she's ready."

Alán's fake pity was worse than his petulant rage. "Unfortunately," he said, voice oozing false sympathy, "the managers of Robado's resources don't have the luxury of waiting. Your mother is on her last warning. One more missed day of work, and her employment with Los Ricos will be terminated." He paused for effect. "Permanently."

Lis squeezed Lucha's hand. She could feel her pulse jumping in her wrist.

"And they sent *you* to deliver the news?" Lucha pointedly ignored the rest. "Seems like a lowly job for the resident occult forest expert."

"Let's just say I took an interest."

Lucha swallowed her revulsion along with the words she

wanted to use. "You'll have to wait until she turns up to tell her, I'm afraid. Sorry we couldn't be more helpful." She started to close the door.

Alán reached out to hold it open. "*I'm* afraid it's not as simple as that. As you know, your family's use of this unit is contingent upon your mother's employment. When she's terminated, the property will need to be vacated. According to the terms of her contract, of course."

Lucha's head spun, worse than it had in the greenhouse. Her world shrank to the feeling of Lis's hand in hers. The warmth and the pressure. "How long will we have?" she asked. "If she doesn't come back. How long until . . ." She couldn't make herself finish the sentence.

"The contract states units must be vacated immediately upon violation of terms. Can't be wasting resources on citizens who don't contribute to the community. I'm sure you can sympathize."

Immediately.

"But . . . we'll be homeless," Lis said. Like he didn't understand perfectly well. "We'll have nowhere to go."

Alán's smile was flat-lipped. It turned Lucha's stomach. He knew exactly how the houseless fared in Robado. Exposed to the olvidados at night? Two young women with nothing? They'd be lucky if they survived their first week.

"How much?" Lucha asked, doing the math quickly. She'd have to take the risk even after last night's developments. She'd do two bounties a day. Lis would be at loose ends, but at least she'd have a roof over her head. "To rent this place. How much?"

"Oh, I'm sorry," Alán said. "The units in this complex are for the use of Los Ricos employees exclusively. No exceptions."

So not even the bounties would save them.

"I'll work for you," Lis said. Her chin was jutting forward like it had during so many childish arguments. "In the greenhouses. I'll start today. Now. Whenever you want."

The shock of this provided a momentary distraction. Lucha sized up her sister. When had Lis ever done anything she hadn't been bribed to do? And here she was, offering herself up for a life of indentured servitude to save them.

But Alán was already shaking his head. "Seventeen is the minimum age for employment with Los Ricos," he said. "We're not in the business of exploiting children, after all."

"You hypocrite," Lucha said. "As if you didn't sell yourself to them long before you came of age."

Alán shrugged. "There are less-official avenues of employment, of course . . ." He eyed them both. His lecherous gaze left a slimy trail on Lucha's skin. "For those with *particular* skill sets."

"*No*," Lucha said, pushing herself in front of Lis. She could almost hear the drums that played at Pecado. Feel the soldado's iron grip as he dragged Lucha toward the west gate. "Never."

Alán spread his hands in front of him. "That leaves you rather short on options, doesn't it? I do hope your mother remembers her duty *very* soon." He glanced up at the sun, now staining the mulched path with late-morning light.

Lucha wouldn't give him the satisfaction of seeing her beg. "I know you did this." Her tone was as level as she could make it. "I hope it was worth it."

"I have a feeling I'll be seeing you tomorrow," he replied. "Some of the boys and I will be supervising the eviction."

One thing was for certain, Lucha thought as she watched him walk away. She didn't plan on giving him that satisfaction either.

5

Lucha and Lis sat together for a long time. The only thing that changed was the light through their single window.

Around midday, Lis retrieved the scattered pagos from the floor. She pocketed two and stacked the other twelve neatly on the sill. When she walked out the door without a word, Lucha didn't stop her—what could she do?

It was her return, less than a quarter of an hour later, that was surprising.

Lis held a little string bag in her hand. She gave Lucha a shadow of a smile before she unpacked it: a cake of soap she used to wash the dishes without complaint. Ground cornmeal to which she added water, cooking on low until it became something resembling porridge.

Lucha joined her at the table when called, and watched Lis scatter deep red jacara berries into each bowl. Sugar wasn't a forest export. It would have been much too expensive. Lis brought down a gnarled cinnamon stick instead, shaving a little into each bowl for flavor.

She finished her meal first, and when Lucha met her eyes they were inexplicably sparkling.

"What?" Lucha asked.

The light behind Lis was red, the sun setting early behind the trees. The greenhouses would let out soon and it would all begin again. "Let's leave," Lis said.

"That seems . . . inevitable," Lucha replied as tactfully as she could.

"No, I mean *leave* leave." Lis scooted closer. "Leave Robado. Cross the river. See what else is out there."

There were a hundred obstacles in their way, Lucha wanted to tell her. They had no money. No family. No support or prospects. As far as Lucha knew, no one ever left the Scar unless it was to go somewhere worse.

But that sparkle was still present in her sister's eyes, and Lucha suddenly understood. Lis was daydreaming. Distracting herself like a child playing pretend.

"What would we do out there?" Lucha scooted closer herself, trying to get lost in the game. To ignore the door that didn't open. The windows going dark.

"We'd have a traveling flower cart." Lis smiled. "We'd go into the forest and hunt for magical flowers that would never wilt. Then we'd walk them into the cities. Sell them to people looking for something beautiful and exotic."

Despite her lack of experience with children's games, Lucha found she could see it so clearly. A little blue-painted cart, overflowing with blossoms. A snow-white burro to pull it.

"We'd start in Puerto de Sal, of course," Lis went on. "It's not far from the crossing. We'll blend in, I bet. We're lighter than most Puertanos, but only because of all these gloomy shadows. I bet we'd brown right up after a few days in the sun."

Lucha laughed at her fair sister, her dark hair and eyes. It was easy to picture her sun-kissed and healthy, too. "But we won't stay?" she asked.

"We'll follow the salt river to the coast, of course."

Lucha was a little awed. When had Lis become such a fanciful storyteller?

"A few days in the Gilded City, walking through the marketplaces. That's when we'll be noticed by one of the queen's handmaidens and invited to the palace."

Lucha had heard of the Gilded king. An old man, skin as rich in color as forest soil. His beautiful queen. "Aren't there princes in the palace, too?" Lucha teased.

Lis nodded. "They're supposed to be the handsomest men in all of Elegido, you know. And none of them are married . . ."

"One of them would ask you for sure." Lucha smiled wistfully. "The youngest one, with the kind eyes." She wasn't sure where this detail had come from, but Lis seemed to like it. She preened at the thought of a prince for a husband.

"An older one for you," Lis said. "One with a serious face and a smile he only shows to you."

Lucha tried to picture this, too. For Lis's sake. But she couldn't. A man was nothing like a flower cart. Furthermore, even the least awful of the ones she'd met hadn't interested her. Not in the way she understood a husband should interest a wife.

"No?" Lis asked, reading her face. "Maybe a princess, then? A studious one who likes to gaze out of high windows and dream..."

Lucha's cheeks flushed. She brought her fingertips to her jaw. "She spends her time in the oratory, making offerings to the goddesses. Or tending to plants, maybe." This time, she knew exactly where the detail had come from. But the princess in her vision kept her high-collared shirt buttoned to the top.

"Very good," Lis said. Then the sparkle in her eyes faded a little. "They say all you can see from the Gilded Palace is golden wheat fields and the aquamarine sea. We'd never have to come back to this mud pit again."

Lucha nodded, but her gaze returned to the window. Twilight gathered in the corners of the south ward. The blue-and-gold fantasy faded away.

"She's not coming back, is she?"

Lis deserved hope, but Lucha couldn't give it to her. Night was falling. Olvida merchants were opening up shop in the market. If their mother wasn't here now, it was already too late.

"Do you want the truth?" Lucha asked at last. "Or a story?"

When Lis looked back, there was nothing childlike in her gaze.

Lucha took a deep breath. "After this long, there are only two places she's likely to be. Encadenar or the Casa del Perdido. Either way, it's not good news."

Lis kept her face impassive, and it broke Lucha's heart. She was barely thirteen. She shouldn't have been so good at burying her fear. "If she were in prison, Alán would have told us."

She wasn't wrong. Lucha just didn't have the heart to confirm it.

"Where will we go?" Lis asked, when minute after silent minute had passed. "What will we do?" Lucha could hear the tears now, held stubbornly in her throat.

"We'll be okay," Lucha said. It meant less than nothing, and they both knew it. "We've come this far, Lis. And we've done it together. As long as we take care of each other . . ."

Lis started to cry then. She'd been a chin-jutting, naysaying troublemaker since the moment she'd been old enough to speak. Her first words had been *no* and *don't*. Lucha had hated her, envied her, and resented her by turns. But she'd never pitied her. There'd been no need. Lis had never seemed broken.

Our mother did this to her, Lucha thought. Everything went deadly still and calm inside her. Lydia Moya had never chosen them, and Lis and Lucha had been forced to grow strong into the emptiness she left. Too strong. Like trees scarred by fire that kept standing but never grew tall.

"I'm going to fix this," Lucha said, deciding as she spoke. "*She's* going to fix this. We're not going anywhere." Her fury burned the fear away as she stood, igniting all the dark places.

Anger burned bright until it burned out, she knew. But tonight, she'd take any fuel she could find.

"What are you going to do?" Lis asked. She joined Lucha on her feet. Her eyes were bloodshot, but the tears had ceased. "Let me go with you. Let me help."

Lucha, in the heart of the flame, barely heard her. "You need to put this chair against the door when I leave. Don't open it for anyone, understand? I'll be back before morning."

"Don't, Lucha, please," Lis said. "We'll survive losing the house, but not each other. You said it yourself, we have to stay together!"

"We will," Lucha said. "As soon as I get back. Just promise me you'll stay inside until I do." Lucha didn't wait for Lis to promise before sliding out into the gathering crowd. She took the road north at a run, not stopping to see if Paz was singing. Not stopping at all. If she didn't let this anger carry her as far as it could, she'd go back.

Crawl into bed with her sister and wait for morning like a scared child.

But Lucha wasn't a child. She'd never gotten the chance to be.

To the west of their ward, there was nothing but treacherous mud.

The salt river was capricious: tumultuous and high one day, waves lapping against the westernmost greenhouses until the workers had to bail the water out with buckets. On nights like tonight it was low and quiet. It waited.

Most Robadans preferred the quiet nights. Lucha knew better. The cursed river never rested—it only bided its time.

She left the packed-dirt road behind, fighting the muck for every step. There was a reason olvidados favored this place. The mud had claimed the bones of enough of them that even the patrols avoided it.

The stories said the gateway of the goddess had once stood here. A monument marking the entrance to her sacred forest. In the dark, Lucha could almost picture it—even though a tree had never stood here in her lifetime. The ancient stone archway guarded by green-robed acolytes. Silvery gold-eyed forest cats at their sides.

A bird called somewhere in the gloom—a shrieking sound that shook Lucha from her fantasy. If the goddess had ever walked these banks, she was long gone. A story. A forbidden one Lucha had only heard passed between women in whispers as they washed their clothes in salt. Lucha recalled Paz and her proud tattoo, in service to Los Ricos like all the rest. What kind of goddess gave up her home and her people to men like the kings?

Some protector, she thought, and the ancient stone edifice she'd constructed in her mind's eye turned to dust. La Casa del Perdido was close. She could feel it.

Lucha had been out to the salt swamp only once before. An eleven-year-old, terrified of the dark—more terrified of her mother's empty bed. She remembered the men passing her on the path. The way they'd leered. There was no one on the road tonight, but the single, guttering torch was still mounted on the front of the dilapidated structure. It made the place look as if it were floating. The only real thing in all this humid, stinking darkness.

A cough sounded from inside. Lucha closed her eyes, steeling herself.

I won't be back, she told herself. *This is the last time.*

And with that promise burning in her chest, she pushed aside the sheet blocking the doorway and stepped inside.

6

The first thing she noticed was the smell. Unwashed bodies. Decay. Something astringent that made her eyes water. Lucha pulled the neck of her shirt over her mouth and nose.

There was no furniture in the large living area—none left whole, anyway—and no light, save a fire someone had lit in an Olvida transport drum. It had burned down to embers, making reddish silhouettes of the bodies huddled around it.

Four, Lucha counted. *Maybe five.* In the corner, one of them moaned. None of them noticed her. Her mother wasn't in this room, but Lucha could feel her presence. Did it ever fade? she wondered. That bright filament that connected mothers and daughters at the heart?

She picked her trembling way through trash, puddles she didn't care to identify, and bodies that shivered or coughed as the only sign they still lived. The narrow hallway was crooked, the floor sloping to the left as Lucha passed a filthy bathroom with no one inside.

In the next room, a man much taller than Lucha's mother lay prone, a hooded figure kneeling over him. Lucha pushed on. A locked door to the left wouldn't budge. When Lucha pressed her ear to the door, all she could hear was a faint humming sound.

Who had something valuable enough to lock up in a place like this? Lucha wondered. She couldn't help but imagine some talisman of the forest goddess. *Don't be childish*, she chastised herself. Hadn't she learned by now?

And besides, there was only one room left.

Lucha stepped inside, the floorboards creaking ominously. The lack of catastrophe thus far had begun to lull her— the feeling that she was the only living person within these walls . . .

The darting of a skeletal arm from beneath a stained sheet cured her quickly of her delusion. It latched onto her ankle before she could step aside. Its grip was surprisingly strong. Lucha stumbled, kicking out as it squeezed tighter, yelping in surprise and pain: "Let go of me!"

"I know you have it." The voice was low. Desperation serrated its edges. Lucha felt the danger like a charge in the air; a warning quickened in her chest. "Give it to me." A man's face emerged from the filthy cocoon, pale as a sombralado's glade and surrounded by matted hair.

"I don't have anything to give you." She wished her voice wouldn't shake. Once again, she pulled away, but the grip held fast. "I'm just looking for someone. I don't have anything . . ."

Lucha had gone looking for her mother countless times. She'd always emerged unscathed back then. But at sixteen, her body leanly muscled from hunting crows and meager meals, she looked like an adult. A threat in the way her childish self hadn't been.

"They said someone was coming with it." The man rose from the filthy floor. The blanket fell. He grabbed her arm before letting go of her ankle. He was at least half a foot taller than her, and his eyes burned in his hollow face. Emaciated from forgetting, his shoulders were still wide, his clawlike hands brutal against her skin.

"You give it to me," he growled. He sounded more animal than human. "If you don't, I'll kill you. I don't care who paid for it. I'll kill them, too."

Lucha's fear took her away from herself as he threatened her. It had often been this way in her younger years. She'd just float away, watching from near the ceiling as her mother raged and stormed . . .

"I have nothing," she heard herself say. Her free hand turned out her pockets. "Nothing."

It was true, after all. She had no mother. No money. Soon she would have no home. It had been a mistake to come here.

Both Luchas—the one in her body, and the one watching from above—could tell that her words meant nothing to this man. He was past understanding. So she would die, she thought, a little clinically. And that would be that.

Perhaps Lis would run. Start that traveling flower cart. Perhaps . . .

"Walk away, hombre."

This new voice was harsh. Ragged from disuse or screaming. Regardless, there was no mistaking it. Unfolding like a skeletal insect from a bedroll Lucha hadn't seen on entering, raven hair tangled to her elbows, Lydia Moya got unsteadily to her feet.

It was enough to bring Lucha down from the ceiling. Enough for a painful, dazzling crash back into her own body. Hope flared too bright. Too hot.

Her mother was here.

Lydia's eyes were filmy and unfocused. Her words too loosely bound to one another. Was there enough of her here to do the saving for once?

If there was, Lucha swore silently, she would take her mother home. Get her better. She would forgive her for everything that had come before. She swore it to the shining gods in their temples across the rivers. To the whispers of the goddess still stirring in the leaves. Even to the dark, pale eyes of the ghostly figure who had stalked her through the wood.

Please, she thought. *Just this once.*

Lydia stepped closer. The man turned to face her. Lucha was unattended then, for a brief second, and she knew she should run. Choose life, and leave this dying place behind. But that bright filament was alive. She stayed.

"I *said* walk away." Lydia stared the man down without a glance to spare for Lucha.

"And if I don't?" the man slurred, lurching toward her mother.

"You don't want to find out."

The man only sneered at her before turning back to Lucha. He was ready to lunge, she could see it in his eyes. He was calling Lydia's bluff. The time to run had long passed. The three of them hung in some horrible balance, the tangled vines of fate weaving and separating between them.

A crunching sound filled the room. The man was face-down at Lucha's feet before she could register what had made it. The chair leg. The man's skull. Lydia, standing over him, still holding the jagged thing high.

Lucha's knees gave way. Her mother had never been more terrifying—eyes half shadowed, the bloody weapon in her fist.

"You saved me," Lucha said, her voice trembling.

Lucha's mother did not reach down to offer her hand. She did not drop the weapon. "Give it to me," she said. "I'm not stupid like him, I know you have it and I need it. I need it, give it to me!"

The pain bloomed like a flower, white-hot petals unfurling in every part of her. Still, Lucha pushed herself to her feet. For Lis. For the tomorrow that wasn't promised. "Mama?" When was the last time she'd called her that? "It's me, Lucha. We have to go home."

Her mother stepped closer. "Sit back down," she said. Her eyes darted from Lucha to the door and back again. "You give it to me." Her feet tangled in the prone man's legs; she nearly fell. "I know you have it."

Lucha took a step forward, praying the forgetting on her mother's face would part like a predawn fog. That she'd remember in time.

Instead, Lydia pressed the splintered, bloodstained weapon to Lucha's neck.

The tears came then. How could they not? One for each

unanswered prayer. "Please, Mama," she said, reaching out a hand. "Please, come home. We're in trouble, Lis and I. We need you. Please."

"Don't you dare move!" The pressure increased. A long splinter broke the skin. Lucha could feel the blood—not much. But enough to trickle into the hollow of her throat.

Her entire world shrank down to the two of them, alone in this terrible place. The feral darting of her mother's eyes. The pain of the jagged wood against her neck. She had spent every moment of her life trying to save this woman—could she fight her now? Abandon her? Die?

She could not choose. The tears continued to course silently down her cheeks.

And then, when it seemed they might stay locked this way forever, Lucha heard footsteps in the hall. "Is everything all right in here? I—"

The shadow of a girl fell across Lucha's feet. She tore her eyes away from her mother's and followed it to the figure standing in the doorway.

"Lucha?"

"Paz?" Lucha's voice was hoarse, tear-filled.

Before she could ask what Paz was doing here, the other girl had turned her gaze to Lucha's mother. It was there again, that harsh sadness in every line. Lucha could barely stand it. "I'm going to need you to set that down."

"She won't give it to me!" Lydia's eyes flickered from Lucha to Paz now, sizing them up.

"If there's something you need, I can help," Paz said,

walking forward with even, measured steps until she was within reach of the chair leg. "No one has to get hurt."

Lucha could see the desperation in her mother—feel it in the way the weapon dug more deeply into her flesh. "Careful," she said. To which one of them? She wasn't sure.

"I'm here to help," Paz said again, the repetition soothing. "Let's just put this down and talk."

It was like magic, Lucha thought, the way her energy transformed the room. Lydia's eyes went from desperate and angry to confused, almost childlike. When Paz reached out for the chair leg, Lydia didn't resist.

"I need it," she said, pitifully. "Please, just tell her to give it to me."

The past few days had been rough on her mother. Lucha could see clearly now that the danger had passed. Lydia was gaunt. Her pretty face wasted. Dark circles ringed her eyes.

"Why don't you lie down here," Paz said, her back to Lucha now. She guided Lydia to the cleanest-looking patch of floor, lifting the filthy blanket without recoiling, turning it, pressing it flat. "Let's see what I have that might help you feel better."

Unnoticed by either of them, Lucha pushed herself to her feet. Her whole body trembled. It felt as though someone were reaching into her heart to pull out something vital. It didn't matter what magic Paz worked here. Her mother wasn't coming home. And even if she did, she'd be in no condition to work tomorrow.

It was over. It was all over.

And there wasn't even enough of her mother here to say goodbye to.

Lydia was lying down now. Paz bent over her, saying soothing things as she pulled tins and bottles out of the pouch at her waist. Lucha backed slowly toward the door, the pain in her chest intensifying. A sob, trapped in the cage of her ribs, would not break free.

But she was in the hallway, her boots pointed toward the exit. She was running. Flying. Through the filth of La Casa del Perdido and out the curtained door. She was gulping down the humid night air by the lungful.

Slumped down just a few yards from the door, Lucha didn't let herself look back at the house. Didn't let herself wonder, or hope. Hope was dead. Lydia had nearly killed her tonight—would have, if a stranger hadn't intervened. It should have been so easy to let her go.

Instead, Lucha found herself rooted to the spot. Unable to walk away from the place where she'd last had a mother. She remembered snatches of early childhood—a whispered story, a soft lullaby. How had it come to this?

So lost in her thoughts, Lucha didn't notice Paz until a sharp sob broke the silence. Paz was just outside the door, her face in her hands, shoulders stooped as if the weight of the world rested on them.

The sight of her made Lucha abruptly furious. How dare she cry? Some missionary, her heart breaking for the hypothetical lost? What did she know about their suffering? "What are you doing here?" she asked sharply.

Paz jumped, uncovering her face. "I thought you were gone."

"What are you *doing* here?" Lucha repeated. She didn't care what it looked like, this time. What her presence here at the edge of the world would mean to the girl now stepping closer in the guttering light.

What did it matter if Paz thought she was an olvidado? What did anything matter now?

"I come to help the olvidados," Paz answered. "I bring them herbs for sleep, for pain. Do what I can to ease their suffering."

"But why?" Lucha pressed. She needed to believe there was nothing here worth saving. How could she ever leave if she didn't? "There's only death and nothingness in there. You have to know you're wasting your time."

"It's *not* a waste of time," Paz said, passion bubbling up through her exhaustion. Tears were still sparkling in her eyes. "People come here because they're lost. Because they have no one. Because this terrible place has convinced them that they're beyond hope. But if I can just help them . . . if I can just save *someone* . . ." She dissolved into sobs again, hiding her face as if her empathy were some affliction she was embarrassed to show.

This wasn't the detached charity of some goddess cult. Lucha had raged helplessly at the trees enough times to know how it looked. The torch burned low on the front of the house. A silent, dying world, and Paz the only other thing living.

"Who couldn't you save?" she asked when the other girl's sobs had become hiccups.

"My uncle," she said after a long moment. "He raised me after my parents died, and . . ." She shrugged, as if to say it was in the past.

"Is he alive?"

Paz shook her head. "We lived in Puerto de Sal. It was an expensive city. He started working for a dealer to make extra money—just pickups and drop-offs on the pier, at first." She took a shuddering breath. "But it escalated from there. He started using at some point—the stress got him, or the temptation . . . who knows? They killed him when his deliveries were light. Just like that. Before he even had a chance to heal."

Lucha nodded, seeing her own mother, racked by grief and burdened by two mouths to feed, reaching for some peace. It was providence that Lydia was alive and Paz's uncle was dead. Nothing more.

For an awful moment, Lucha envied this girl the clean pain of her grief. The wound scarring on her heart instead of tearing open again and again. Paz wouldn't have to walk away. The choice had been made for her.

They sat in silence as the shadows deepened. The darkest part of the night settled in the sludge. Soon it would be time to move on.

"Will she be all right?" Lucha asked now, unable to help herself. "The woman inside."

"I did what I could," Paz said. "The same as I do for all of them. Made her comfortable. Helped her sleep. I know she attacked you, but she's a human being. She deserves the help she needs." The rest was there, unspoken: She had helped

Lucha's mother, but Lydia had been wearing her uncle's face. Just like the men in the night garden. Just like all the rest of the olvidados she'd tried to save.

And perhaps Lucha should have understood this impulse, after everything she'd been through. Only she didn't. She couldn't.

"Nothing's going to bring him back, you know," she said, getting to her feet. "But what you're doing here? Flaunting that tattoo? Pretending this is all selfless charity? It's not really to help us. It's only to make you feel better."

Paz's eyes went wide, like Lucha had slapped her in the face. But Lucha didn't care. She was so angry, so tired of being helpless and alone.

"That woman in there?" she said, gesturing back through the doorway. "She has a family. Most of them do, whether they remember or not. And they don't need someone making their lives in this hellhole so *comfortable* that they never go back to them."

"Lucha, I—"

"No," Lucha said, turning her back. "I don't need your sympathy. None of us do. Why don't you just go home to your goddess and leave us alone."

"What did you just say?" Paz asked, getting to her feet as well. Lucha expected to find anger in her expression, but there was only naked disbelief.

"I said *leave us alone!*" Lucha turned and ran, tears blurring the path, making every step treacherous. Behind her, she could hear Paz calling her name, telling her to wait. But she couldn't go back.

The tallow torch grew smaller in her wake until it was no more than a pinprick. When the bright cord in Lucha's chest finally snapped—she almost convinced herself she didn't feel it.

Lucha ran until her body ached. Until sweat poured down her face. Until she'd lost the road completely. She didn't stop until she saw something more haunting than the memory of her mother: a grove of dead, pale trees reaching out of the sludge like a corpse's bloated fingers.

There, in the palm of this ghostly hand, Lucha let herself feel it. Let herself be racked by the memories and the hole in her chest and the horrors to come until all that was left to do was scream.

So she did. A full-throated, animal thing full of the pain. The longing. The fear. She screamed until she felt empty— but even then, the grief remained. "Where are you now?" she called, voice hoarse and ragged. If ever there was a place for a monster marking your steps, it was here. "You want my soul? Come and fight me for it!"

But the grove did not answer. The man did not come. Lucha was alone.

Before she left, she removed his portrait from her pocket and threw it into the mud.

* * *

Dawn was approaching by the time Robado came into view again. Lucha's throat was raw, but the wound in her chest felt cauterized. She knew what she had to do.

They would be gone, her and Lis, before the clock ran out. Many had died while crossing the salt river—perhaps they would join that number. But Lucha chose instead to imagine a blue-painted flower cart.

With the housing complex ahead, she broke into a jog. Her heart—the pieces of it, at least—light for the first time in longer than she could remember. The rest of their lives were before them. All they had to do was begin.

She pushed hard on the door of their unit, expecting the resistance of the chair she'd told Lis to leave on the other side. Instead, she flew right through. A shrill alarm began to sound in the darkest part of her mind.

"Lis!" she called. "I'm home! You were right. We don't have much time, but I . . ." She trailed off when she walked into the bedroom. Empty. The bed neatly made.

Lucha turned around, half dazed. *She just went to blow off some steam*, she told herself. But the warning bell was louder every second.

The worst blow didn't come until she saw the note sitting on their little table. Lucha's name scrawled across the front. Tears in her eyes, she picked it up. Too afraid to read the words. She focused instead on the beautiful flower her sister had drawn. The kind of magical bloom that might have attracted a queen's handmaiden in the Gilded Marketplace.

The first tear fell beside three words that would not be ignored.

Don't follow me, the note said. *It's my turn.*

7

Lucha made her way to the north ward fence. Her anger filled every space her fear had once inhabited. It would be ruination now. Nothing less.

The road was mostly empty this time of morning. The majority of the workforce was already in the greenhouses and manufacturing buildings for the day. Lucha made it as far as the market in record time, blowing past without a glance to spare for the stalls.

You should have known, she told herself. Alán's slimy gaze traveling over her sister's body. The way Lis had jumped to volunteer for a life in the greenhouses. Lucha had thought she knew her sister better than anyone. But that certainty had fixed Lis in her mind—forever the spoiled, whining, ungrateful girl. If she had allowed her sister to grow, to change, perhaps Lucha would have seen it in time.

She passed through the mushroom grove, drawing her anger close. A second skin. She would need it, she knew, when she reached Pecado. The forest stirred, as if she were an approaching storm and not a girl.

To save her sister, she would have to be a storm and more.

When she pushed her way past the early-morning guard, he made no comment. Lucha didn't have time to wonder why. Perhaps Alán had told him to expect her—perhaps the guard was still too hazy from the night before to care.

It didn't matter which. He hadn't forced her to kill him, that was something. Right now, she felt capable of it. Of worse.

La Casa del Pecado was the northernmost place in the compound. Another large metal structure boasting its power, the expense paid to construct it. However, this one had a special feature that set it apart. A door that opened to a dock on the salt river.

There was no other way to access this dock—from which Los Ricos shipped Olvida to the rest of the continent. It was from here that Lucha meant to escape with Lis.

Two of Los Ricos' private bodyguards stood in front of the doors, armed to the teeth. These men were of different stock than the soldados—who were usually hungover and trading chisme. These men looked ready for war.

"Alán is expecting me," Lucha said. "And if he's not, he should be."

The doors clanged against the metal walls as the men pushed them open. He *had* been expecting her, then. Perhaps he'd even wanted her to come. It meant he underestimated her—her first lucky break in days.

The room was low-ceilinged. Dark, even in the light of

morning. The furniture was cushioned in red—the dye imported, of course. This early, there was no music, and many of last night's revelers were still asleep. Some weren't alone. Some weren't even dressed.

Lucha drew her knife to cool her cheeks, and as she did, she spotted him.

Alán was draped over a red satin armchair, his eyes deceptively slitted. It was an act, Lucha knew. No one stopped her as she made her way toward him, but when she noticed the thin, pale girl tucked under his arm she stumbled.

It was the same outfit Lis had been wearing with the dregs. Only in this room, with her hopeless eyes, it no longer looked like a costume.

"Look who it is, Lis," Alán drawled. "Your big sister. Here to rescue you from evil old me."

Lucha wasn't sure how she crossed the cloyingly perfumed room to stand before them. But she did.

"Get dressed," she said to Lis. She refused to meet Alán's eyes. Hid her hands so he wouldn't see how they shook. "This isn't how it ends, Lis."

If Lucha had expected gratitude, or even compliance, she was disappointed.

"It's not up to you." Lis's eyes were empty. She'd always been good at hiding her fear. "The unit is ours. Mom won't lose her job. I came here so you could have a life, Lucha. Go have it. Leave me be."

"No!" Lucha said, no longer hiding her rage. "No, Lis."

"We own her," Alán cut in. "So your protest, entertaining

78

as it might be, is too little, too late." He stood up, leaving Lis with her folded arms on the chair.

Lucha spat at his feet. "You don't own her. And I won't let you take her from me."

"It's much worse than taking." He glanced dispassionately at the saliva speckling his shoes. "She *offered* herself to me. So unless you'd like to join the party, I suggest you go home. Your sister was kind enough to make sure you have one to return to, after all."

The guards advanced as he finished—a response to some unspoken signal. This was Alán, showcasing his power. Who needed stature or weapons when you could control men with both?

"Don't," Lis said to Alán, getting to her feet. She looked like herself for a moment, before she recoiled from the expression on his face. "I'm sorry. I just mean there's no need. She'll go."

Alán turned without urgency. The guards moved with him. "You're new," he said to Lis. "So I won't kill you for that." He backhanded her across the face without warning. Blood beaded up on her lip. "Don't forget your place again."

Everything stayed very still for a heartbeat, the moment trapped beneath glass. Lucha remembered, like a haunting thread of song, the way Alán had cried when the soldados came to tell him his parents were dead.

She didn't give her body permission to move, but she found herself on him all the same—punching, kicking at every inch of him in reach. Her memories shattered like bottles at her feet.

Lis was screaming, pulling at Lucha. Her sobs were close enough to be heard even over the pounding of blood in Lucha's ears. "He'll kill you! He'll kill us both! Why couldn't you just let me save you?"

Alán had been surprised by Lucha's attack. His guards were still standing down on his orders, but he recovered from the shock too quickly—before Lucha had a chance to turn the knife on him. Grabbing her by both wrists, he headbutted her hard in the nose.

Immediately, Lucha's eyes were streaming, pain radiating from the point of impact. Her nose was broken, at the very least. Blood splattered the floor at her feet and kept coming.

In the chaos, Alán took out a handkerchief and blotted his lip where she'd split it.

He was laughing.

Still struggling through the pain, Lucha crouched in front of Lis. She was more creature than human when she pulled her lips back to show Alán her teeth. *He won't take us alive,* she promised silently.

Lis was crying behind her. Alán stepped forward, towering over them. "You could have left well enough alone," he said. "But that's not your strong suit, is it?"

"She'll never belong to you," Lucha snarled. But her voice wasn't the only one that spoke. There was another, like a harmony in a song, speaking with her. A growling, low timbre that brought rattling bones to mind.

Alán hadn't noticed the change. "This is Robado," he said.

"You've always belonged to us. The only question was when we would take possession."

As Lucha's anger built, the air itself seemed to change. She could suddenly taste every spore and speck of wood dust on the air. Could see them, even, floating like tiny, vicious blades.

In the stories, aid was never given for nothing. There was always a price to pay. *Whatever it is*, she thought to these new apparitions in the air, *I'll pay it. Just save us, please.*

There was no answer.

"Take them," Alán said. Lis cried harder at Lucha's back. "They'll get their manners lessons in Encadenar if they won't learn them here."

The two guards crossed the space in seconds. Lis was shouting for Lucha to run, but there was no running from this.

A tinny, whining sound filled her ears, like she'd stood too close to an explosion.

The blades floating in the air became sharper. Everything else grew dull.

As one of the guards took Lis's arms, the floor began to shake.

Everyone froze. Alán's eyes flew to Lucha, locking intently on her face while the other guard looked uncertainly between them. "What are you waiting for?" Alán asked him. "You have your orders."

"I wouldn't, if I were you." The double layer to Lucha's voice was more pronounced now. The guards' eyes widened. The floor shook harder. Drinking glasses leapt from tables and broke. Around the room, sleeping bodies began to stir.

"I said *take the bitch!*" Alán cried.

The trembling in the room filled Lucha's body as it intensified. It ground at her bones. Twisted in her veins. The pressure built in her head until she thought she would scream, or be sick.

And still the guard didn't move. Alán, furious now, stepped forward and took Lis's arm. Wrenching it until she cried out in pain. He was shouting at her. At the guards.

Lucha couldn't hear him anymore.

All she could hear was the movement in the air around her as every speck of wood dust sharpened. A sound like the river on a flooding day. Of everything coming together in a terrible rush, toward a terrible end.

He appeared at the height of it—when Lucha thought her skull would crack down the middle. A shade of a man. Tall and slender, like a blade. Lucha could no longer pretend she didn't know him by name.

You said no cost was too high, his eyes seemed to say. Inside her chest there was a fluttering like birds' wings. What did it feel like, she wondered, when your soul left you?

It won't matter, as long as Lis is safe.

There was no goddess, Lucha had known that for a long time. No savior. There was only what you were willing to do for the people you loved. Only what you were willing to pay for their freedom.

When *he* opened his mouth to whisper, Lucha's voice spoke with him. It was a tongue she'd never known. A language of rot and decay and the roots that grew within it.

Lucha didn't have time to wonder what was happening to

her. *He* raised his arms to his sides like a twisted scarecrow, and Lucha's stretched with them, wider still.

Where was Lis? Where was Alán? All Lucha could see was him. His voice poured from her mouth like dirt into a grave and then ...

The windows shattered. Someone was screaming. Every wood-dust mote and spore in the air rushed together, and their collision was the tolling of a funeral bell.

Someone was screaming.

Someone was screaming.

The sound was too loud in her head. There were hands taking her face between them. Ragged fingernails dug in, drawing blood from her cheeks that dripped down the man's face in vivid ribbons.

When it stopped, Alán was standing where he'd been a moment ago, an unfathomable look on his face. On the ground, both guards lay slumped, wrapped in white vines. The smell of lye and dying was thick in the air.

All was still.

The man was gone.

Had he used her to do this? Lucha wondered. Or had she used him? And when would the payment be due? Those birds' wings in her chest were still fluttering. How long until they stopped for good?

"You've been holding out on me, Lucha." She had expected fear. The look in Alán's eyes was twice as dangerous as that. A frenzied sort of joy, barely contained. "I always knew you had an aptitude, even back then. The way you found paths no one else could see. The way the leaves seemed to bend to you . . . and of course, your gift with the beasts. But I never knew . . . never could have dreamed . . ."

Lucha let him mutter himself into silence. This stillness, the shock, was what she had bought. Her one chance to get them free.

"Come on, Lis." Lucha could barely feel her body—everything tingled, ephemeral and strange. "We have to go, come on."

Lis was still on the floor. She shook her head wildly, peering up at Lucha—a small animal gazing into the face of a predator. Lucha tried to pull her sister up. To lift her. To get her out by any means. The minutes ticked by.

"Please, don't be afraid," Lucha begged. "I would never hurt you."

Still, Lis's mouth remained open. A silent scream. And their time was up.

The double doors in the back of Pecado—the ones leading to the boat at the center of their escape plan—were obscured as at least twenty armed guards poured into the room.

They ignored the bodies on the floor, looking to Alán for orders. They were not afraid.

"We have to go, Lis," Lucha said. They didn't need a boat. They would make for the forest. Hide. Find another way.

But Lis made no move to join her. Her face was a mask of fear. Unmoving, unseeing.

"Take them," came Alán's voice from behind them. The sound of boots marching across the glossy floor of Pecado drowned out Lucha's next words. The ones that would have convinced her sister.

This time, the floor did not shake. The air did not sharpen. But Lucha knew how to buy them time. She stood fast, stretching her arms out at her sides.

When she was a child, Lucha had hoped for true magic. The savior returned. The Scar, teeming with life. The kind of power that helped things grow. Perhaps such power did exist. Somewhere. But not in Robado. Here, there was only the monstrous. The profane.

Lucha had already reached into the shadows. Who was left to care if she did it again?

The men kept advancing. Lucha felt empty, like a jacara pod with the seeds scooped out.

Where are you?

Lis whimpered behind her.

Alán's insidious grin grew wider.

Lucha closed her eyes, reaching for the motes in the air. The smell of the white vines. The decaying tongue and its strange language, guttural in her throat.

She opened her arms wider still.

Nothing moved. No one came.

"Treat this one gently until I arrive," Alán said. The soldados drew nearer. "I have a grudge to settle with her."

It was very nearly too late, and Lucha had only one line left to cross.

El Sediento, she thought. She let the name she'd feared for a lifetime fill her thoughts, pound alongside her pulse. What use was her soul if she couldn't save her heart? If she lost Lis, she wouldn't need it.

"EL SEDIENTO!" Lucha cried when the air remained still and empty before her. She didn't care who heard, or what conclusions they drew.

The boots reached Lis. A man lifted her like a rag doll, and Lucha forgot the vines. The man. The mushrooms and the stories. She flung herself into the knot of soldados, kicking and tearing and biting at whatever she could reach.

But she was nothing now. The power had deserted her. She was just a girl who'd been up all night. A girl whose knife had skittered across the floor when she'd believed she had better weapons. A girl who had overvalued her own soul.

One girl, against the might of Robado's greed and the men who protected it best.

Of course she fell.

Of course.

8

When she came to, Lucha was alone.

The first thing she did was cry out for Lis. Her throat was rough from screaming. She called until she could feel it tearing. The only answer was her own voice, echoing off the metal walls.

She remembered the scene in Pecado as if she were viewing it through fogged glass. The dust motes, sharpening. The man with the pale face. *El Sediento,* she'd called him. Said no price was too high for Lis's freedom.

The stories all agreed: Trading with monsters was a double-edged blade. Even when you won, you lost. Lucha had been stupid, she knew. But it didn't matter now.

Eventually, sleep came. Fitful and writhing with nightmares. A sombralado, demon-red eyes locked right on Lucha's. She backed away, weak-kneed and stumbling, until the frame of a looking glass came into view. When she screamed, the bird's beak opened. The dark tunnel of its throat went on and on ...

She woke choking back a scream, sure she'd seen *him* in the shroud of dreaming that still lingered. Coming to collect his due. She would kill him, she vowed, before she let him take her. But when her eyes cleared, there was no one there.

Lucha marked time by the gnawing in her belly. There was a slot in the door. Nothing had passed through it. Hunger was a creature on the periphery at first, but it came closer as time passed. A gnawing beast.

After it tore into her belly, the walls of her cell began to swim. The metal swirled and parted like the cursed river's current—reminding Lucha of all she had failed to accomplish.

We should be crossing, she thought. A tiny, stolen boat cutting through the river's swells. Lis wedged in the bow, eyes fearful but exhilarated. *I could have saved her.* Lucha closed her eyes against the tide of regret rearing up to swallow her.

When she opened them again, she was no longer alone. In the corner, *his* dark eyes were fixed on her. He emanated a chilly glow—one that allowed her to see his features clearly, even when she could scarcely see her hands in front of her face.

He had come to collect. There was no question now. The fluttering in her chest was back—weak, but still hers.

"You won't take me." She was shocked by the sound of her own voice. The rasping growl her futile screams had left her with.

He didn't speak, only watched with those ravenous eyes. Eyes that said she wouldn't stop him when it was time. Lucha lunged at him with all her remaining strength, delirious with hunger and fury.

By the time she reached him, he was gone again.

* * *

When she had lost the strength to stand, the slot in the cell door opened at last. A wooden tray, pushed through before the metal flap snapped shut again.

Lucha dragged herself across the floor with her arms alone. Stale tortillas, greasy broth—she tore and slurped like a wild animal. The meager meal was gone in seconds, the water in the tiny clay cup barely enough to wet her lips.

But she was alive. And now she knew they intended to keep her that way.

It wasn't much, as power went, but it was something.

Lucha slept again, and awoke to a boot in the ribs.

"Get up."

Another kick landed before she could push herself up. Her head pitched and rolled. It took a moment for Alán's cruel smile to come into focus.

"Where's my sister?"

A blow to the stomach next. Lucha coughed, spitting something warm and wet onto the ground at his feet.

"Where is Lis?"

He grabbed her shoulders roughly, picking her up only to throw her back down. Bones collided. She felt them all, too close to the surface of her skin. "She'll be safe," he said, dusting off his hands. "As long as you cooperate."

"If you want cooperation, I want proof." She coughed again. "I want to see her. Alive. Unharmed."

"Where's all your power now, Lucha?" Alán asked. "Your tongue speaking, your vine twirling, your mushrooms? Perhaps they've heard you belong to me now."

She didn't bother to answer. The power was gone. It had been a liability, like all power was. She'd been a fool to trust it. To use it. But it was gone.

"Remember the stories?" Alán asked, pacing back and forth before her. "We read them together as children. Monsters and mushrooms. Sombralados. We used to wonder which one would come to life next. What new horror would enter our city after a hundred years convinced the world they were only fiction . . ."

Lucha remembered. Of course she remembered. Days crouched over makeshift compasses. Drawings of monsters. The way they'd clung to each other when the first sombralado came into the city.

"I should have seen it," he ranted on. His eyes danced with a mad eagerness. Barely human in the harsh light from beyond the doorway. "The way you melted into the trees. You were never lost. Not even when we left the path. I've been chasing the source of these strange, terrible happenings for years—and all along it was right next door."

She roused at the accusation, her half-broken mind struggling to turn it over.

"Don't bother denying it." He didn't wait for her to try. "The people already know. Over a hundred years we've been safe from the horrors of the forest—and then little Lucha Moya is born and all hell breaks loose."

He came closer. Too close. She could smell some kind of spirit on his breath. Alán had never been one to indulge before.

"I told them it was you all along," he whispered, the words hot on her face. "The mushrooms, swallowing land and people. The screeching in the night. The skeletal birds disemboweling people in the town square."

"How . . . ," Lucha began, her dry throat less an obstacle than her terror.

"They came up with their own sins to lay at your door once they knew," he continued, ignoring her. "Illnesses, disappearances, deaths and madness. People are predictable that way."

"I didn't," Lucha said, hating the note of pleading in her voice. "It wasn't me." But if they thought it was, she would never be free. She thought of the tattooed woman in the plaza—accused of worshipping a forbidden goddess. Imprisoned for life, and there hadn't even been proof of her misdeeds.

If they believed Lucha had been responsible for the sombralados, the mushrooms . . .

Lucha wouldn't escape with her life. Especially not once they realized the power had abandoned her.

"My mother," she said when all hope was gone. "She can tell you . . . I was just a child . . ."

"Your mother has yet to return," he said. "It seems she's forgotten you for good. And *if* she ever remembers, memories are all she'll have."

Of course Lydia hadn't come back. Not to save their home, then. Not to save Lucha's life, now.

"I told them I killed you," Alán whispered. "There's no one left to look for you."

"Lis." She said it more to herself than to him. Lis would know she was innocent.

"Yes, poor girl." Alán got back to his feet. "Her beloved sister, eyes rolled back in her head, calling for El Sediento with trained soldiers dead at her feet. She's grateful for our protection. Grateful you can't hurt anyone else . . ."

"If you harm her in any way, I'll kill you." Lucha wished the double timbre would return to her throat so Alán could hear the yawning of his grave. "I'll make sure you suffer."

"No," Alán said, already near the door. "You won't."

"Remember what I said." Lucha was desperate now. Unwilling to admit how much she feared the utter solitude that would replace him when he left. "You'll get nothing from me until I see her alive."

"We'll see about that." His back was already to her.

"When will you return?"

"It's complicated, visiting a dead girl," he said, opening the cell door wide enough to pass through. Lucha was too weak to even attempt escape. "Don't expect me soon."

The pale specter of El Sediento returned again with the hunger. When the food slot had gone unused too long. When

Lucha's lips had begun to crack like old leather and she'd lost track of the days.

"You won't take me." It was a whisper. A rasp. Nothing more solid.

"I'm not here to *take* you, like some monster in a story." His mouth moved, but his voice seemed to come from the very air around her. "Haven't you learned?"

If she was shocked by this, if she was still too weak to stand, she refused to show it. "You think I'll give my soul to you willingly? You've underestimated me."

His face was sharp against the darkness. The only thing in focus. A smirk twisted his surprisingly full lips. A contrast to the rigid angles that made up the rest of him. "Every story ends that way. The villain, trying to steal the soul of the pure, innocent heroine. Boring, if you ask me. We should have come up with something better by now."

"But . . . if you don't want my soul . . . why are you here?" Even the effort to maintain this conversation was nearly too much for Lucha's wasted body. Her heart raced; the words she wanted swam just out of reach.

"I'm here because I can help you, and I've already seen you're the kind of girl who's willing to strike a bargain."

"And if I say no?"

"Before you've heard what's on offer?" He stepped closer, peering down at her. "Sounds like a mistake to me. What's the harm in knowing your options?"

His eyes were mesmerizing. The last embers of a dying fire.

"I trusted you before," Lucha managed. She remembered the taste of his voice in her throat. The way she'd opened her arms to him. The emptiness, when he didn't come. "You left us to die."

He shrugged, as if the matter of two mortal lives were of little consequence. "A trial. To see if the power at full strength would shatter your mind. I had to be sure, of course."

"Is this a game to you?" Lucha croaked, thinking of Lis terrified at her feet. Lis, who had refused to run because Lucha had been more frightening than life in a cell.

Another shrug. "When you've lived as long as I have, the urgency fades. You roll the dice again and again. In that way, yes. It's a game. But a high-stakes one—does that make you feel better?"

A small pinprick of resistance needled at her now, but when he spoke again she didn't silence him.

"Fortunately for us both, your mind—if frustratingly juvenile—seems to be intact. That means you can be of use to me."

"I won't," Lucha said. An instinct. She stared at those smoldering eyes, waiting.

"Ah, what have I said about knowing your options? You'll listen." His gaze intensified. "Because as good as you try to convince the world you are, you crossed a line back there. And I think you'll do it again. Care to roll and find out?"

"I crossed the line for my sister," Lucha said. "For Lis. For her freedom. Which you couldn't deliver."

El Sediento paced before her. His steps clicked on the metal.

"Your sister barely knows her own name. When they hit her, she doesn't cry out, because it's better than the alternative."

"Stop," Lucha said, the word catching in her throat. "Please."

"She doesn't sleep anymore. When they do let her rest it's in some filthy corner of their depraved clubhouse, and she can't dream. Not of escape, or of rescue. There's only one thing she wants, and it eats through her joy and her memories like an acid."

His words bored into the emptiness created by Lucha's ceaseless, gnawing hunger. Her isolation. Her failure to save the one thing that mattered to her. They tugged on its edges, pulling the yawning void wider until it threatened to swallow her. "Stop," she said again.

But mercy wasn't in his nature.

"When they call, she responds. When they command, she obeys. When they miss a dose, she begs."

At these words, something caught within Lucha. A tiny flame that burned in the void of her chest. The heat coursed through her body, reviving her. She got to her feet.

"I told you to stop."

But he only smiled. That half-mad grin immortalized in a thousand storybooks. "Your sister *begged* the men who put you in here for her next dose of Olvida not an hour ago."

The heat had reached an unbearable point. There was no-where to release it. It searched for any crack large enough, and when it could not find one it split Lucha in two. "ENOUGH!" she cried, to El Sediento or this torturous heat, she did not know.

A flash of light in the cell. She covered her eyes—too long accustomed to the dark—and fell back to the floor.

When she opened them again, a mushroom stood where El Sediento had seconds before. Its lacy white cap reached for the ceiling, but black spots were already blooming along its flesh, eating through anything they could find.

Lucha watched it with awe. With terror. Was this why he wanted her? Because she could do this? He had tested her. She had passed.

But now . . .

"*Yes*," El Sediento said. The light in his eyes danced as he took in her creation. "Now we can begin."

Lucha should have said no. Then. Before he was ever allowed to tempt her.

She didn't.

"Begin what?" she asked instead, unable to tear her eyes from the mushroom.

"To save your sister."

"How?"

The smile was back, cruel, bright as a distant star. "We'll destroy the thing that keeps her in chains. That keeps so many helpless and compliant. We're going to destroy Olvida."

A new hunger was born in Lucha the moment she heard these words. Unlike anything she'd ever felt, even after days of starving here. *Destroy Olvida.* Free her sister. Robado. Her mother . . .

"What's in it for you?" she asked, but already her mind was still building a glorious future. One without the drug that had fettered everyone she'd ever known or loved. One where she'd freed them all. She'd never even dared to dream of it before.

"All will be revealed in time," he said. "Suffice it to say our goals are aligned here—and you, with that fledgling power of yours, can be of some use to me along the way. For now, all there is to do is choose."

"You won't force me?" Lucha asked, surprised.

El Sediento threw his head back and laughed. A sound on a saw's edge between human and monster. It bounced off the walls of the tiny cell. It multiplied.

"That would be so much neater, wouldn't it?" he said when he was finished at last. "The monster, here to steal your soul for some terrible end." He shook his head. "I've learned a little something about the nature of human will in all my long years—shall I share it with you?"

Behind him, the mushroom caved in on itself—a pile of black jelly where moments before there had been a tall, proud column of flesh.

"To bind your will—weak as it is—to force it or subjugate it, only serves to make you desperate. In desperation you're capable of much, and more than anyone would expect. History isn't made by fate, girl. It's made by choice. So no, I won't force you. I won't take pieces of you. I'll simply make you an offer.

"Come with me, and destroy Olvida. Or stay here in your cell. Rot away. Take your chances."

It was madness, she knew. Even considering it was madness. But her mother was gone. Her father dead. Lucha imprisoned and Lis wasting away . . . Lis *forgetting*. And it was more than just the four of them. More than even Robado.

Lucha thought of Paz—her uncle in Puerto de Sal, killed by dealers. The sickness and rot of Olvida running through the veins of Elegido like some death curse . . .

If she stayed here, she was doomed. Alán would kill her or worse—and Lis? Lucha couldn't even let herself think of that. Olvida and the kings had ruined all of them. And Lucha, evidence of her fledgling power still decomposing on the cell floor, could make them pay. Did it matter what she had to sell to make sure they did?

"How do I know I can trust you?" Lucha asked.

El Sediento laughed again, softer this time. "You don't. But you can trust one thing: With me, you will never be *imprisoned*. Never locked away. Never again."

There was a hint of confession in these words. He sounded as if he spoke from memory. From a place of anger and fear. Lucha filed it away for later use.

"Make your choice, girl. There is work to be done."

There would be no easy answer. The lines of his face told her that. And perhaps the right thing to do was remain in this cell. Take her chances with starvation, or the madness of isolation. But Lucha's hatred for Olvida burned brighter than her fear. Brighter than anything.

Still too weak to stand, she struggled to her knees. "I'll go with you," she said, in a voice that didn't sound like hers. "I'll help you along the way. But the moment Olvida is destroyed, we go our own ways. You will have no claim on me. Is that understood?"

This time, he did not laugh. Only nodded. The solemn gesture of one ready to strike a bargain.

"And I won't go without Lis," Lucha said finally. She felt her last demand stretching the fragile fabric woven between them, but this was nonnegotiable. She would rot in this cell and let Olvida destroy the world before she left Lis to the kings.

He waved an impatient hand, long and pale. "In her condition, she'll only slow us."

"I'll take responsibility for her," Lucha insisted. This part was as familiar as breathing. "But if you want my help, that's the price."

His eyes bored into her for a moment, a physical pressure. "Your freedom and your sister for your aid," he repeated. "That's the bargain."

"My aid in the destruction of Olvida," Lucha replied. The stories were full of trickster demons—best to close all paths but the one she planned to travel.

El Sediento's eyes hadn't left Lucha's. "Deal," he said, and she nodded, unable to look away.

"You remember how these bargains are sealed." It wasn't a question.

Lucha wanted to deny it, but the memory was visceral. It showed in the gooseflesh on her skin, the color rising in her cheeks. There was no point in pretending she did not know.

She remembered the feeling of opening her arms to him.

Her mouth moving as he spoke. Marks of the bond her consent had made between them. The emptiness it had left when it was gone.

Instinctively, Lucha spread her arms again. Weak and malnourished, they trembled as she held them aloft.

It happened at once. A feeling like a lightning strike in the center of her chest. Her wasted muscles tightened, her bones went rigid. Her face, she knew, would be a mask of grief and pain.

The end of Olvida, she repeated to herself again and again. *The end.*

She saw it there, at the white-hot center of her agony. Robado, empty and burning. The warehouses collapsing in on themselves. The kings' massive continental enterprise ruined. Every Pensa plant in the forest shriveled and dead. Dust on the wind that stirred the trees . . .

Salvador's end of the bargain fulfilled.

Lucha's body writhed and spasmed. Her mouth moved once more in that tongue she did not speak. Could not understand. She saw herself, more wild and more terrible than in life. The architect of this ruin. Creator. Destroyer.

After a minute, or an hour, or a day, the lightning strike subsided. Lucha's first thought was that they had returned: the weapons she had once sensed on the air. She reached for them, but her arms dropped to her sides. One by one, her muscles began to fail her until she collapsed on the cold metal floor.

The darkness, as it swallowed her, was a mercy.

9

Days passed. El Sediento's form no longer faded away, but burned bright and clear in the corner he favored.

He stayed as Lucha ground her madness on the whetstone of his promises. Olvida, gone. Lis, safe. Perhaps she would never be the savior she had dreamed of as a child, but there was more than one way to be free.

She grew stronger. Despite the gnawing hunger. The ever-present thirst. Despite the trays that came rarely, if at all. She made splinters of the wood dust on the air, then sharpened them like knives. Her awareness of the place this magic originated from grew subtler as she used it.

He had awakened it, but it belonged to her. It obeyed her.

"What is your name?" she asked him one day.

"You know it."

"That's not a name," Lucha insisted. "That's a story. What's your real name?"

He stared a long time before he answered. He knew the power of names. Perhaps he believed she was too much at his

101

mercy to make use of his, because eventually he said: "Salvador is what they called me, before I was called all the rest."

"Salvador," Lucha said. It sparked a little against her teeth.

In the corner, he shuddered. But he did not speak.

In the silence, Lucha moved on from her splinters. In the cold metal box of her cell, she grew mushrooms. She watched them with awe and wonder. Each single spore contained a whole world. Infinite possibility.

They sought out the dead and dying. Broke down the weak and made life from it. She fed them her old life, scrap by scrap. A feast of decay. They thrived as she whittled away everything that was not necessary within her. Honed herself like a blade.

"He will come soon." Salvador hadn't spoken for hours— maybe days. "He will bring the girl."

"How do you know?" Lucha's voice had grown stronger, too. The breathlessness was gone, though a rasping edge remained.

"The currents of men's thoughts have been well worn through the ages. He has much to gain from using you. Nothing to lose, or so he believes. Men always go where the greatest power is—unless the price is too high."

"He won't know the price until he's bleeding." Lucha felt for the knives she'd made, reassuringly solid against her thigh. "By then, Lis and I will be long gone."

* * *

He was right.

Alán returned after two more trays. Lucha was leaning against the wall of her cell, growing mushrooms almost idly.

Salvador watched from the corner as Alán opened the door. Lucha found she didn't mind Salvador's presence now—any more than she minded the dark, or the hunger. It was just another thing upon which to feed.

She finished the row of ghostly fungi in time to get to her feet. They nearly filled the room, waist-high. She'd left a path from the door to where she stood, for effect.

"A touch melodramatic, don't you think?" Salvador asked.

Lucha ignored him.

Alán was visible now, backing into the cell, but when he pulled Lis in behind him Lucha's knees buckled. All her preparation had been a joke. How could anyone prepare for this?

Her sister was barely standing—only Alán's grip on her upper arm kept her on her feet. She was dressed in black, but barely. A skirt that skimmed her wasted thighs. A top that showed midriff and shoulders both. The jutting bones of her lowermost ribs protruded, jabbing at her sallow skin.

In the front of her hair—lustrous and black like their mother's—was a white streak, wide as three fingers.

Lucha seethed. The mushrooms stretched toward the ceiling.

It took Alán a long moment to speak. His eyes were on the mushrooms. Lucha watched him decide not to mention them. To swallow his fear. "Are you ready to discuss your future?"

Lucha didn't bother to answer. Lis's presence here was all the assurance he needed. She fed her mushrooms instead, letting them grow to her elbows. Alán's eyes widened.

"I'm listening," Lucha said.

"She's useless to me now." His voice was a half octave higher. Lis sagged in his trembling grip. "We'll put her on a boat for the crossing. She'll be on her own after that, and you and your unnatural powers will remain in my service until you die, or your debt is paid. That's the offer. And it's the only one you'll get, so I suggest you consider quickly."

For a moment, Lucha saw what her life would be if she agreed. Lis would die in the crossing, or shortly after. This deep in forgetting, she could not take care of herself for even a day. Lucha would be forced to treat with the sentient forest. Use its gifts against all who opposed Los Ricos.

The curse of Olvida would fester and spread, and Lucha would be the engine at the heart of it all . . .

"And if I refuse?" Lucha surveyed him. How she had ever thought this pathetic man a threat was a mystery to her now. His sniveling bargain. As if she hadn't moved much greater forces than this to secure her sister's safety. Robado's future.

"I kill you both, here and now."

Lis groaned. Lucha longed to run to her, to collapse sobbing against her shoulder. But she had been alone so long. She was afraid of what it might unravel inside her.

"Do we have an agreement?"

Lucha nodded. In the corner, unseen, Salvador nodded with her.

"I'm going to put these on you for my safety, and hers." Alán unhooked chains from his belt and stepped toward Lucha, into the path through the mushrooms. They'd begun to glow faintly. Alán tried to ignore them, but his eyes darted like a rodent's.

"You really think chains would stop me if I wanted you dead?" Lucha heard her voice as Alán must have heard it. The rasp. The madness at the edges where the isolation and the starving had eaten away the girl she used to be.

His eyes darted back to the mushrooms. To Lucha again. He tossed the chains at her feet.

Unable to support her own weight, Lis collapsed. Her eyes rolled back. Across the arm Alán had been holding, a ladder of scars became visible. Some were shining and white against the tan of her skin. Some were much newer, barely scabbing over.

Lucha saw the time she'd lost passing in those scars. In Lis's vertebrae jutting through her skin. Salvador's words had outlined every moment of this torture, and Lucha had hoped he was wrong . . .

"Cooperate, and she'll be free," Alán reminded her. Lucha, with the senses of a predator, heard the skittering terror beneath the smoothness. "All you have to do is put these on." He gestured to the chains at her feet.

Lucha picked them up. The cold weight of the metal dulled her senses. "Chain myself?" Her pride swelled a little at the thought. He feared her too much to approach. He would not touch the thing she had become in here.

"Unless you'd rather I had some soldados come down and do it."

Lis's eyes were rolling. She hadn't looked at Lucha once. For a moment, in the glow of the mushrooms, Lucha saw her mother's empty expression.

The light in the room turned red.

From the dust Alán had tracked in on his shoes, long wooden fangs began to grow strangely from the floor. In the corner, Salvador's eyes were closed. Was this his doing? Or had Lucha's anger taken on a mind of its own?

"You won't call the soldados." Lucha's voice filled the space like noxious fumes. "They think I'm dead. They think *I'm* the curse that woke hundred-year-old monsters and worse."

Alán watched her, the mushrooms reflected crimson in his eyes. His jaw was tight.

"You counted on me being weak," Lucha said. "On this little cell of yours breaking me." She stepped toward him. The chains fell loudly to the floor. Alán backed toward the door, but the splinters stopped him. A barbaric gate, turning the tables.

"Listen," he said, his borrowed confidence failing him at last. "Listen to me . . ."

"You won't make a puppet out of me." Salvador's mouth moved along with Lucha's. The double timbre of their joined voices echoed in the room. "Not for any price."

The mushrooms took Alán's feet first. They had Lucha's hunger. Before he could even struggle he was waist-deep, kicking and thrashing. He broke the skins of the nearest caps, but more grew in their place. Ravenous.

Once he was trapped she saw it. Hanging from his hip like a trophy. The bone knife of Lucha the cazadora. She took it before the mushrooms swallowed it; the weight of it in her hand grounded her. Reminded her who she'd been.

"D-don't do s-something you'll regret," Alán stuttered. "We can make a new deal, Lucha. A better agreement, all right? I understand. Just let me go."

"There are no agreements between captors and prisoners," Lucha said. "There's only freedom. At any cost. By any means."

The mushrooms had Alán to the shoulders. She could feel them pressing into his hot, wet throat. He began to choke.

Lucha stepped forward, reaching Lis at last. She weighed next to nothing as Lucha looped one arm around her shoulder. "You'll be safe soon," she promised. "Just hold on."

Salvador stepped out of his corner as Lucha carried her sister to the door of the cell.

Alán's breathing grew more labored. His eyes—wide in horror—tracked Lucha's movements across the cell.

"We both know no one will look for you here." Lucha's voice was ringing and clear. "I have your ingenuity to thank for that." She took a deep, shuddering breath. "I wanted to kill you. I've fantasized about it every second I've spent down here." She held his gaze for a long moment. "But we're old friends, after all."

She closed the door behind them with a clang. A sliver of

wood wound around the lock, end meeting end like a snake eating its tail. She drew all the moisture out, calcified the wood until it was hard as stone.

From inside, Alán screamed.

Lucha smiled, hoisting her sister up. Then she turned toward the sweet taste of outside air.

10

All told, three men lost their lives in the halls of Encadenar as Lucha Moya made her way toward the light.

In the stories they'd tell, she was a sorceress. Vines for fingers. A mushroom carpet unrolling at her feet. She poisoned everyone who dared to approach.

In the paintings they made, she held a fragile girl to her side. In some, later burned, a man walked behind them—black cloak open like wings.

But art never told the whole truth.

The truth was that when Lucha turned the prison's final door to dust, she was panting. Half weeping. The weight of her sister was almost too much to bear. The shadow of the man behind her was so much darker than it had been in her cell . . .

The truth was that when she finally felt the sunlight on her face, it burned. She cried out. Collapsed. Cast an arm over her eyes as it threatened to blind her.

No one would ever know that she considered surrender

then. Thought longingly of the cell she'd crawled out of—returning there to die. To end the pain. To kill the broken girl she had never wanted to be, and this terrible bargain along with her.

But she did not.

Encadenar was the northernmost building in Robado—separated from the city by a tract of cleared forest. It was heavily guarded on the best of days. Lucha entered the glade freckled in soldados' blood. Wreathed in the stories Alán had spun too well. Her face was gaunt, her skin impossibly pale. Her filthy clothes were torn, her feet bloody and bare.

Later, they'd say she had clawed her way out of her own grave, and she'd half believe them.

In the clearing, the roots seethed under her feet, still living beneath their stumps. They'd seen brutality. Fed on blood and fallen brothers. Lucha positioned herself at the center of the three largest as the five remaining guards spilled out of the prison, weapons drawn.

She had expected more.

The one who stepped forward first got the closest. Lucha held tight to Lis's limp form, offering vengeance to the roots that had felt the severing of their trunks. The guard didn't have a chance to scream before they pulled him, struggling, beneath the ground.

The second came more slowly, avoiding the stumps. He underestimated the network of the roots, the width of their spread. The long days and nights they'd waited.

He was allowed a scream. After that he was gone.

The remaining three men hesitated, eyes darting to one another's, tongues flicking out like those of nervous snakes. They tasted their deaths on the air. Lucha looked each of them in the eye. Her promise was as clear as if she'd shouted it: If they followed her, she would make sure they met the same fate.

When she turned away, they stayed.

No one watched Lis and Lucha Moya leave Robado, but stories had never needed witnesses to thrive. The tales sprang up like mushrooms themselves, thick and fast in her absence. She and her sister had ridden on the backs of skeletal horses. They'd laughed as they went, the blood of the fallen soldiers dripping down their chins.

The most common was that the trees had parted to greet them—the forest, welcoming its daughters home.

The truth was that someone did greet them at the forest's edge. But it wasn't the trees.

Paz waited at the mouth of the western road, her chin jutting proudly, a rucksack on her back.

"Lucha," she breathed as they came into view. "You're alive. I've been waiting . . . hoping . . ."

They faced each other across the road. The yawning emptiness Lucha had come from told her she could not trust the look on Paz's face. The relief. The concern. People didn't wait, after all. They left. They forgot.

"Why?" Lucha asked. She could hear the broken edges in her voice. She hoped they would scare Paz away. "Why would you wait for me?"

Paz stepped forward. "When I heard what happened I . . . I didn't believe you were dead. I couldn't."

Lucha stepped back off the road. Half feral. Skittish at the closeness. She stumbled, and Lis's unconscious weight pulled her down into a tangle of vines and limbs. Something ached at her temple—a wound? Or just the effects of the power she'd used? She had to get up. If anyone from Robado had followed them, this was over before it could begin.

Only she didn't have the strength to get up. She barely had the strength to draw another breath. Lis was moaning beside her, still lost in a world Lucha could never follow her to. Lucha had believed Salvador when he said she could destroy Olvida—but where was he now? How could she help him when she couldn't even get up?

And then Paz was there, kneeling beside her. She smelled of jacara flowers—sweet and bitter both. Her eyes were liquid with some emotion Lucha couldn't identify as she reached out a hand.

"Please," she said. "You were right at the Lost House. I've been doing this for all the wrong reasons. Trying to assuage my own guilt about my uncle. But I want to do better. Let me start here."

It was something out of another life. Lucha could barely remember the words they'd exchanged. But when Paz leaned closer, Lucha's body remembered what her mind could not conjure. Heat, in her cheeks. A quickening of her heartbeat.

Closeness that did not hurt. Closeness that was not a deadly bargain.

Lucha took Paz's hand and allowed herself to be pulled to her feet. Together, they lifted Lis, who groaned again, eyes darting wildly beneath closed lids.

"She's had a very high dose," Paz said, checking her pulse. Lucha envied her competence. "It'll be a day or more before she's even conscious."

In her condition, she'll only slow us, Salvador had said. Where *was* he?

"We don't have a day," Lucha said. "I have to get her out of here."

"Where are you going?" Paz asked.

Lucha suppressed a shudder, remembering the mad, desperate voice in which *he'd* told her the way. West, he'd said. Until they reached a massive lightning-struck tree. A place of power. There, they would have what they needed to begin.

Of course, she could share none of this with Paz. The girl with the holy tattoo. Devout believer. Living saint to Robado's lost. She would understand the mission, perhaps. But never the means.

"There's a place," Lucha managed. "A few days' travel west. Into the forest. We'll be safe from the kings there."

Paz had finished examining Lis. She took the girl's slight weight from Lucha's shoulders, holding her up without showing the strain. Lucha's body screamed in relief.

"When she wakes she'll be disoriented, possibly even violent. She won't . . ." Paz paused. "She may not remember who you are."

Lucha's hand darted to the tiny scar she still bore. The place where her own mother had threatened to open her throat. "I can handle it."

"Not alone."

I won't be alone, Lucha thought, thinking of Salvador. Of his promise, and their plan. But he wouldn't help her. He would abandon them the moment they grew too heavy a burden, agreement be damned. She had no illusions about whether she could trust him.

"Let me go with you," Paz said. Her eyes were on Lucha's again, but this time there was no quiet tenderness. Her gaze burned like some distant star.

The intensity there prickled at the back of Lucha's neck. A warning.

"Why?" Lucha asked, too aware of the minutes slipping past. Enough time for the men she'd spared to run to Pecado, to rouse the kings? Enough time to amass an army to hunt them through these woods?

Paz did not look away. "Because you told me the truth, even when I didn't want to hear it. You helped me. Let me help you."

It didn't seem enough of a reason to leave everything you knew. But Lucha's arms trembled at the thought of taking Lis's weight. Her sister whimpered in her deep trance. When she woke, veins screaming for another dose, bearing her weight would be the least of Lucha's worries.

Could she trust Paz? Perhaps not. But that didn't mean she couldn't use her help.

"It will be dangerous," she said, glancing back over her shoulder. All was still. For now.

"I understand," Paz replied.

"We won't be returning."

"I wouldn't expect you to."

"I don't believe you've told me the real reason you want to help me."

Paz smiled. A sad smile that said her uncle's death wasn't the only tragedy she'd lived through. "If you give me time, perhaps I can convince you my motives are honest ones."

"If we don't get eaten by something first," Lucha said, gaze already drifting back to the forest. To the unknown they faced—together, now.

"We?" Paz asked. The burning stars were gone from her eyes. They were kind. Bright. As if this were some adolescent lark. For a moment, Lucha wished it could be.

"I won't blame you when you want to turn back," she said, stepping into the shadow of the trees at last.

Paz, still holding Lis, was close behind.

They traveled through the night, leaving Robado as far behind them as they could. They did not speak for fear that their voices would carry.

Lucha barely noticed the forest thickening, growing wilder around them. She had no strength left for anything but a single step. Then another. Then another. Paz trudged silently along, asking no questions, making no complaints.

Salvador did not return. Lucha tried not to wonder whether she had followed some hallucination into the trees to die. She had to believe—in him and herself. She had no other choice.

Before the sun rose in earnest, Lis had begun to sweat through her clothes. Her moans became more frequent as they walked. Louder. The pain of remembering was just beginning to fight to the surface.

"Let me take her," Lucha said. The first words she'd spoken since they left the road.

Paz, breathing heavily, transferred the girl without comment.

But in another hour, it was clear Lis could no longer be safely carried. Her muscles had begun to spasm. Her breath came in rattling gasps. Once, Lucha nearly dropped her among the stones at a creekside. Her own limbs were growing weak. Adrenaline had carried her this far, but it was fading now.

"Crossing the creek should make us hard to track," Paz said, scouting ahead. "We'll travel up the rocks. Find a place for her to rest."

Lucha did not argue, and when at last they found a moss-covered glade she lowered her sister gratefully onto the ground.

The relief didn't last.

Lis looked far worse here than she'd looked by torchlight in Encadenar. The shadows beneath her eyes were a stark contrast to her sallow skin, beaded with sweat. She was so thin. So frail. Lucha couldn't bear to look at her, but she couldn't look away.

We'll destroy the thing that keeps her in chains . . .

Before her, Lis's face wavered as if heat distorted it. Lucha saw her eyes as empty sockets, her mouth full of wriggling worms.

Robado's warehouses burning. The empty city, left off every map . . .

We're going to destroy Olvida . . .

Lucha swayed on her feet. Exhaustion made its demands, but she could not obey. Not now. Not when Lis was fading away.

"We have to keep going." The words weighed down her tongue. Came out garbled and strange. Pain, in her knees. She'd fallen. No matter, she could rise again.

Paz's face swam near. Not heat, now, but water. Ripples and waves. Her fingers on Lucha's cheek, cool as rain.

"We have to keep going."

The lightning-struck tree. He would be there. They would go together.

We're going to destroy Olvida . . .

It was the thirst that woke her. A dream that she'd swallowed fire and her body turned to smoke.

She was on her belly in the mud, hands cupping creek water, before the forest came into focus. The trees stirred, restless in the wind. In their glade all was quiet.

Water ran down her chin, soaked the filthy rag of her shirt. Lis slept, and Paz, and for a moment Lucha was the only flickering candle in a vast darkness. She felt the filth of Encadenar coating her. Defining her.

She pulled her shirt off. The shadows of the night made a ladder of her ribs. Black trousers met the gravel of the bank as Lucha slipped naked below the surface of the inky water. Tonight, she didn't care what lurked beneath.

With fistfuls of sand from the creek's bottom she scrubbed her skin raw, felt the sting of the air and the water. She was alive. The dying washed away on the current. The trees continued to toss, each leaf sharpened by moonlight.

When she was clean, her clothes drying on a flat rock, Lucha floated, her dark hair fanning behind her. She did not know this body, its bones barely encased by her skin. She watched it drift as if from a distance.

Paz stirred as the moon kissed the treetops, startling Lucha back into her flesh, unaware of how much time had passed. She was abruptly conscious of her nakedness, their proximity, and felt ashamed of the heat that writhed in her belly.

You've been alone too long.

Her clothes were stiff and damp, her body still dripping, but she struggled into a state of more modest dress before returning to the imprint her body had made in the moss.

The glade was small. Barely wide enough for the three of them to lie shoulder to shoulder. Lis breathed evenly on the far side. Paz had chosen the middle. The moss beneath Lucha was a luxury compared to the metal floor of her cell—yet still she struggled to find a comfortable position.

She had been so utterly, terribly alone for all those months that to be this close to another person felt unspeakably intimate. The flush of Paz's cheek, the rise and fall of her breast—too shallow to suggest sleep.

Paz cleared her throat, but she did not speak. Her imprint in the moss was no slight thing, no needle or knife. She made a luxurious, decadent shape. In the moss that held them both, Lucha felt the ways they were different. The ways they were the same.

Lucha fought to control her heart rate. In isolation, her body had been an enemy. A doomed and starving creature. She'd been forced to distance herself from it—its hungers and urges—as a matter of survival. But tonight, they were free. Alive.

Around them, the forest and its peaceful night-sounds seemed to grow louder. The very air between them felt charged. Every particle that made up this cradle whispered of hunger. Of need.

Of a power Lucha had never been allowed to glimpse or claim.

It coursed through everything—not only these two girls feigning sleep in a glade.

As Lucha returned to her body, bit by bit, she realized that this force was everywhere—seething and writhing and altogether too much to bear.

Pinned down like an insect on a board, Lucha was unable to do more than breathe tiny, shallow breaths. She felt the soil, teeming with life. Below it, a vast network of roots connected each tree, bush, and vine for thousands of miles. Branches, reaching wide. Leaves fluttering in the wind. Each element of each living thing seemed attached to an invisible string that led straight into Lucha's chest.

Her shallow breathing became ragged. The pressure built. If she let it, Lucha knew, the forest would claim her. Take all she had to give. She had practiced. Prepared with spores and wood dust in a controlled environment where her will was the only factor.

She had not been ready for this.

Paz, Lucha was dimly aware, had risen. She bent over Lucha's body, peering down. Her mouth moved in the same shapes again and again. Lucha couldn't hear the words in the riot of sensation overtaking her. All she could do was hold on.

And even that wouldn't be possible for long.

"Help me," she whispered. She could not blink. Could barely breathe. "Please. Help me."

"Lucha?" Paz was saying. The tension around her eyes betrayed her fear. "Lucha, what can I do?"

But it wasn't Paz's help she needed.

Lucha pictured *his* arms folded across his chest. Hair in his eyes. Those sharp cheekbones; that perpetual scowl. If he did not come now, she would die here, before they could ever achieve the purpose she had staked everything on.

"Lucha, please. Tell me how to help you."

"*Precious,*" came another voice. "*The mortal thinks she can help.*"

Salvador circled her, outline sharp against the seething green. His smile was sinister.

Lucha turned toward him, rigid with fear. The forest told her she was part of its hierarchy. That her connection to it made her beholden to its needs.

"Please," she said again. A ragged gasp. "Please."

"Well, since you've asked so nicely." He knelt down beside her head. Lucha whimpered—a small, pathetic sound. She expected him to taunt her. He didn't.

"A tree has bark," he began. The pain—like holding your breath underwater—threatened to split Lucha open. "The root has skin. Every leaf has an edge. Why?"

I'm going to die before this lecture is finished. Lucha gritted her teeth, tears streaming freely down her face. *I'm going to die while he gives me a botany lesson.*

"They're *boundaries*," he said, when it became clear she could not answer. "Boundaries are what allows each piece of a whole to work together without forgetting their individual identity and function."

Lucha whimpered again.

"Are you a root, girl?"

Beneath her, a thousand acres of roots pushed at her feeble dam. They claimed her power as their own. They shouted their *yes* into the earth so loudly it quaked.

"*Are you?*"

With the last of her strength, Lucha shook her head. *No.* She was not a root. She was a girl, with skin and bones. Hair and nails. She was not a root, and she would not allow the roots to claim her.

Gradually, the pressure lessened. The roots went quiet. She could still feel them there—a part of her, but separate from her, too.

"Good," said Salvador. "Now, are you a trunk?"

The trunks, with their many millions of rings, shouted their claim as well. They stored memories within them— millions of years of life. Their *yes* was definitive. It rang with authority, threatening to shake Lucha's own history loose and claim it for their own.

This time, her *no* came easier. She was not a trunk. She was a girl.

The leaves tugged at her next. Then the vines. Then the rest. Each time, Lucha whispered her quiet *no*. She remembered her body, her mind, her soul. She told them her name until they retreated at last. Not gone; they were ready. Waiting for her to claim them.

Limp and shaking, Lucha sat up—herself again. A girl in a glade.

Paz hovered off to the side with shock and pity painted across her face in broad strokes. She would think the ordeal of Lucha's imprisonment had finally sunk in. Lucha would never have to confess to more . . .

But a small part of her mourned the loss of that earlier closeness. The kindling of heat before the roots and the rest took hold.

Lucha looked away, back to *his* pitiless smirk. His face seemed to glow, phosphorescent in the shadows.

"Remember our bargain," he said. "You and I have an injustice to correct. A world to reshape. Everything else"—he looked pointedly at Paz—"is a means to an end."

Trembling from head to toe, Lucha barely managed a nod before he let the shadows in the glade embrace him, disappearing from sight. Like the roots and the trunks and the leaves, Lucha knew he was not gone.

She would find him at the lightning-struck tree—no matter what she had to sacrifice to reach it.

11

When Lucha woke again, the sun was high and Paz was gone.

It's only a few hours back to Robado, she thought as she rose on shaking legs. *Last night was probably plenty to send her scurrying home . . .*

Lucha tried not to be disappointed. Tried not to hope. A means to an end, Salvador had called Paz, nothing more. Perhaps he'd been right. But a small weight settled on Lucha's chest beside the rest.

Regret. Loss. What did it matter? She would face far worse before this was done.

Lis slept fitfully, a crease between her eyebrows. Lucha would be no use to her or anyone else if she didn't find something to eat. Pure necessity had carried her this far, but as much as she wanted to stay, to watch Lis until she woke, she wouldn't make it farther without fuel.

Especially not alone.

Despite growing up at the edge of Elegido's most diverse forest ecosystem, Lucha had never learned to forage. To hunt game. She'd stood in line with the rest of Robado's workers for rations, trading any pagos she had to spare for small luxuries like cinnamon and fresh fruit. But here, surrounded by a vast wilderness that fed countless life-forms, she was at a complete loss.

"What was I thinking?" she muttered as she searched the ground and low branches for anything that looked familiar. These violet berries could be sweet or poison. This pungent weed with its tuber-like root might fill her belly or turn it inside out.

From up ahead, a bird took flight, wheeled around, and cut purposefully through the sky to the west. Lucha imagined how its fleshy breast would crackle, fat dripping as it roasted on a stick. But she was no closer to catching it than to taking wing herself.

Beneath her, the roots sang their deep weaving song. Above, the leaves flashed, cutting the air. A few fluttered to Lucha's feet. If only she could drink the sun and rain. Create her own sustenance.

This thought, warped and fractured by her hunger, ventured into the teeming life around Lucha like a curious mouse. She could feel it around her now—the power that had nearly destroyed her just last night. That would have if Salvador had not intervened.

At Lucha's feet, the violet berries seemed to sing. A bright and curious song. Sweet on the air. Beside them, a red variety chimed low, a resonant warning. Metallic, like blood.

There were more songs. More whispering voices. More

scents and tastes. The forest wanted her alive, Lucha realized. They shared something. Some bright thread like the one that had once connected her to her mother. She suspected she could call on this connection, tap into its power as she had before . . .

She had barely thought it before she remembered. Dead soldados. Lis's wide, terrified eyes peering up at her. Blood and death and rot.

All around her now, the forest's whispers eased her out of her waking nightmare. They told her that the power they shared was more than destruction. That it could help her. Save her. Lucha tried desperately to reel herself in. Ground herself in the present. Forget the death and the whispers and the temptation.

I am not a root, she remembered. *I am a girl*. And this girl knew enough about power not to go seeking it if she had any other choice.

With enormous effort, Lucha closed her mind to the forest's songs. Its whispers. She had lived without seeking power all her life. She would find another way to survive.

As if in answer to this inner declaration, something rustled in the trees to the west—where just a moment ago she'd seen the bird take flight. Was it the wind, perhaps? Or did she dare hope for prey? Lucha took her knife in her hand, thinking of rabbits and foxes. She would not commune with the forest, but if it saw fit to deliver her a meal, she could hardly refuse . . .

When Paz pushed through the thick boughs, it was hard to

tell who was more surprised. Hastily, Paz slid something into her rucksack. When she turned back her smile was too bright. Lucha, who'd believed her gone for good, was so shocked by her appearance that she forgot the knife in her hand.

"Waiting for me?" Paz asked mildly. Her eyes traced the bone blade's sharp edge.

Lucha sheathed it hastily, her mind on whatever Paz had hidden. Did she dare ask?

"Hunting," she said, when she decided she did not.

"Mind some company?"

For a moment, Lucha's thoughts strayed to the night before. Her rail-thin body floating naked on the water. Paz, feigning sleep. Salvador crouching between them, whispering instructions as Lucha's life force bled into the rocks and roots.

Everything else is a means to an end . . .

"Depends," Lucha said at last.

"On what?"

"On whether you know what you're doing."

Lucha had a cazadora's reflexes. Paz had a keen eye and knowledge of the forest's bounty. They shared an instinct for avoiding detection that made it possible to creep up on unsuspecting prey.

"On your left," Paz whispered. Her breath barely stirred the air. "Whitetail."

The cotton puff stuck up in the air as the rabbit drank from a narrow, trickling stream. Lucha kept to the shadows.

She walked on the balls of her feet. The rabbit didn't even have time to widen its eyes before blood ran red between Lucha's fingers.

The questions between Paz and Lucha melted away in the thrill of the hunt, along with the lingering embarrassment of the previous night. The second rabbit darted at the last moment, causing Lucha to step knee-deep in mud and Paz to hoot with laughter.

When she tested a berry, Paz's teeth turned blue, and she made gruesome faces as Lucha attempted to track a fox without success.

Within an hour, however, they had amassed a feast. They walked back to the glade together, flush with their victory, not minding if their shoulders touched on the narrow path. Three rabbits hung from Lucha's belt. Paz's pockets overflowed with roots, greens, and berries.

A flat river stone at the creekside made a decent butcher's block. Lucha's elbows bumped Paz's companionably as they skinned and peeled and diced, sharing the knife. In a quarter of an hour, the rabbits crackled over a small fire. The vegetables steamed in clever pouches Paz had made of leaves. They rested then, watching the flames as Lis slept on and on.

For a moment, it was easy to forget the silhouette of the lightning-struck tree. The terrible bargain Lucha had made. The destiny she had chosen, and might not survive. For a moment, they were two girls who had tasted freedom, and found it sweet.

When the meal was finished Lucha insisted on feeding her

sister first. She mashed roots into a paste with the butt of her knife, dripping grease from the rabbit in and spooning it a little at a time into Lis's mouth.

The sleeping girl moaned, batting at Lucha's patient hands until at last, she swallowed. Three bites. Four. A little cold creek water dribbled from a large pointed leaf.

"Your turn," Paz said when Lucha's body quaked with hunger and relief.

Washing had made her human again, but this meal brought Lucha back to life. The rabbit was tender, and its meat was earthy beneath the char of the flame. The pale tubers Lucha had been so skeptical of were creamy when cooked, accentuated by the bite of the herby greens Paz had dressed with the juice of tiny citrus fruits.

Lucha's stomach filled quickly, yet she continued to feast until her ribs felt uncomfortably compressed. The silence that followed was peaceful—the first peace Lucha had felt in longer than she could remember.

"I thought you left," she confessed when the meal had made her limbs heavy, her tongue lazy and loose. "This morning. I thought you'd gone back to Robado."

Paz leaned against a tree across the dying fire. The afternoon sun was sinking, staining everything russet and gold. Her eyes were heavily lidded, and Lucha thought she looked sated and glorious, like a lustrous, sunbathing cat.

"You thought I'd abandon you so soon?"

Lucha didn't say what she wanted to say, which was that leaving was human nature. That she'd expected nothing more.

Instead, she said: "Where did you go?"

Paz took a long time to answer, and Lucha remembered the hasty way she'd reached into her rucksack. The too-bright smile. The feeling on the road when they'd first encountered each other: that Paz had her own agenda—their causes only temporarily aligned.

"My uncle always dreamed of seeing this forest," Paz began. Her tone lingered somewhere between dreaminess and sorrow. "My mother was the devout one, but when she died he took up her mantle. He promised to bring me here one day, no matter the cost of the crossing."

Lucha looked for an answer in her words and found none. She waited.

"He taught me to hunt and forage. Questioned every Olvida runner who landed in Puerto de Sal about the Bosque and the crossing. That's . . ." Her voice caught. She cleared her throat. "That's how he first got started running Olvida. One of them convinced him it was the best way to get to Robado."

Lucha tried to picture one of the pale, rat-faced boys who risked the crossing in sunny Puerto de Sal. Talking to a handsome man with a sparkle like Paz's in his eye.

"He changed so much over those months. Lost weight. His hair turned white. He started forgetting for longer and longer. I had never even heard of Olvida, I had no idea what was happening to him. But he never stopped talking about the Bosque de la Noche. Not even at the end."

This part, Lucha had no trouble picturing.

"In Puerto de Sal we give our dead to the fire," Paz

continued, still staring into the flames like she saw her uncle's face there. "They found him on the dock, burned him before I had a chance to say goodbye and brought me his ashes. Nothing more."

"I'm sorry," Lucha said. The world had shrunk again. Herself and Paz. The sun setting early behind the trees.

"Thank you," Paz said quietly. She wiped at her eyes. "When you become a devotee of the goddess they make you leave all your personal effects behind. They want you to start a new life in her service, free of the burdens of your past." Paz reached into her rucksack and pulled out a tiny silk purse. "But I couldn't leave him. I told myself I'd take his ashes on the crossing. Into the forest. Leave them there so part of him could make the journey . . ."

Like a wick catching fire, Lucha understood. Paz's solitary journey into the woods. The object she'd hidden. Her false smile.

"You couldn't leave him."

Paz's expression was rueful. "I've carried this bag for years. I'm finally here. I don't know why I can't just . . ." Her voice was thick with emotion. For the first time Lucha pictured her, a little girl. Orphaned and alone. The last person who'd loved her already dust.

"The woman who tried to kill me at the Lost House was my mother."

She hadn't intended to say it. It landed like an offering between them, and Lucha found the rest coming up like black bile from somewhere deep down.

131

"The first time she came home sick I was nine. My father was already dead. I thought I'd be an orphan, alone with Lis. It's forbidden to pray in Robado, but that night I did. All night. Just begging some distant god or goddess not to take her from me."

Paz's eyes still sparkled. The flames died down to an orange glow.

"She disappeared so many times. Leaving us alone. Spending our ration money on Olvida. She came home still in the thick of it. She lashed out. Hit us. Called us names and left again."

"Lucha . . ."

Her name was heavy in Paz's honeyed voice. It said she had enough room for Lucha's grief as well as her own. That Lucha hadn't leaned too hard.

"That night I was going to find her because she'd lost her job. We were being evicted. She was our last chance, and she didn't remember me. She knocked that man out with a chair leg and held it to my throat thinking I was a dealer, and I still couldn't leave. She had forgotten me, she could have killed me, and I couldn't leave."

Lucha's eyes burned, her throat shrank around this toxin as she purged it at last.

"The only thing heavier than a parent's presence is their absence," Paz said into the weighty silence. "I suppose they'll always be with us, whether we can leave them or not."

Lucha looked up across the glade. Paz's eyes were round

and wide, reflecting the dying light. For a long time they stayed that way, reflecting this last warmth toward each other.

"When you're ready to let him go, you will," Lucha said, feeling the pain of it all over again.

"You too," Paz said.

A remnant of last night's heat rekindled in Lucha's chest as they looked at each other. Two spots of color appeared in Paz's cheeks. She dropped her eyes. Her tongue swept her bottom lip, leaving it glistening.

The forest, which Lucha had tried all day to tune out, whispered again. Some distant promise Lucha thought she might want to keep. But before she could name it, Lis screamed.

Paz was closer. By the time Lucha reached them her sister's eyes were rolled back in her head, Paz bracing her neck as Lis's back arched against some imagined attack. She cried out again, batting her hands at assailants no one else could see.

Lucha grabbed her sister's hand, letting her squeeze until her own bones ground together. She deserved this pain. How dare she forget, even for a moment, what had brought them into these woods?

On Paz's face was that same desperate longing Lucha had seen during their first encounter. She knew now that Paz was seeing her uncle. In pain. Fading away.

We're going to destroy Olvida . . .

Though her expression was tortured, Paz's hands were capable. Steady. She reached into her rucksack for a brown-tinted glass bottle and shook the clouded liquid inside. "It seems frightening," she said. "But this is a good sign. She's fighting the drug."

"She's in *pain*," Lucha said. Lis's hand crushed her own with more strength than her wasted body should have been capable of. "What do I do?"

Paz pressed an ear to Lis's chest as the frail girl drew a great, shuddering breath. "Her heart is strong," she said, returning to her little bottle. "I can give her this. It's a tincture that should sedate her through the worst of the withdrawal."

"Is it safe?" Lucha asked. She eyed the bottle suspiciously. More drugs in Lis's system hardly seemed the answer.

"It's mild. Easy on the body. Without it, this could continue for days, and it'll only get worse from here. Fever. Hallucinations. The body will do whatever it needs to purge itself."

The lightning-struck tree flashed in Lucha's mind—a dark silhouette splitting the pale sky. How many were suffering? Dying, while she ate and rested and frolicked after rabbits. And how long would the Robadans look for them? How long until they found this place?

"We don't have days," she said. "Just promise me it won't hurt her."

Over Lis's spasming body, Paz gripped Lucha's wrist. "I'll never do anything to hurt her. Or you. Please, believe that."

Lucha didn't. Not entirely. But she gave a short jerk of her head anyway. They couldn't afford to dally any longer.

Paz tipped a few drops of the tincture into Lis's mouth, holding her chin when she thrashed. "Another good sign," Paz said. "The tincture is very bitter. She can taste it. She's here with us."

Bit by bit, the color receded from Lis's face. Her breath slowed. Her body relaxed into the moss. Lucha used the sleeve of her shirt to wipe the cooling sweat from her brow.

The memories of her mother crowded in like mushrooms after rain. The relief that chased the fear. The hope. *It's not the same,* she told herself. *Lis didn't have a choice.*

But in a place like Robado, how much of a choice did anyone have?

"We need to get going," Lucha said abruptly, pushing these questions aside. She didn't have time to wonder. She had to keep moving.

"Now?" Paz asked, her eyes wide. Darkness had settled in the glade. The forest was alive with the sounds of encroaching night. "Wouldn't it be better to wait for morning? It's dangerous to travel at night."

"It's more dangerous to sit here and wait for them to find us," Lucha said. "I need to get her to safety." She didn't mention her ghosts. Not this time. It was already too easy to get lost in this camaraderie. Too easy to forget what Lucha had promised, and what was at stake.

"I'll put out the fire," Paz said.

Between them, a door that had barely begun to open seemed to close.

Better now than later, Lucha told herself as she stalked the glade, doing her best to erase any sign that they had been here at all.

12

Travel through the woods at night was far from easy. Lucha and Paz fought through tangled vines and brambles they couldn't see until they were snared in them. The path (when there was one to follow) was barely visible.

The forest's whispers were louder at night. A chorus from above and below. The woods opened paths for Lucha, and she refused to walk them. The woods lighted her way, and she took another. She had allied herself with Salvador for a purpose, but she did not trust him or this power he had awakened in her.

But fighting came at a cost. Lucha was exhausted after less than an hour. Her body had been confined to its cell for so long, her muscles were ill-adapted for long stretches of exertion. She pressed on, regardless, stubbornly choosing her own way.

Phosphorescent moss grew on the north side of every tree, casting a greenish pallor over their skin. Night-blooming flowers clustered from vines overhead, pale petals and stigmas like eyes that followed as they passed, heading west. Always west. Spores from glowing mushrooms drifted on breezes like a creature's breath. Little as she trusted its language, Lucha found herself unable to resist the rhythm of the night forest as it came to vivid life around her.

Paz seemed to have understood the closing of the door between them. She did not bring up her uncle again, or Lucha's mother. But from time to time she gasped at some new glowing revelation, some tiny, otherworldly creature in their path, and Lucha couldn't help but imagine it all through her eyes.

Paz had fought, and lost, and sacrificed to reach this place, Lucha thought in the darkest part of the night. Could it be that her only ulterior motive was to be here? Immersed in the fantasy her uncle had dreamed for her?

If that's the case, why did she wait so long?

The questions had no answers. The night seemed endless. Once or twice Lucha thought she saw Salvador, his face pale against the shadow of a tree, but eyes played tricks in low light. And the stories said the forest had tricks of its own . . .

Hours passed. When Lucha faltered, Paz carried Lis without waiting to be asked. When a bramble caught Paz's skirts, Lucha cut her free. In this way they pressed westward with dogged determination until the glow faded from the wood and dawn began to gild the tops of the trees a hundred feet above.

They would have to rest, and soon. Exhaustion pulsed in Lucha's limbs. It hollowed out her mind, making room for dark thoughts to steal in and breed. The pull of the lightning-struck tree was inexorable.

She pushed on; she ignored the pain. If the only thing under her control was this forward movement, she could let nothing stop her. If Paz wondered about the details of their destination—this mythical safe place Lucha had invented—she did not ask.

But even forward motion became difficult as the first rays of sun filtered through the tree-lined horizon. Whatever Paz had given Lis was wearing off. It had been nearly a day since Lis's last dose of Olvida. Even with herbs to keep her peaceful, she would be awake soon.

It was impossible to predict who Lis would be when she returned to herself. Lucha knew that better than most.

She was about to break the night-long silence to discuss her concerns with Paz, when Lis began to seize in her arms.

Lucha managed to lower her sister carefully to the ground. Lis thrashed and moaned there—the trees offering little cover—as Lucha stood helplessly by. "What do we do?" she asked.

Paz was in her rucksack again, her eyes wide and serious. Her usually full lips she held in a thin line. "It's a severe case of withdrawal. Not common, but not unheard of. Can you hold her shoulders, please?"

Grateful to have a task, Lucha crouched at her sister's head, pressing Lis's shoulders into the ground as she continued to thrash against the pressure. Her eyes rolled again. Blood trickled from the corner of her mouth where she'd bitten into her cheek or her tongue.

"If I could just get her mouth open," Paz said under her breath. "The herbs will help, but . . ."

Lis's shaking intensified. Tears sprang to Lucha's eyes. "Is she dying?"

"She's not dying." Paz sounded so sure that the edge of Lucha's fear could not help but soften. "Her jaw is clenched too tightly. We need to get her on her left side. It'll help her breathe."

Together, they turned her. When Paz moved her hands, Lucha's took their place. When Lucha's grasp faltered, Paz took Lis's weight. It was a slow process, but its effects were immediately visible. Color returned to Lis's cheeks. Her jaw relaxed; her breathing deepened.

Paz moved quickly when Lis was still, and Lucha held her sister once more as the loosening of her jaw allowed the tincture through. Within a few minutes she was boneless.

Even Lucha knew there could be no more travel today. Paz found a place off the path to settle—not as comfortable as their glade, but it would do. In silence Lucha cut long, supple branches and stripped them. When they'd been placed, Paz covered them in a canopy of moss and leaves.

Not sophisticated, as shelters went. In turns their eyes darted to the storm clouds gathering above. Hopefully they had done enough to stay dry.

Paz seemed poised to speak, but Lucha turned away. "Sleep," she said. "I'll keep watch."

The other girl's mouth opened, then closed again. She settled in the small shelter with her back to Lucha, Lis breathing softly between them.

* * *

Barely an hour passed before Lis began to toss and turn. The heavy clouds did little more than threaten, rumbling above the trees.

Lucha lifted her sister easily, carrying her some distance from Paz. Tomorrow, she would tell Paz she hadn't wanted to wake her. The truth was more complicated. Lucha could feel her heart opening to this girl. Responding to her kind words, her capable hands, the ease she created in any place they called home even for a moment . . .

But Lucha could not let herself forget why she was here. The bargain she'd made for Lis, and Robado and herself. Paz was kind, and perhaps she truly wanted to help—but she was also a marked devotee of the forest goddess. She would never accept Lucha's bargain with El Sediento. And Lucha would not be able to hide it once they arrived at their destination.

A sundering was inevitable. The less Lucha relied on Paz—the less she cared—the easier it would be for them both.

Still lost in thought, Lucha nestled her sister in a bed of freshly fallen leaves. She dripped condensation from a leaf between the girl's cracked lips. She hummed without skill or melody—something comforting she remembered from childhood.

Lis's breathing grew harsher. Against her ribs, her heart fluttered, then slowed, then pounded. Shadows pooled beneath her eyes, and in the shape of her bones Lucha saw death. Threatening like rain.

From her blood, racing through her veins, Lucha heard the whispers. Olvida was of this forest, after all. It spoke to her like all the rest.

"No," Lucha said aloud. She would do anything to save her sister, but to use this power on Lis was too great a risk. Lucha closed her eyes against the images of white vines. Wooden blades. Mushrooms, filling Alán's gurgling throat. Could it heal Lis? Perhaps. But it could kill her just as easily.

"You know you're very boring when you're scared."

Where a silvery tree trunk stood in the shadow of a mammoth evergreen, he appeared. This time, Lucha was not startled. He belonged here, in the dappled light of dawn.

"I don't need your magic to care for my sister," she said. "I've been doing just fine without it her whole life."

"You're boring when you say things like *magic*, too."

"What else would you call it? Whispering forests. Vines that choke guards. Mushrooms that consume men. The very fact that I can see you standing there is proof of it."

"Every tree in this forest transmutes sunlight and rain into sustenance, allowing them to grow to gargantuan heights. Is that *magic*? When you think you'd like to move, electrical impulses in your mind send signals to your limbs, directing them to dance. To leap or twirl or march. To embrace a lover or attack an adversary. Is *that* magic?"

"Will she die?" Lucha asked bluntly. There was no time for semantics.

"Undoubtedly."

"Will she die soon? From her withdrawal?"

141

"Her body is weak. The toxin is unforgiving."

"Illuminating," Lucha snapped. "I'm only helping you to save her, you know? If she dies I'll have no reason to go on. If you still want my help, it might be in your best interest to tell me what to do."

Salvador heaved a sigh that expressed all the exasperation of his hundreds of years. Around them, leaves quaked on their stems, sending chattering ripples through the air.

"I'm not an oracle, girl. I can't tell you the future. Only the past. Plenty have died, and from lower doses. Plenty have given up rather than face life beneath the crushing weight of want unfulfilled. If you want to save her, save her. But don't dawdle. We have work to do."

"How do I save her?"

"Even a myopic novice should be able to answer that question easily enough. The drug is of the forest. The forest obeys the call of the gift. Connect to it. Remove the toxin. Restore her. The rest is a question of her own will."

"But . . . couldn't I kill her? Couldn't the crash kill her?"

This time, he did not answer. When Lucha looked up, the silvery tree stood alone.

The old fears returned in a rush, like a river's wild current breaking a dam. Lucha, alone. Lis, helpless. The only person with the power to protect them was indifferent, and she didn't even know where to find him. A familiar story. Her hands began to shake.

Lucha had never been able to save Lis, only to stave off

disaster for a minute, an hour, a week. She'd been a child with an adult's burden and none of the agency.

But now, the whispers said, she had both.

Laid out fragile, translucently pale before her, Lis gasped. A horrible, rasping sound. She clutched at her chest, eyes so wide Lucha could see the whites all the way around her irises. When Lucha leaned over her they locked gazes for the first time since their escape from Encadenar.

Lis knew her. Lucha could tell by the way she gripped tighter, pulled closer. She couldn't speak, but her body language screamed: *Save me, or kill me. Just take the pain away.*

Closing her eyes, Lucha thought of mushrooms. The way they absorbed decay, transmuted it into life. The mushrooms would make a feast of Lis—so close to death. They couldn't be trusted to leave her whole.

She allowed her strange new sense to range out around her. Listening to the roots. The leaves. The mycelium webbing through the soil. Nearby were blood-orange flowers on stalks as big around as Lucha's wrist. Their color was a warning of the poison they contained.

But in their roots, Lucha felt it. A cleansing process. A purifying one.

These flowers were cleaning the soil. Removing traces of metals and toxins. Restoring life. They didn't thrive on decay, they filtered it. Made room for more sensitive plants to take root and grow . . .

Lucha carried her sister's body to the place where they

clustered and laid her among them. She did not think of white vines. Of the mushrooms. Of the dead or the dying. Instead, she put her hands on the ground and beseeched the roots beneath it.

Save her. Please.

The roots remained still. They did not want pleas, or gratitude. They obeyed the call of the gift. And Lucha was too afraid to call them.

But could she coax the Olvida free of her sister's veins? Show the roots where to find it? Give them a taste and trust their nature to do the rest? It was worth a try.

Lucha closed her eyes, listening. The mushrooms had wanted all the decay in her mind. But Olvida's whispers asked for something different. Something infinitely more precious.

The drug fed on memory. Life. That was what it was drawn to. What it stole.

Tentatively, Lucha offered it her history in Robado. The image of the forest's edge. The name of the girl beneath her hands and the way her arms folded when she was being especially stubborn. The Olvida in Lis's blood was ravenous, and Lucha felt the trickle of her memories become a stream in response.

She brought forth more, as quickly as she could call them: Alán, a boy again, his gap-toothed smirk as he beckoned her into the trees. The tattooed woman, breasts bared to the taunting crowd. Lucha's first glimpse of a sombralado. The fear tunneling into her bones. The weight of the pagos in her pocket.

From the scars on Lis's arms, a pale green liquid beaded up. The Olvida was responding. Lucha watched as, curious and searching, the first of the flower's pale roots broke the surface.

Lucha plunged back into her memories. Paz's fingertips, pressing cool against her cheek as she stitched. The little blue flower cart, snow-white burro hitched to its front.

Salvador's slim figure against the dark metal of her cell.

The pale, stringy roots found Lis's scarred arm. They probed until they found the place where the toxin was oozing from her wounds. Slowly, they began to wrap around her arm, covering the scars. It was working.

Sweat collected at Lucha's hairline. She pressed her fingertips deeper into Lis's chest, a sob building up in her own. She had to make sure the drug was purged entirely. That every last bit was absorbed by the roots.

Lucha swayed on the spot. She could not fail her sister again. This time, there would be no bargain to save her. No second chance.

She reached for the most potent of her memories now. Her father's face. The sound of his laugh.

Her mother, then. Eyes bright and lucid, dancing in the tiny kitchen. Spinning Lucha until she was dizzy, then catching her with a kiss on her cheek. The lullabies she'd sung when nightmares kept them both awake.

My darling, my sweetheart . . .

The Olvida made for all this remembering like a dowsing rod to water, escaping through the one door open to it. The roots of the vivid blooms wound tighter, drinking every drop. Cleansing Lis's blood.

Exhaustion threatened to take Lucha. The Olvida was nearly gone. But when she looked down at her sister she cried out in despair. The roots had taken her arm, fingertips to shoulders, and were winding around her neck.

"No!" Lucha cried. Lis's blood was clean, but the roots were not human. They continued to feed. Lucha dug her fingernails frantically into the cocoon of plant matter that had once been her sister's arm.

Above her, the orange petals of the strange flowers glowed vivid green. Transformed by this new poison.

Roots snapped, loosened, only to be replaced by more. Lucha's arms ached. Her fingernails left scratches on Lis's skin as she tried desperately to keep the roots from overwhelming her. Choking her.

The forest obeys the call . . .

But she couldn't command them. Not when she had seen what using the power could do. She felt the shadows within her surging. She could not trust herself to heal.

Then suddenly, when Lucha's despair threatened to blot out every last memory, she was no longer alone. A second set of hands tore at the roots, exposing Lis's pale flesh. Paz's eyes were strangely unfocused, sleeves rolled up over sepia wrists. Her lips moved soundlessly, as if in prayer.

There was no time to question. The burden of fear was lighter now, and Lucha tore faster than ever. Soon the ground was littered with stringy, pale roots. Inert. Cut off from the source that gave them life.

And then Lis was free. Breathing. Her blood was clean.

Lucha hauled Lis as far as she could from the sinister flowers. They peered indifferently down at the scene. Sweat soaked Lucha's clothes. Even now that her sister was safe, the world was slow to come back into focus.

When it did, Lis's eyes were closed, her brow furrowed. Her heart beat wildly inside her chest. A hummingbird's wing. The scales of fate weighed her strength. Was there enough of her left, after the ordeal of her detoxification, to survive on her own?

Minutes passed like hours. Like years. Lucha was aware of Paz nearby.

Lis's heartbeat slowed and strengthened. Her breath evened out.

She was alive. Lucha had not failed her.

The relief was like an animal trapped in Lucha's chest. It was too strong to take on alone. Paz was there, a look of awe on her tearstained cheeks, and Lucha did not wonder, did not doubt, only threw herself against this girl's chest and wept.

Paz's arms encircled her without hesitation. A strong and steady pressure that kept the creature at bay. In time its thrashing subsided, but Paz did not let go. Lucha could feel the other girl's heartbeat against her own chest.

To feed the Olvida in her sister's blood, Lucha had dropped

all her defenses. She felt terribly light and free. Paz's arms drifted from their bracing position against her back to a gentler one. Lower. Movement so slow it made room for an answer.

Lucha tipped her chin back, feeling their cheeks graze each other. Eyes met, dropped, met again. She had never felt more painfully present in her skin. Her pulse pounded at the tip of every nerve.

Paz released her, moving a hand to her cheek. Lucha leaned into her fingerprints—not cool this time, but feverish against her skin.

All around them, the forest held its breath.

But there, creeping above the collar of Paz's shirt, were those branches again. Proof of the futility of it all. Lucha dropped her arms. "I'm sorry," she said.

Paz shook her head, as if to dismiss the need for an apology. The tension faded between them, leaving something melancholy in the air that refused to fade long after they'd parted.

They didn't rest for long before Lis awoke in earnest.

From her first groan, Lucha was abruptly and painfully aware. She had dreamed that Paz stole away as she slept, but the girl was beside her, already alert.

"Do you want me to stay?" she asked when Lucha met her eyes.

Yes, said Lucha's traitorous heart. "That's all right," she said instead. "There's a lot to explain, and . . ."

"It might be easier to talk without the presence of a stranger."

Lucha allowed her brief silence to speak for her.

"I'll find us something to eat."

"Thank you." Formal. A little awkward, but that couldn't be helped. *A means to an end*, Lucha reminded herself. It didn't matter if the places they'd touched still burned. Nothing mattered now but Lis.

As Paz departed, Lucha turned toward her sister.

Lis's eyelids fluttered. Her hands cast around at her sides, coming up empty. "Lucha . . . ?"

"I'm here, Lis. I'm here." She knelt beside her sister's wasted body and took her hand. It was warm. A good sign, even if Paz wasn't here to read it.

As Lucha waited for Lis to return to her, her thoughts raced. She replayed that night at Pecado. The last night her sister had seen her. Lucha had spoken in a strange tongue— she'd strangled the life from two guards. In the moment she'd bought them, Lis had been too afraid of her to escape.

Lucha had been so fixated on getting Lis healthy, getting her to safety, that she'd forgotten to worry about the moment now barreling toward her. The moment when she'd have to account for all she'd done to get them here.

Not to mention the bargain she'd made in the aftermath. The one that would free them from the clutches of this awful drug for good.

Lis had never liked having her choices made for her—even before she'd been fed a steady diet of Alán's lies about who Lucha was. *What* she was . . .

Lis moaned, her eyes opening, closing, opening again. In a moment of panic, Lucha considered turning away. She was afraid to see fear in her sister's eyes. The fear that had nearly been the end of them . . .

"Lucha?" Lis's voice was gravelly, and it wavered. Somehow, it was more childlike for all this. Lucha stepped forward as her sister struggled to sit. "Lucha?"

"I'm here," she said. She squeezed Lis's hand. "I'm here, and you're safe."

Lis's eyes were wide when they found Lucha's—lighting

only briefly before they darted around the clearing. "They told me you were dead."

"They lied. I never would have let go until I knew you were safe. It just . . . it took me some time to get us out of there."

There were new lines bracketing Lis's mouth. Combined with the white streak in her hair, the weary slump to her shoulders, she looked as if she'd aged ten years in the time Lucha had been imprisoned.

But her eyes were still a girl's. There was hope.

"Where are we?" Her gaze darted around the clearing again, as if trying to make sense of it.

"We're a couple of days' journey from the city now," Lucha told her, as gently as she could. The very air seemed charged with anticipation. Any minute, Lis would remember. Would blame Lucha for everything. "I'm taking you somewhere safe."

Lis's eyes widened in fear. "We can't! I have to go back." Her arm shot reflexively to the place where the newest cuts were just beginning to heal. "I can't . . . Lucha, you have to take me back."

"We can't go back. We can only go forward now."

Lis's face looked like a tiny animal's, searching for a predator whose scent was already on the air. "If I don't go back I'll die. He said . . . he said if I missed a dose it would kill me. Lucha, please. Please, take me back." She began to cry, bitter, hopeless tears. Nothing like her childhood tantrums. "I don't want to die."

Lucha scooted closer, wrapping her arm around Lis's thin, shaking shoulders. "You're not going to die," she said fiercely.

151

"I will." Lis's sobs were racking, awful things. "I'll never get away. Never."

Moving in front of her sister, Lucha took Lis's face between her hands. "Look at me, Lis," she said. And when she couldn't: "*Look at me.*"

Finally, Lis's tear-filled gaze met her own.

"I need you to listen to me: It's been two days, Lis. Your blood is clean. Whatever he gave you, we fought it together. You're free."

Slowly, the words seemed to sink in. The shaking stopped. "It's really gone?" Lis asked.

Lucha nodded. The silence stretched between them until all the specters from before Lis had woken returned.

"You must hate me," Lucha said, voice breaking on the last word.

"Why?" Lis whispered.

"Because this is all my fault." Lucha turned away, overwhelmed by her failures. "I left you, Lis. And I couldn't bring Mom back, and I tried to save you, I did *horrible* things to save you, but in the end *I* did this to you. And now you're on the run with me even though you've done nothing, *nothing* wrong. All I've ever done is—"

Before she could continue, arms were encircling her shoulders, Lis pressing her frail body into Lucha's. Surprising her into silence. "You saved me," she whispered into Lucha's hair. "You saved me again."

Lis was crying once more, but the hopelessness was gone. And Lucha was crying too, clinging to her sister, so alive despite everything. It would be worth it, Lucha knew, to eliminate the thing that had done this to them. The *people* who had done this.

When the time came to destroy Olvida, she'd do it gladly, no matter what price Salvador demanded.

After a while, the reunion took its toll. Lis slid into a half sleep and Lucha lowered her to the ground, shirt stained with tears, heart aching and full.

She was just straightening up when Paz reappeared. She'd made a basket of her skirt to carry roots and mushrooms, and her legs were visible beneath, all the way up to the curves of her thighs.

Lucha turned away with some effort.

"How is she?" Paz asked.

Lucha wanted to tell her everything. To break down and weep again for all Lis had been through, and all she would face now. She wanted to lean on this girl, who had stood so steady for her. But she couldn't. Not without lying. Not without hurting them both.

"She'll be all right once we get where we're going."

A silence, full of all she had wanted to say. Paz arranged her bounty on a rock and settled her skirt. "Lucha," she said. "Can we—"

"Would you mind examining Lis while I get the food prepared?" Lucha cut in. "There's no time to waste with this storm on the way."

Paz's eyes showed her hurt, but Lucha turned away from this, too. A little sting now, to prevent devastation all too soon.

A few raindrops scattered the ground between them. It was time to get moving. To find better shelter than the feeble one they'd built together.

With Lis awake, travel should have been much swifter. When they set out after a long, cold night in a shallow cave, Lucha expected they'd make the lightning-struck tree by the following day.

The forest, it seemed, had other plans.

They'd been traveling west from Robado for three days now. The going had been difficult, but not impossible. But whatever cease-fire the forest had previously granted, it seemed to have withdrawn.

The farther in they delved, the less human influence there was. No paths. No convenient glades. This was true wildness in a way Lucha had never experienced.

A part of her thrilled to witness it.

Another part of her recognized that it simply did not want them here.

Whenever Lucha found a promising way forward, it was blocked within yards. When she tried to force her way, to hack at thorned vines or kick nests of brambles twice her height, the forest fought back. Again and again, she cut down obstacles only to swear they had regrown the moment she turned aside.

For Lucha, the rejection only doubled her determination. Salvador had sent her west. Her quest to destroy Olvida had sent her west. She *would* go west.

But determination wasn't enough. After spending a sweaty, cursing quarter of an hour hacking at a cluster of densely woven vines, Lucha threw down her knife, groaning in frustration before flopping onto the ground.

Lis was exhausted from the travel. Her face was wan and pinched, though she refused to complain. More than once, Lucha had seen her wince. Seen her gaze travel into the underbrush, where undoubtedly there was Pensa to be found.

During these moments, Paz would engage her in light conversation. Steer her along the slow, hacking paths Lucha made.

But the hours of forging through appeared to have come to an unceremonious end. These vines blocked the only possible way toward the lightning-struck tree. They hung from a canopy Lucha couldn't see, and their ends had burrowed into the ground, forming roots that held fast even when she dug and yanked and kicked and swore.

"Don't suppose your *goddess* has any stories about how to hack through indestructible vines," Lucha grumbled as they made camp a frustratingly short distance from where they'd begun.

"And here I thought you didn't trust her," Paz said. She glanced at Lucha sideways from the small fire pit she was surrounding with rocks. This deep in, among trees this densely packed, there was no risk of the light traveling more than a few hundred feet. They'd hear the Robadans before those bastards ever saw the light.

"I don't trust her," Lucha said. "But I'm desperate."

"You could always try asking nicely."

It had been a joke. But the stirring of the leaves grew stronger. The whispers swirled around Lucha. Asking for her attention. Her acknowledgment.

She shut them out forcefully, but it was harder this deep in. Whatever the source of this place's primal power was, they were drawing nearer to it. Lucha took deep breaths. She heard Salvador's words in her mind as the forest tugged at her resolve.

Are you a root, girl? Are you a leaf?

"I'm not," she muttered under her breath.

A few feet away, at the base of a trunk twice as wide as Lucha's former kitchen, Lis was sitting with her knees drawn up to her chin. Her eyes were wide, unfocused. Lucha thought she was fighting her own battle of wills.

"Hungry?" Lucha asked. She offered Lis a handful of berries Paz had deemed safe to eat, but Lis only shook her head. "You should get some rest. We'll have to try again at first light."

Lis nodded, but her eyes didn't focus. After a few long minutes she curled up at the base of the tree and closed her eyes. Lucha clenched her fists, helpless. The only thing that could cure her was time.

"Are you tired?" Paz asked, settling in beside the fire.

Lucha shook her head. She was physically exhausted, but she'd never felt less like sleeping. The puzzle of the forest gnawed at her, making her restless.

"You?" she asked.

"A little," Paz admitted. "But I can take the first watch if you want to rest. Or . . ." She trailed off. "We could just talk?"

Awkwardness stole in like a chilly mist. Talk had come so easily before. Sitting beside the fire, bellies full. That night Lucha had told Paz more than she'd ever told anyone. Things about Robado. Olvida. Her mother . . .

But tonight, for so many reasons she'd been over and over in her mind, she couldn't.

"Do you think Lis will be all right?" Lucha asked. The only safe topic. Lis's care, after all, was the reason Lucha had allowed Paz to accompany them.

"Her color has improved," Paz said. "She seems to have more energy. Physically, she's doing fine." She paused. "The . . . cravings can be intense at this stage. It'll take a while before they subside."

"How long?" Lucha asked before she could think better of it.

"It depends. Sometimes a week. A month. Sometimes they never do."

Silence crept back in. The cheerful cracking of the fire did not detract from it.

"What can I do to get you to trust me?"

It was the last thing Lucha had expected. Paz's eyes were steady on hers across the fire, but Lucha could not meet them. Not when the only answer she could give was so dissatisfying.

"I trust you with Lis," she said simply. "That's something."

"It is," Paz agreed. "And I appreciate it. But . . . we're out here alone. We're facing things neither of us can predict or control. Isn't it better if we can depend on each other?" She tugged her sleeves down. A nervous habit. "I just . . . I want to know you, Lucha. I want you to know me."

These words reached for a soft place within Lucha. A place that had rarely been seen by anyone. She wanted to say yes. She wanted to tell Paz everything.

"Give me time," she said instead, looking away. Pretending for a moment that what Paz asked for wasn't impossible to give.

"I will." Paz leaned forward. The fire flushed her cheeks. "I'll be here. When you're ready."

Lucha wondered how Paz would feel about saying these things when she learned the truth of Lucha's bargain and the monster she'd made it with.

"Why don't you get some rest," Lucha said, when the tension crackled louder than the fire. "I'll take first watch."

Paz sat for a long moment, as if hoping Lucha would change her mind. The silence stretched. The flames died down.

"Good night, Lucha," she said at last, getting to her feet.

Paz's eyes were closed in minutes, but it was a long time before her body relaxed into sleep. Lucha, for her part, felt more restless than ever.

When she was sure Lis and Paz were soundly asleep, she got to her feet, padding on bare soles to the wall of vines. This time, she didn't bother with the knife.

With her feet in the moss and her hands tangled in the vines, Lucha closed her eyes and followed her thoughts like they were vines of their own. Olvida had destroyed Lucha's family. The entire city of Robado. Olvida was the reason Lis cried out in her sleep, and traveled with dark circles beneath her eyes.

Olvida was the enemy. Lucha had believed no price was too high to destroy it. So never knowing this beautiful girl was one more offering. Hadn't others paid more and worse?

But her sacrifice wouldn't be worth a thing if she couldn't get past this wall of obstinate greenery.

The forest obeys the call of the gift, Salvador had said. She almost expected him to appear here. To instruct her in that wry, condescending way of his. But no one came. Lucha was alone as the forest's voice began to fill her mind like the buzzing of bees.

It was the vines who pulled on her first. Lucha recoiled instinctively from their intrusion, but she found she could withstand it. *I am not a vine,* she told them. *But I'm here.* How long she stood still, experiencing the rising, falling music of the forest, she didn't know. The vines danced. The roots sang their low, mourning song. The leaves chattered above.

Weaving through it all, the electric pulse of mycelium webbing. Connecting every disparate piece of this incredible biome. Defining its edges. Giving it a language.

As long as she stood, feeling her way into this world (so much and so little like her own), Lucha never detected the sinister force she had expected to find at the heart of its power. Neither did she find something shining and pure that could transform her into a champion the way the stories claimed.

What she found was much more terrifying than that. It was potential. Ready for the call of the gift to shape it. To command it.

To reach the tree, the whispers seemed to say, would require more of Lucha than she'd been willing to give so far.

The forest obeys.

Lucha closed her eyes. She slid her hands between the tangle of vines, feeling the rough and the smooth of them. The old and the new. Last night she had been afraid to use the gift, afraid she might kill the girl she was trying to save. But tonight there was no body beneath her hands. No fragile heart. Just vines, Lucha thought. And she pictured them parting. *Willed* them to part . . .

The buzzing stopped. The whispers. Enfolded in the most perfect silence, Lucha waited.

When the forest allowed her through at last, every vine was still green. In the moon-drenched glade on the other side, Lucha was more herself than she'd ever been. More sure. More alive.

Her destination couldn't be far now. They would find out what came after, at last.

Lis stayed close to Lucha as they passed through the vines at the first light of dawn. Her sister's steps were steady, her grip strong, but her eyes still looked inward. Fighting perhaps the only battle Lucha could not fight alongside her.

Paz followed close behind. She looked up at the parted curtain of vines (which only yesterday would not yield) with a mixture of awe and trepidation. Did she think this a miracle, too? Lucha wondered. Another blessing from her goddess?

Lucha forged ahead. The forest was no longer against them. Or perhaps it was Lucha who had acquiesced. When the wood opened paths, she took them. When it presented obstacles, she understood their warning, diverting her route. Trusting that she would eventually make her way back to the westward road.

In this way, they traveled more quickly than they had since the start. In fact, they made twice the progress of the day before by the time the sun crested the trees.

Lis's energy appeared to be flagging, but she didn't complain, and Lucha knew better than to coddle. Paz had been quiet all morning. Perhaps it was for the best.

But the deeper they moved into the forest, the less space there was in Lucha's mind for concerns like these.

Just ahead, her surroundings seemed to whisper. *Just a little farther.*

Any minute, Lucha thought, they would round a corner or break through a dense thicket and there it would be. The lightning-struck tree. She could almost see Salvador, pale and determined, leaning against it. Ready for what came next.

"Lucha," Paz gasped. She and Lis trailed behind.

Lucha barely heard her. They would rest when they had

reached it. When their job had been done. When Lis was safe, when Los Ricos were destroyed, when her mother . . .

"Lucha, *stop!*"

Lis, this time. With some effort, Lucha remembered herself. She was a body. Separate from the forest surrounding her. *I am not a root. I am not a leaf.*

"Are you all right?" she asked Lis. She heard the strangeness of her own voice. A double timbre like the one that had preceded the deaths of Pecado's guards.

Lis didn't answer. Nor did Paz. Impatient, Lucha turned to face them, seeing the source of their alarm at last.

Behind them, filling in gaps between the trees that had not been there moments before, seven pairs of luminous eyes emerged from the dark.

14

Paz and Lis caught up to Lucha, panting, exhausted. Together, they looked ahead. A moment before, there had been a path, leading them westward through a dense thicket of trees. It was gone. In its place was a small clearing, glowing golden in the late-afternoon light.

Lucha felt dizzy with the strangeness of it. Vines parting, paths widening—these were subtle-enough mysteries to digest. But this transformation was so complete that it expelled Lucha at once from the understanding she'd reached with the forest. It left her alone and nauseated with dread.

She didn't have to approach the glade's far edge to know there was no way out.

So fixated on her destination, Lucha had allowed the forest to corner them. It seemed impossibly naïve now, that she had believed them to be aligned in purpose. The only question was what machinations the forest had been working *while* she believed it.

"I'm sorry," Lucha said quietly. Her companions stood on

either side of her, shoulders pressed to hers. "I thought . . ." But how could she possibly explain?

They watched in silence as the creatures entered the clearing. They moved with the slow, regal pace of predators that had no equal.

Cats, Lucha realized—caught between terror and awe. They had piercing green eyes that glowed with the light in the clearing. Slate-gray fur, a black stripe down each back. Tufts of fur stood straight up from the tips of their ears, making them look sharply pointed. Alert.

Had Lucha been brave enough to stand beside one, its head would have been as high as her waist.

Shocked out of her connection with the wood, Lucha could not feel their intentions in their footfalls, but they did not seem poised for attack. They surrounded the three awestruck girls, like a tribunal prepared to make their final judgment on a matter of great consequence.

"What's going on?" Lis whispered. Lucha could see the whites of her eyes all the way around. "Are we about to get eaten?"

"No." The answer came from Paz. She did not, apparently, care to elaborate on how she knew. Her eyes were fixed on the cat directly in front of her. Where Lucha expected fear, there was something infinitely more mysterious. A kind of desperate longing she recognized from the greenhouse a lifetime ago . . .

"Your friend is kind of strange," Lis said under her breath.

Lucha was so relieved to hear Lis sounding like herself

that she momentarily forgot the danger. A reluctant giggle made its way past her lips.

The closest cat let out a low, warning growl.

Lucha turned back to Paz. "Do you know something about them?" she asked in an urgent voice. "About what's happening? Because if you do, now would be a great time to speak up."

Paz's eyes never left the cat in front of her. "They're compañeras," she whispered. "Here. Right in front of us. I never thought . . ."

She trailed off, but Lucha did not need to hear more. Goose bumps erupted across her arms, though the afternoon was warm.

"The companions of the goddess?" Lis asked. Her own features were touched with a fraction of Paz's wonder. "From the stories? But they aren't real . . ."

And yet here they were. No other explanation made sense. These were no common forest beasts, nor monsters like the sombralados. These intelligent, beautiful creatures were wreathed in divinity.

Was this what the forest had been steering her toward? Lucha couldn't help but wonder. She remembered her childhood fixation with the Bosque. The forbidden goddess. The hidden sanctuary where her acolytes supposedly still awaited their promised savior.

Did the forest want to show Lucha that the stories she'd believed had been true?

And what would it mean for her, for the path she had chosen, if they were?

As if in answer, the clearing seemed to grow more vivid. Gilded sunlight descended in loops and swirls. The moss at their feet sprouted tiny white flowers.

A gift. The word sprang unbidden into her mind. This was a glimpse into the world as it had been. As it could be. She wouldn't have been surprised to see the goddess herself step into this pool of light . . .

But it wasn't the goddess who appeared, when someone did. It was Salvador. And every one of the predators surrounding them bared their teeth.

"What's happening?" Lis asked, reaching back to grip Lucha's wrist. "Why are they angry?"

"I don't know," Lucha lied. "We need to stay very still."

Paz's gaze found hers, and in that moment the things Lucha had not told this girl were louder than anything she could have.

"You need to get out of here before they kill you." The urgency in Salvador's voice was a harsh contrast to his usual bored arrogance. "Do you want to get rid of Olvida or not? I promise you, if you stay here, everything we've done will be for nothing."

Lucha had never trusted Salvador. Had seen him since the start as a terrible means to a necessary end. But against the backdrop of this golden grove, with all her childhood hope stirring in her chest, she felt rebellion begin to bloom for the first time.

"Lucha?" Lis's voice was panicked. The hissing, growling beasts began to close in. "What do we do?"

"You do what I command," Salvador said. His words sparked with anger. His eyes bored into Lucha's like he had heard every one of her rebellious thoughts. "Leave this place by whatever means necessary. Before you have worse than cat scratches to contend with."

Beyond the creatures, in the direction they'd come from, the way was open. The steely glint in Salvador's eye said he knew it would be impossible for them to escape without bloodshed. He wanted her to prove her allegiance to him. To kill not just the creatures before her, but the hope they had brought into the glade with them.

Even riled by the malicious presence in their midst, the creatures were regal. More person than beast. Lucha could not make herself draw her knife. Not even if it meant breaking the bargain she had staked everything on . . .

"Lucha!" Lis's voice was sharp with fear. "Snap out of it! These things are going to kill us!"

Lucha did not respond. Could not. Her eyes were locked on Salvador's. A standoff, and everyone's life hanging in the balance.

I won't kill them, Lucha told herself. A promise. *And if he tries to force me, I'll find another way to do what I came here to do.*

The forest roared its agreement in her ears—no longer a whisper. A high wind tossed the branches above them. For the first time since Encadenar, Lucha could feel the weapons of the wood as if they were placed on a rack before her.

Not dust motes, this time. Not single spores. An entire

seething forest churning with life. Offering its power to her if only she dared to command it.

Lucha closed her eyes. A memory came to her. Salvador, his eyes livid and burning, swearing she would never be imprisoned. Never chained. *Let him taste his fear,* she thought. *Let him see that I read it in his voice.* She was no disobedient child, and she would show him now.

To the idea of confinement, the vines were drawn. Turning toward Lucha as if she were the rising sun. Reaching for her. Her instincts (or her fear) screamed to close the connection. But Lucha did not.

Opening her eyes, she saw the forest bending toward her. The vines brushed her fingertips. They asked her where she would send them. What she would bring about with their sacrifice.

Bind him, she thought. *Chain him.*

And they did.

But no sooner had the vines encircled Salvador than an earthshaking roar shattered the clearing. His eyes smoldered. The heart of a flame. And the flame caught in Lucha's chest, sending her to her knees. The vines fell lifeless to the forest floor. The giddy, electric connection had closed, and Lucha was alone. Alone and burning.

Lucha scrabbled at her chest for flames that were not there. The agony went on and on.

She screamed. The pain was unbearable. A white-hot

poker pushing into everything soft and vital. It began right in the place where she had first felt the pull of her power. At the place where her agreement with El Sediento had been sealed in that cell a lifetime ago.

He wouldn't stop, she realized. Not until she had done as he demanded.

Perhaps not even then.

Lis was on her knees beside Lucha, tugging at her arm, yelling something unintelligible. Paz rummaged in her rucksack, not knowing there was nothing there that could save them.

Salvador's words echoed in the clearing, unheard by anyone else.

"I've played your little game. I've shown you why you need me." The pain intensified. Tenfold. Then a hundred. "Let me show you now, what happens when you defy me. When you attempt to *chain me*."

She would die here. She knew it the way she knew rain was wet and sugar was sweet. No body, weak and human as hers was, could withstand this kind of agony. Not for long.

This torment was a dark tunnel with no end. No light. It would go on until there was nothing for it to feed on.

And then, as suddenly as it had begun, the pain was gone. Lucha's body trembled. A single leaf in a rattling wind. The glade was fuzzy in her vision, splotches of green and gold. Someone's hands were on her cheeks. Cool, like a drink from a spring . . .

Lucha pushed herself up, blinking hard until her surroundings clarified themselves. Lis and Paz were still on either side of her, but the creatures that had seemed so hell-bent on destroying them seconds ago had gone.

Her first thought was that Salvador had taken matters into his own hands. Lucha cast around wildly for any sign of him, for the carnage she imagined he'd make of these noble animals given half a chance.

But Salvador was nowhere to be seen.

Head pounding, Lucha turned to face her companions, not at all sure what she would say. What she *could* say. The silence stretched on as she imagined what it must have looked like to them. Lucha's focus on something they could not see. The screams, though no assailant was visible.

"Are you all right?"

"Lucha, what happened?"

But how could she answer when she was still reeling from Salvador's punishment? Still seeing him in every shadow, waiting for the fire to return . . .

Only moments ago, Lucha had been so sure she was on the path toward destroying Olvida. That the bargain she'd made with *him* was the only way to accomplish that goal.

But now the agony of his retribution echoed in her chest. He had been slippery, certainly. His charisma an obvious veneer. Was *this* what lurked beneath it? Not a sly trickster spinning double-edged promises, but a monster, demanding complete obedience. Willing to torture, and even kill, to achieve his end.

What was the next thing he would demand? Lucha wondered. And to what lengths would he truly go if she refused to carry it out?

"Lucha?" Lis asked. Her voice trembled.

Paz quieted her. "Let's give her a minute. Come with me." They moved away, but not far, and the feeling of expectation was still heavy in the air. Paz and Lis had followed Lucha here. Would follow her farther still.

But where to lead them now?

The lightning-struck tree had been a destination from the start, pulling her onward. The place where he was waiting. The place where Olvida would be destroyed. But the fire had burned away these delusions. It would not be as simple as that, and she knew it now. The tree would be the place where he expected her to fulfill her end of the bargain.

What would the cost be now that she'd defied him?

This is what you get for treating with a monster, she told herself. For underestimating the stories. For grasping at power without understanding the consequences.

Around her, the forest was quiet. But not inert. It waited, like Paz and Lis, for Lucha to decide. But still she lay on the ground, heart hammering, curled around the place where he had hurt her.

The light of Lucha's desire to destroy Olvida had not dimmed. It beckoned her on, even now, in her most uncertain moment. She saw the fires Salvador had shown her. Robado, burning. Production ceased. A new world waiting to bloom.

She couldn't do it alone. But if she was going to honor her

bargain with Salvador, she needed to stay strong. She couldn't fall apart. Eventually she would need to make some demands of her own.

Lucha pushed herself up to her feet, arms trembling. Paz and Lis were beside her in seconds.

"We need to find food," she said with some effort. "And then we press on. West." Lucha held out a hand and her sister squeezed it. "On the way, Paz, I need you to tell me everything you know about those creatures and the lore of the forest goddess." The compañeras had looked at Salvador like an enemy. The forest had obeyed her when she called it to bind him.

If worse came to worst, Salvador's foes could be the only friends she had left.

Paz looked surprised. "Of course. I'm not sure what good it will do, but I'll tell you everything I know."

"Thank you," Lucha said. She took care not to hold Paz's gaze for long. This skirmish in the clearing had only been further proof of the fathomless distance between them. Paz, face turned to the light. Lucha, writhing in the shadows.

Their separation was close at hand. Lucha did her best to pretend that this knowledge didn't cause its own kind of agony.

15

Every muscle in Lucha's body ached. Her bones were weary. After half an hour of foraging they had nothing more than a few berries. There was nothing to hunt. Not even a squirrel rustled the underbrush.

"We'll do the best we can with this," Paz said bracingly. Her concerned eyes returned again and again to Lucha's face. "I'm sure we'll find more as we travel. Don't worry."

Lis stayed close to Lucha. She asked no questions, though the mystery of Lucha's screaming agony must have plagued them both. Were they giving her space? Were they afraid of her? She couldn't ask. Not until she was prepared to answer the questions that came after.

They walked back to the clearing, an air of malaise hanging around them like fog. They would eat their meager meal and they would go on, Lucha told herself. They had all pushed on through worse.

Up ahead, Paz gasped as she entered the clearing, shaking Lucha from her gloomy thoughts.

"What is it?" she asked wearily. Expecting the worst.

Paz didn't answer. She didn't have to. As Lucha joined her between two trees, the source of the other girl's amazement became immediately clear. In the center of the clearing where the compañeras had surrounded them, where Salvador had scorched Lucha's heart, a single shaft of sunlight illuminated a bright-white hare.

"Shh," Lucha whispered to Lis. "Don't startle it."

"It's a sign," Paz said in her own tearful undertone. "The white hare is a symbol of the goddess."

Lucha's weakened body knew the hare was their best chance at recovering their strength before pushing west, but she couldn't bring herself to move toward it. Even the thought of killing it turned her stomach. She watched it instead, trying to draw a different kind of sustenance from its beauty against the dark backdrop of the wood.

The hare twitched its nose. Its dark eyes stared straight at them. It did not appear to be afraid. They stood suspended for an endless moment until at the animal's feet, the ground broke, and a thorned vine crept out toward the light.

"No!" Lucha said, instinct sending her sprinting forward. But before she could reach the hare, the vine had reared up like a snake and plunged through the creature's heart.

Lucha arrived just in time to cradle its impossibly soft body in her hands. It was nearly three times the size of the scrawny rabbits that had made up their first forest dinner. Its heart fluttered for a brief moment before it fell still.

Silent tears coursed down Lucha's cheeks. It was all too

much. The parting vines, the compañeras. Salvador. Now this innocent creature, struck down in a moment of peace.

Footsteps, on either side of her. Paz's hands lifted the hare from Lucha's. On her face, when Lucha could bear to look at it, was a beatific smile. "It's a blessing," she said. Her eyes sparkled. "The goddess is offering us aid."

Lucha's tears dried as Paz took the hare to a nearby stump. Her hands moved reverently over its lifeless body as she prepared it to be eaten. Lis's eyes were so big they nearly swallowed her face. Could it be true? Lucha wondered.

Her nature was to distrust, of course. But what other explanation could there be?

Paz built a fire in no time. It crackled merrily as the meat cooked. The smell sent saliva flooding into Lucha's mouth. Not the smell of the gamy rabbits they'd caught their first night, but something infinitely richer.

When they gathered to eat, Paz looked skyward. Lucha thought she might say some kind of prayer, but when she opened her mouth it was not to speak. It was to sing.

Her voice floated upward toward the treetops, husky and curved like the very first time Lucha had ever heard it. It had intoxicated her then. But now, with the knowledge of Paz she had gathered through this journey together, it was sweeter still.

The song went on, the words in a language Lucha did not speak. Still, she felt she understood. The threads of music wove through the grass at their feet. Reached for the branches above them. The song stirred something in Lucha that was far beyond her feelings for Paz.

Something like the forest's whispers when they called to her.

A thank-you, she knew somehow. And a promise, too.

When the song was finished at last, the final note seemed to hang on the air for a long time. Lucha bit into the meat, letting her own silent gratitude flood her. The goddess, if she was truly weaving these threads, had every reason to leave Lucha on her own.

But she hadn't.

In the stories, it was always good versus evil. In life, things were rarely that simple.

Lost as she was in her thoughts, Lucha's meal was half gone before she glanced up to find herself alone.

She noted this without much concern, continuing to slurp until even the marrow was gone from the hare's bones. Everything around her felt hazy and distant. Lucha got to her feet and stretched. Was there something she was supposed to be doing?

Lis, said a distant voice in her head. *Paz.* They had been here, hadn't they? Just a minute ago. Paz had been singing, the notes of her song weaving through the trees . . .

But this place was much larger, and the trees here were different. They shone as if lit from the inside. Their otherworldly foliage was almost translucent. Delicately spun gold.

The place was still in a way that felt intentional. A holy

kind of quiet. The sunlight filtered through the faded leaves, sending shimmering light scattering everywhere . . .

Into the silence, into Lucha's dreamy, drifting thoughts, came a sound. Some kind of cry. It was full of a despair that was no less profound for the clarity and beauty of it.

Lucha, thinking of Lis, made for the sound at once.

But it wasn't Lis she found when she drew closer. Nor Paz. Instead, there was a woman Lucha had never seen before. A beautiful woman, her sepia skin seeming to generate its own light. Light that rivaled the grove for brilliance. Her hair fell in inky waves down her back, her dress like shifting moonlight on a pond.

As Lucha approached, the woman cried into her hands, her face hidden from view.

"Are . . . you all right?" Lucha asked. Her tongue felt strange and heavy in her mouth.

The woman didn't respond. Didn't cease her musical sobbing. The wind kicked up, whistling hauntingly through the trees.

"I think we'd better leave," Lucha said, struggling to remember what she was doing. Where she was supposed to be . . . "It's not safe here." That much, she was sure of. But still the woman didn't look up, just continued to cry.

Short of physically pulling her to her feet, Lucha didn't see how she could help. She had no choice but to leave her behind.

She'd only made it a few yards when the temperature

dropped. The silvery grass at Lucha's feet began to shrivel and die. An unnatural night fell over the grove. Lucha froze. In the center of her chest, the skin was tingling. A memory of pain, or the anticipation of it.

Salvador. His name swam to the murky surface of her thoughts. The air tasted of him. If he was coming, Lucha thought, she needed to run. She'd barely escaped him alive last time.

The shadows deepened until Lucha couldn't see anything at all. Not the deathly white that spread through the trees. Not her own hand in front of her. Nothing but the woman, faintly glowing, still crying inconsolably into her hands.

And then, before Lucha could run—toward her or away— *he* was there. Pale and thin as a sliver of bone, wreathed in the shadows that cloaked a sombralado's wings. Lucha's body went rigid with fear.

She reached out to the forest, knowing it would not be enough. It didn't answer. The woods around her were as cold and lifeless as stone. Their power could not help Lucha here, even if she could surrender to it.

I'm sorry, Lis, she thought as the cold and the shadows threatened to overtake her. He was close now. Any moment the pain would begin. Any moment.

He drew level with her. She closed her eyes tightly. But then, another miracle: he passed without a word. Lucha opened her eyes, relieved for the split second it took her to realize what he was doing instead.

He made for the crying woman with swift, purposeful

steps. She had not looked up, even to notice the dark. She would be no match for him. Lucha knew she had been given a reprieve. That she needed to use it to put as much distance between Salvador and herself as she could . . .

But she also knew what it felt like to be at his mercy. She couldn't let someone else go through it. Not while she was here to fight for them.

"Salvador!" Lucha called out, before she could convince herself to run.

The wind changed in the grove. Restless, now. He did not turn. Did not even slow.

"I defied you," she said, stumbling after him, tripping over roots in the dark. "I tried to bind you with the power you taught me to wield. You can't tell me you mean to let that go unpunished."

It was then that Lucha knew he could not hear her. Could not see her. The Salvador she knew would never let a slight against him pass. Whatever this place was, she was a spectator here.

The thought did nothing to comfort her.

Up ahead, the swirling shadow of him approached the glowing figure. He stopped, and the woman uncovered her face at last. They faced each other like something out of a storybook. The shadowed prince and the queen of light.

"I told you to be gone from this place." His voice was writhing snakes, a surging river of them. "Unless you were prepared to defend it."

"I know what you've done." Her voice was all musical

sorrow, mourning bells echoing for miles. "The devastation you've wrought. The people this will kill . . . Help me understand."

"What can I say? You taught me well."

"I did *not* teach you this." There was something beneath the weeping, this time. Something steel-hard and unyielding.

"You gave me life. Gave me power. You had to know you could not control the outcome of such an experiment."

"I taught you balance!" She wasn't crying now. She stepped toward him. "The equilibrium at the foundation of this world and all the power in it. You refused to learn."

"It was a faulty lesson. My power does not grow things. It does not nurture, or nourish, or feed. It only destroys. You could have been my balance, brought life to the decay as was intended. But you've always been too weak." He spat the last word.

Lucha watched, equal parts confused and awestruck. Was she seeing into Salvador's past? Who was this weeping teacher who had tried to save him? What would—or *had*—become of her?

"The balance exists within each of us," she insisted. "Your unwillingness to see that created this monstrosity. You have pursued your own power above all. You have forgotten your duty."

"*Your* duty," he said, dismissive. Scornful. "A mantle you hoped I would take up. I have made a different choice."

"An evil choice." It pained the woman to say this, Lucha

could see it in the heaviness that settled on her shoulders. "A choice that threatens all things living."

"Kill me, then." A hiss; the tide of snakes returned. "If you're strong enough. But remember: You created me. You taught me. And then you allowed me to surpass you. Failed to hold me in check as I have held you. Your precious balance was upset by your *weakness*, not my strength."

The tears were back, sparkling in the light from the woman's skin. They no longer made her look weak. "I value the lives I create," she said. "I value yours still. Let me help you. Let me teach you."

"Death is part of life," Salvador said. He moved toward the woman once more.

"But life is so much more than only death."

"You've drawn your line," he said, impatient. "And I mine. You knew what to expect when you came here tonight. Defend yourself or die. *Kill me*, or die."

Lucha was frozen in anticipation—even though she knew the outcome. Salvador would not die. He would live to horrify generations of Robadan children. To stalk a hunter through the forest at night. To bend her to his will with promises of vengeance. With torture and pain.

The woman pressed her palms together. The light emanating from her grew brighter. "Goodbye, my son," she said, her voice full of sorrow.

"Goodbye, Mother."

Mother . . .

Lucha could not have said whether they fought for an hour, or a year. Light pushed against shadow. Shadow swallowed light. Mother against son in this haunted place that would never be the same when they were done.

In the end, Salvador howled from within a glowing prism. It looked like honey, or amber, and there were no tears on the woman's face as she lowered it into the earth. Lower, and lower, and lower until the earth closed over it. Trapping him beneath it.

His words came back to Lucha now. His vicious anger at being confined.

As Lucha watched, from the place where his prison had been buried, a horrible nothingness spread. It swallowed everything in its path. Every blade of grass was white and brittle. Every creature a pile of bones.

In the end there was no life left here but the woman's. She lowered herself once more to the ground, the salt of her tears watering that which would never grow again.

At the place where he was buried stood a tree much taller than the rest. A giant, split in half. It appeared to have been struck by lightning—but now Lucha knew better. No simple lightning could have killed this majestic elder.

Only a monster could have done that.

16

Groaning, Lucha found herself on the ground. Her head throbbed. Her stomach tossed like an angry sea. A restless buzzing seemed to fill her chest cavity and spread through every vein.

She wrapped her arms around her chest. She shivered, though the evening was warm.

"Lucha?"

Fingers on her cheek. Cool. She kept her eyes shut tightly as the memories returned: the hare. The song. The vision she'd seen—Salvador's mother. Her tears. The fight that had gone on and on.

"Lucha?"

A pair of burning eyes. A tree, split in two, jagged end piercing the sky.

The buzzing grew louder. A mouth full of vicious teeth seemed to open wide at Lucha's center. Hungry. *Craving . . .*

"You're on a sandy beach," came the voice again. There were fingers combing gently through her hair. Grounding her in her body. "You're lying in a hammock and it's swaying in a warm breeze."

It took a moment for the image to appear, but when it did Lucha clung to it like a lifeline.

"The sun is setting over the ocean. The sky is so wide. Orange and pink easing upward toward the lavender of twilight. The waves are rolling in, frothy at the top. They whisper on the sand."

Fingers massaged circles on Lucha's scalp. She could hear the waves. The yawning mouth closed, then disappeared.

"You lean over the hammock and trail your fingers through the sand. It's soft like velvet. Tiny grains cling to your fingertips. A world inside each one."

Lucha's heart slowed. Her breath came evenly. She unwrapped her arms from around her body and opened her eyes.

"Better?" asked Paz, peering down at Lucha, whose head was resting in her lap.

"Thank you," Lucha said. She straightened up, already missing the feeling of Paz's fingers in her hair.

Everything was back where it should be. The clearing. The fire, burning low. Even the stump where Paz had prepared the hare. It was almost as if none of it had ever happened. As if it had been a very strange dream.

"Are you all right?" Lucha asked. She brushed the dirt from her clothes. She chanced a look at Paz, who was still peering at her. A tangled mess of emotions warred in her expression. Concern. Wariness. The same longing that had been there the night Lis awoke. And last night, across the fire.

It was too much to process, armorless as Lucha was. Instead, she dropped her eyes, focusing on a bird's feather that clung to Paz's sleeve.

"I'm all right," Paz said. They got to their feet together. "I woke in the grass a few minutes ago. I saw . . . I saw you, Lucha. I saw us, and . . ."

She was interrupted by the sound of retching. A few feet away, Lis was bent over a scrubby bush, emptying the contents of her stomach.

Lucha ran to her, but a part of her stayed in that moment, waiting to hear what Paz had seen.

"What did you *feed* us?" Lis groaned, straightening up at last, wiping her mouth with a shaking hand. "Some goddess to go around poisoning people who sing her songs."

If she hadn't been so acutely aware of Paz in that moment, Lucha might not have seen the way her eyes widened. The way they darted back to the stump. To the fire.

Lis swayed on her feet before Lucha could make more of it, her eyes rolling. Lucha stepped forward to brace her.

"I'm fine," Lis said through gritted teeth. The circles that had ringed her eyes since Encadenar were darker now, her face pinched and pale. "It was just a dream, wasn't it?" She looked up at Lucha. "It wasn't true?" Her eyes flicked to Paz, then back to Lucha.

"No," Lucha assured her, thinking of her own vision. "Just a dream."

But Lis did not appear comforted, and Lucha didn't blame her. She could still see the weeping woman like she was here in the clearing.

Paz stepped forward then. She looked as if she was on the verge of confessing something, but before she could, a terrible scream split the sky.

A scream that could only have come from one nightmare creature. A scream Lucha knew all too well.

"No . . . ," she said, stepping in front of Lis. Her eyes were already scanning the sky. "It can't be. Not here . . ."

"What's happening?" Paz asked as Lis leaned heavily against Lucha. "What is it?"

"Something I hoped I'd left behind," Lucha muttered. The scream sounded again. Closer now. Around them the forest came alive again, awakening from the sacred hush that had held it in stillness. It rolled and writhed now in an anxious wave. As if it might get up and run, if only it could.

Lis clapped her hands over her ears and moaned. Paz kept her eyes fixed on Lucha, waiting for an explanation.

For the second time that day, Lucha found herself unable to give one. The sombralado's shadow passed over the grove, plunging them into darkness.

She could feel the bone blade strapped to her thigh. But this wasn't Robado, and she was not the girl she'd been when she last fought one of these monsters. She was no longer invisible.

No longer alone.

The sombralado proved her point by circling the glade. Zeroing in on the place where they stood. When it screamed

186

this time, the sound rattled Lucha's teeth. But she did not forget herself.

Instead, she surveyed the glade. The woods around them. The thing would land in no time, and it would be fight or flee. But Lis was fading; whatever vision had claimed her after their meal seemed reluctant to let go. Could she run fast enough? Could any of them?

Paz stared up with her mouth open wide. The compañeras seemed a lifetime ago. That had been Paz's forest—full of magic and wonder. This was Lucha's. The one she had always known.

"I can fight," she said as the massive creature's wingbeats stirred the leaves. "I can kill it. I've done it before."

If this revelation startled Paz, she didn't show it.

"You'll need to get her to safety." There was a lump in Lucha's throat, and she spoke the words around it. "As far away from here as you can." She swallowed, hard. "If anything happens to me—"

"*Nothing* will happen to you," Paz interrupted fiercely. She grabbed Lucha's hand and squeezed it. "We'll be waiting for you."

Lucha nodded. Her words had failed her at last. The warmth of Paz's hand in hers seemed like the only real thing in the world.

And then the warmth was gone, and Paz had taken Lis's weight, and the two of them were disappearing toward the tree line. Lucha stood in the center of the glade, wind whipping her hair from her braids as the monster descended.

* * *

It was the largest sombralado she'd ever seen. At least twice the size of any she'd fought in Robado. Its dark, swirling center was so far beyond her reach it seemed comical. Her knife had never looked more like a child's plaything than it did now. The only thing between Lucha and death.

Not the only *thing*, the forest's whispers seemed to say.

But how could she trust the forest after it had led her into *his* trap? After it had failed to save her from his retribution?

When the sombralado landed, the earth shook. Lucha could feel every tree straining against its roots. Away from this place and the white death that was already spreading.

She would have to do her best, Lucha thought. Her and the slender blade, the way it had been so many times before. Paz and Lis were already running. They would be safe, even if the worst happened.

The creature's red eyes locked onto Lucha's as they had only once before: in the western tract of forest outside Robado. When Lucha had seen her mother's eyes staring out of a monster's face and begged it to look at her.

She didn't have to beg, today. The sombralado raised its wings, beating the clearing into a frenzy, shrieking again before it dove for her with talons and beak alike.

Without the invisibility that had kept her safe during her cazadora years, Lucha was no match for this creature. She knew it right away. The first minutes of the fight all she could do was dart out of its way, anticipate its movements and dodge as all around her the clearing succumbed to the white rot creeping through it.

Lucha felt the death of each unique life in this place. She wanted to avenge them all. Only how could she?

The sombralado stalked her relentlessly. It swiped at her every time she paused for breath. Once, it caught the back of her leg, which was wet with blood in seconds. The pain made every step slower, and she could not afford to lose time.

At least Lis and Paz would get away, Lucha thought, as if from some great distance. She could distract it that long.

As if in answer to this comforting thought, a second scream split the sky. A second silhouette passed overhead. Lucha's heart plummeted. She had never seen more than one sombralado before. Had never even imagined it.

And now the sky was filling with them. Passing over the clearing and scouting beyond. Even Lis would not be safe. They would find her. They would . . .

Lucha was running before she gave her body the order to move. She made for the gap in the trees where Paz had disappeared with her sister not nearly long enough ago. Drawing them away was impossible now. She was barely a threat to one of them, let alone an army.

Behind her, the first sombralado screeched again, no longer distracted by the appearance of its fellows. The sound of its talons ripping through the ground behind her told her it was following. That it didn't intend to let her go.

Lucha made her way down the path Paz had followed with Lis. Staying away only guaranteed they'd be defenseless—but what would Lucha do when she reached them? What *could* she do?

The sombralado could not move as easily as Lucha could through the dense thicket of trees. Neither could it take flight without losing her beneath the canopy. This speed of movement was her one advantage. She sprinted with every ounce of her strength, dodging toppling trees, the white death always right at her heels.

Lucha did not know how long she had been running when she saw them at last. They struggled bravely against the underbrush, the dense wood blocking them at every turn.

"Paz!" Lucha cried, and pushed herself harder still to reach them.

"Lucha!"

But it was too late. From the sky, at least four sombralados circled their position. Horror coiled in her belly, reached for her throat. For a moment, her legs would not move, and she crashed to the ground, knees skidding along the soil.

The beast that had been tracking her from the clearing was upon them now. Tears streamed down Lucha's face.

"What do we do?" Paz screamed.

Lucha had no answer. She wanted to tell Paz she would do anything to protect them, but the ground was already shaking again. Sombralados, on the other side of them. Surrounding them. The white death spreading everywhere. Pulling Lis beside her, Paz returned to Lucha, stumbling and crying until at last they collided. They would face the end together, her expression said.

Lucha could not rise. She reached out for Lis's hand, which lay limp in her own. Lis had lost consciousness again, and Lucha was glad. It would be as if she were sleeping. A long, restful sleep, never interrupted.

"I'm sorry!" Paz called over the sound of the crashing trees, the chattering and screaming of the nightmare beasts. "I couldn't save her, I'm sorry!"

"I'm the one who should be sorry," Lucha said, using her free hand to take Paz's. The three of them, connected.

They locked eyes as the shrieking grew louder, as the trees tossed and the ground vibrated with every step that brought the monsters closer.

If these are my last breaths, Lucha thought, *at least I can love her without reservation.*

The warmth of the feeling—unfettered at last—filled Lucha's chest, and spread. Every cell of her felt more vibrantly alive, as if to contrast what was coming. The endless nothingness, or worse.

It was unbearable, Lucha thought, as all her walls came crumbling down. She didn't want to die. Not now, when she finally knew what living meant . . .

And so, she didn't.

From this joyous, vibrant warmth, rays reached out to everything still living in the forest around them. The roots, thrashing in fear, were calmed by it. The branches, sounding their warning to the skies, went still. The trunks stood fast, and the mycelia spread their whispered pulses through the ground.

Within Lucha it all made sense at last. Some cosmic rotation aligning the planets until each sat in the shadow of the one before it.

She would not die. She would not let the people she loved most die.

It was as simple as that.

From the center of that certainty, an explosion. Light. Heat. Intention. Sound. Every disparate part of the wood surged to Lucha's purpose. There was movement everywhere. Cascading, writhing, reaching, grasping. The forest reared up, a tidal wave of green. From below, the undertow, an inexorable current drawing down, down, down.

Paz threw her body on top of Lis's, protecting her. Lucha, on her back, spread her arms wide. She did not close her eyes. Instead she watched as the forest pulled every last sombralado down to the ground, restraining them as vines and moss and ground cover surged forward to envelop their skeletal bodies.

The roots drank the shadows that wreathed them. Flowers burst to bloom through their vacant eye sockets. From the center of each pulsating, shadowed heart, a mushroom ballooned into life. Vivid red with weeping, milky spots.

When the mushrooms were full-grown, stillness fell within Lucha and without.

There was a vague humming emptiness where only seconds ago there had been a riot.

Lucha sat up slowly. Only now did she remember the dead soldados. The mushrooms as they devoured Alán in her cell.

The fear she had carried, that to use the power would mean risking everything she loved. Everyone.

In the moment of doing, there had been no fear. It had been as easy as breathing.

The humming faded. Twilight was gathering at the thicket's edge. Lucha, on her feet, made her unsteady way toward Lis. She checked her sister's pulse. Her fluttering eyelids. Lis was unconscious, but alive. The relief crashed in—another wave—then receded.

Paz had thrown her body on top of Lis's, Lucha remembered. Where was she now?

Lucha's eyes scanned the thicket, unrecognizable now as the place she had believed would be her last. The sombralados' bones were all but hidden in the green hillocks the forest had made of them. Mounds of vibrant, blooming life where once there had been nothing but the certainty of approaching death.

It took her a moment to spot Paz, standing some distance off, watching her.

The forest's electric pulse kicked back to life beside Lucha's own. She was more wild wood than girl in that moment, and perhaps this was why she didn't hesitate. Why she crossed the clearing in purposeful strides to press herself into Paz's body like a brand.

Their lips were spare inches apart: "Can I—?" she began, but she was interrupted by the searing answer.

Paz's hands rose to Lucha's face. Her body found every

space between them and closed it. In her embrace, Lucha found everything she'd sought in the forest's power and more. She was tremblingly, *painfully* alive.

It was over before she could find herself in it. Paz pulled away, guilt etched in every line of her expression.

"I can't," she said, stepping back.

"I'm sorry," Lucha said. Her thoughts were a useless tangle. "I shouldn't have ... I ... The relief of it must have turned my head."

Paz smiled again. A fleeting thing. "Believe me, I want to." Her cheeks were still flushed. "It's only ... the things I saw. Lucha, it's blasphemy for me to want you this way when you're ... you're ..."

To complete Lucha's breathless bewilderment, Paz sank to her knees before Lucha.

"You're the salvadora," Paz whispered, making some sign with her fingers Lucha didn't recognize.

Lucha's mind went immediately to Salvador, fearing Paz was somehow aware of their connection. Their bargain. Then she remembered the meaning of the name in the old tongue. *Savior.* She could have laughed aloud at the irony.

"When the stories about you began to spread in Robado, I wondered," Paz was saying now. "And then, the night Lis got better ..."

Lucha knew what Paz was remembering. The way she had guided the flowers to pull the Olvida from Lis's bloodstream.

"I couldn't prove it," Paz continued. "It felt like a dream— and there have been stories of prayer and faith healing among laypeople. Maybe your love for her had . . ." She trailed off. "In any case, it wasn't proof. Not definitively."

"Proof of what?" Lucha asked, afraid of the answer.

"The gift," Paz whispered. "The goddess's blessing. The mark of the savior." Her eyes were wide and dark again, boring right into Lucha's. But there was something different lighting them now. Not vulnerability. Not desire.

Reverence.

It felt like losing something precious.

"She bestowed it only on her most devoted servants. It hasn't been seen for a hundred years. But it's a sign, Lucha. Of the beginning of the end of this age of tribulation. I hoped I would live to see it, but I never dreamed . . ."

Lucha turned away, taking her head in her hands. Of all the cases of mistaken identity, had there ever been one more twisted than this? Paz thought *Lucha* was the savior from the old stories. The one destined to return abundance to the world after the goddess's departure.

When all the while she'd been locked in a bargain with a monster. Connected to him at the core. Lucha didn't know the source of her power, how much her bargain with Salvador had to do with it, but she was sure of one thing. She was no savior.

Where a moment before there had been light and relief, joy and desire, the chasm between them yawned now more widely than before. All the reasons they couldn't feel these things slithered in to fill the space, settling with alarming swiftness into their old positions.

When the sombralados descended, Lucha had discovered

her true feelings for this girl at last. But something else still burned brighter in her chest. Her hatred for Olvida would always come first. And for Paz it would always be faith.

And as long as Salvador was her best chance of destroying it, Lucha and Paz could never be aligned. Never together.

Paz had gone quiet. She watched as Lucha waged an invisible war in her mind.

Tomorrow, she was certain, they would reach the lightning-struck tree. Everything would be revealed. What was the harm of letting Paz believe tonight? If it made their last night easy?

But how could she lie? After everything they'd been through?

"I don't want to be anyone's savior," Lucha said truthfully. "And I don't believe I am, Paz. The forest has been kind to us, I agree. It helped me heal Lis, it protected us from the monsters. But that could be proof of your faith as much as any doing of mine."

A curious flicker passed over Paz's face, but she did not speak.

"You said you saw me, in your vision," Lucha pressed on, gambling. "What did you see?" If the vision had shown her any kind of truth, it would not have been an image of Lucha the Savior. Perhaps that would be enough to convince Paz for now.

Instead, the other girl's cheeks flushed once more with color. "I couldn't say. Not now. Not if you're really—"

Lucha stepped forward. "I have something I need to do, Paz. Something more than just finding a safe place for Lis and me. Something I believe is important. If I succeed, we'll find out the truth of all this once and for all. But tonight, I'm just me."

Their eyes were locked, now, and the reverence in Paz's gaze had not diminished. It had only changed into something more personal. Something that saw Lucha the girl. All of her.

"You were different," Paz began. "When I saw you. Lighter. That weight you carry was gone. You were laughing, and when I approached you I . . . we . . ." She trailed off, the crease back in her brow. Whatever she had to say, she didn't seem capable of reconciling it with her theory of Lucha as the savior of humanity.

But Lucha had a hunch. Half hope, half fear. "Maybe you could show me instead."

She reached forward as Paz had done after her vision, taking the other girl's wrist in her fingertips. There was barely a world to shrink, but their locked gazes erased even the bones beneath the green.

Paz turned her hand over, fingers tangling with Lucha's. The space between their bodies shrank and disappeared. When their lips met this time, it was not desperate relief. Not impulse or recklessness. It was something decided. Something safe.

And then a dark shape moved outside Lucha's vision, and her heart caught fire again.

17

The burning seared across her chest. Lucha clutched at it, eyes shut tight, afraid of what she'd see when she opened them.

Of course it was him. His broad shoulders and too-long limbs, the black cloak that had once writhed with shadows in a ghostly grove. Lucha's history told her this was the only outcome she could have expected: that all hope was rewarded with disappointment and pain.

"Enjoying yourself?" Salvador asked dryly.

"Lucha, are you all right?" Paz had stepped back when Lucha gasped. Her eyes were wide and worried, her cheeks still flushed.

"Yes," she told them both, sinking down to the floor of the thicket, the rich carpet of moss. "I think I was just more tired than I knew."

The pain was already receding, but Salvador's image was as defined as ever. His expression said he would not be leaving them alone again. Not tonight. Paz stood beside him. The contrast was unbearable.

Lucha patted the ground beside her. "Join me, please," she said to Paz. "I'm sorry I frightened you."

Unaware of the strange juxtaposition, Paz lowered herself down beside Lucha, but there was no reclaiming the moment they had lost. The girl Paz had been beneath Lucha's hands, beneath her lips, was already becoming a memory.

Lis mumbled in her sleep. Salvador's eyes smoldered in the dying light.

"Tomorrow, we make for the lightning-struck tree," he said, carefully enunciating every word. "You will do as I say along the way, or I will make all the pain you've felt before feel like nothing. It's time to deliver what you promised me. No more distractions."

Dread coursed through Lucha's veins. She couldn't show it. Here, with Paz's wide, curious eyes taking in every movement, it would be an admission to fight him, as well as a deadly risk.

But if she didn't fight him, she had to obey. She would be revealed, or she would die.

"I think I've figured it out," Paz said quietly now. Her cheeks had finally returned to their usual color, but her eyes still darted anywhere but to Lucha's face.

"What's that?" Lucha asked.

"Your sister. The hare must have fed on the Pensa plant."

For a moment, the delicate balance of fate was forgotten as it all clicked into place. The visions. The way Lis had deteriorated so quickly. A taste of Pensa, however small, would have made Lis's cravings unbearable.

"You know, the forest priestesses use Pensa to commune with the spirits," Paz said, a sleepy near-whisper.

"Do you think it really shows the truth?" Lucha could still see it. Salvador, corporeal and wreathed in shadows. His mysterious mother, weeping as she lowered him into the ground.

Paz was quiet for a long time. So long, Lucha wondered if she'd fallen asleep.

"I hope so," she said at last, and her fingers found Lucha's again.

For several long moments, Lucha felt the reassuring beat of Paz's pulse against her palm. She thought the other girl might be falling asleep, but then Paz sat up. There was a desperate urgency in her expression.

"Lucha, let's stay," she said. "Forget being a savior, forget whatever path you've been set on, and I'll forget mine. We'll find a place in the woods. Build a little home and grow a garden. No one will ever find us. We can start again."

As she once had in her housing unit back home, Lucha used her imagination: a little cabin with a vine-thatched roof. A garden outside. The whispers of the forest lulling them to sleep each night, and Paz . . . Paz in her arms . . . Paz waking up beside her.

It was the life Lucha had craved for as long as she could remember. A family. Love and purpose.

"We can start again," Paz repeated. "As the people we are now. Leave the past where it belongs." She looked into Lucha's eyes, a pleading expression there that pulled at every fiber Lucha was made of. "We could do it together."

Lucha wanted to say yes. Wanted to scream it in the forest's double timbre so there was no doubt what she wanted. Where she belonged.

But Salvador stood sentry over them, his smirk telling Lucha exactly what he made of this fantasy. And Lis slept off the Pensa fitfully, still beholden to the aching emptiness in her blood. Somewhere behind them, Robado still stood. Lucha saw it again as she had in her cell. The warehouses burning. The north ward destroyed.

Freedom.

"It's a beautiful dream," she said to Paz. She turned her face aside, letting the shadows hide her tears. "But we can't, Paz. I can't."

The longing on Paz's face did not diminish with this rejection. It only settled. Becoming something permanent and steady. Lucha knew that this moment—Paz's offer, and the expression on her face—would haunt her for a long, long time.

Morning came, and Lucha feigned waking along with the rest of them. She ignored the corner where Salvador still stood. He had stayed the whole night. His burning eyes had never left her.

But she had made use of her sleepless hours. All night she'd watched Paz and Lis—the innocence of their sleeping faces contrasted by the cold, otherworldly light on his. She had tried to come to terms with leaving them. Pursuing the destruction of Olvida no matter what it cost.

As she had in the moment of her approaching death, Lucha had found this outcome unbearable. Once, she had believed she alone could protect Lis. Protect herself. She had been wrong. If she was going to do what she needed to do, she could not begin by tearing the three of them apart.

She knew now that Salvador—irreplaceable as he might be in the fight ahead—could not be trusted. But to keep Paz with her, Lucha would have to tell the truth, once and for all.

Her nerves skittered like dry leaves in a breeze. As Paz woke slowly, Lucha wondered for the hundredth time if the gamble would prove foolish. Suppose Paz turned on her when she learned of the bargain? Suppose Lucha lost her anyway?

She shook herself. There could be no room for thoughts like this. Paz, after all, had seen *Lucha* in her vision. Light and carefree. There had to be a reason for that.

"I need water," Lis croaked.

Lucha turned to her immediately, helping her sit up. Paz was beside them in an instant, close enough that her elbow and Lucha's touched.

"I got dosed, didn't I?" Lis asked, rubbing her eyes with one hand once the dew-filled leaf Paz brought had been drained.

"We think the hare we ate had been feeding on Pensa plants," Paz confirmed. "I'm so sorry."

Lis took this news in stride. She stretched her arms over her head and yawned hugely. Her face was still wan, her eyes ringed with shadow, but she was conscious. It was a victory.

Paz helped Lis as she got gingerly to her feet. The younger

girl's eyes were wide now, taking in the violently blooming hillocks that had not been there when she lost consciousness. It would be time to leave this place behind, and soon. The west beckoned.

Lucha, for her part, was rooted to the spot. It was now or never. "I need to tell you both something," she heard herself say.

Lis squinted at her through the haze the Pensa had left behind. Paz's busy hands stilled, and her eyes met Lucha's.

"What are you doing?" Salvador asked. He had not moved from his place. His eyes narrowed to suspicious slits.

Lucha ignored him.

"I've been keeping this from you for a long time," she said shakily. "But I trust you both, and if I'm going to survive what comes next I'm going to need your help."

Now she had their attention.

Salvador, against the thicket's tallest tree, seemed to swell in his anger. "Trust is a dangerous game, girl," he said in a low voice. "When the devotee learns of my existence she will only be an obstacle. And you know what I do to the things that get in my way."

"It started when I tried to rescue Lis from Pecado," Lucha began, pushing through the chill his words inspired. "I couldn't do it on my own, and I had seen things. Strange things. A power in the forest that turned men to fungus and held the sombralados at bay. I needed to harness it, so I asked for help."

"She will never accept you," Salvador said. "She will make you her enemy and I will see her die at your hands before we resume our task. I warn you: Do not do this. The girl is a means to an end and she has served her purpose. Let her go."

"Help from who?" Lis asked, and Lucha knew she was picturing it: the guards, wrapped in white vines. Lucha, speaking in tongues.

"He told me we could destroy Olvida together," Lucha said. "And I agreed. You know what it's done to the people I loved. To our city. I wanted it gone more than anything. I still do." She took a deep, shuddering breath. "But I'm not the same girl I was in that cell. I understand now that people *aren't* a means to an end. You deserve to know the truth of who I am. What I've done. That way you can decide if you want to help me."

"An agreement with who?" Lis demanded, scared and frustrated all at once.

"You know the power of names, girl," Salvador said, stepping closer, his cape brushing against Lis, who shivered. "This is the last time I'll warn you."

Lucha held his eyes as she said it: "El Sediento."

Lis's face fell in an instant, horrified. Lucha's eyes found Paz. There was surprise there, to be sure, but something else too. Something that looked like triumph.

But before Salvador could react, before anyone could speak, a flurry of movement erupted from the surrounding trees. The compañeras were back, charging out from the shadowy spaces between the trees, hissing and snarling.

What are they doing here? Lucha wondered. When they'd arrived before, it had felt like some kind of sign. Now it felt like an ambush.

The power surging through Lucha—the power that had just taken down five sombralados and saved them all—did not whisper from outside now. It lived within her, a warm and steady presence. If she decided to, she could force it to destroy them.

But she remembered the creatures at rest. Sparkling with divine light. If she killed them, she would be setting herself against Paz and everything she believed once and for all.

"No," Paz whispered, as if she'd heard Lucha's thoughts. "Not now, please, not now."

"Listen to me." Salvador, cutting through the rest. "You need to get out of here. Bring down the beasts. Run. You aren't equal to what's coming next—not before—"

He was cut off by a gasp from Lis. Lucha followed her gaze to see a hooded figure standing up from behind one of the hillocks. And suddenly there were more, four of them, five. They were surrounded.

"We need to get out of here," Lucha said. "We need to run."

Paz did not move. Her face was frozen in horror.

"*Paz,*" Lucha said, grabbing her arm. "We have to go *now.*"

A dart whizzed into the clearing, just missing Lucha as she ducked. There would be no discussion, then. Only a fight.

And still, Paz didn't speak. Didn't even move. She was frozen with her back against a tree, staring at the figures now removing their hoods.

"Take them down *now,*" snarled Salvador. "And run as fast as you can. There will be more where these came from, and they won't stop until they have you. You *must* survive, do you understand me? Leave the others if you must, they're disposable, but you—"

"I won't leave anyone behind," Lucha said aloud. "We'll stand together."

"Lucha . . . ," Paz whispered, her first words in several long minutes. "I'm sorry."

"It's not your fault," Lucha said bracingly. "I'm the one who—"

But when the second dart was fired, it hit Lis right in the neck.

"No!" Lucha screamed. She threw herself down at her sister's side, pulling out the tiny, feathered thing as Lis's eyes rolled back in her head. "Paz! Please! You have to help her!"

Before anything could be done, Lucha felt the bite of the third dart as it pierced her own neck.

The effect was instantaneous. White spots danced in her vision, her limbs were weak. Useless. The last thing she heard before she lost consciousness was Salvador's voice. It reverberated around the hollow.

"You fool," he said. "You've destroyed us all."

18

Long before she woke, sounds bled back into Lucha's world.

A cat's feral snarl.

Hooves clopping over an uneven road.

Voices in low conversation.

"You're sure she said his name?"

"Yes. And the cats—"

"I know, I know. But still, they're only animals."

Lucha slept, then woke, then slept again. Each waking brought her closer to her own mind, but her vision did not return. She was on the back of some creature, bouncing along. That was all she knew for some time.

Occasionally, she dreamed, but she was blind even there. The dream sounds merged with the waking ones. The conversations, too.

Once, she thought she heard Lis screaming and struggled— only to find herself bound. Once, she was sure she heard Paz. But nothing she said made sense.

"I told you I needed another day."

"Your orders were clear. He would have intercepted you in another *hour*."

"Listen, you don't know what it was like out there. It's much more complicated than they led us to believe."

"Which is why we didn't kill her on sight. Be grateful."

"I need to be with her. To explain."

"Your role has been played. You will ride back separately, with the sister." This was the other voice, harsh and severe. "We will make sure your . . . *suspicions* are relayed to the appropriate contact."

"You're going to regret separating them." Paz. This time Lucha was sure. "Everyone else has."

Quiet followed.

Lis, Lucha tried to say. Something was blocking her mouth. Half the hoof sounds grew more distant, then faded away. This time, when the poison beckoned Lucha back to sleep, she didn't fight. What was left to fight for?

She was dreaming—or else she was dying, but Salvador was the one who screamed.

Lucha opened her eyes.

They itched and burned, but they displayed him well enough. Alone against a black backdrop. Every line of his face spelled fury.

"Wake up," he said in that smoldering velvet voice. "You need to get yourself out of here *now*, or all will be lost."

"I'm tired." Her mouth wouldn't move, but she heard her words as if she'd spoken them aloud. From the way he scoffed, Lucha knew he could hear her too.

"You swore to work with me. To save them all from Olvida. This is the moment that agreement matters most. I will not be able to destroy it if you reach their destination, girl, and neither will you. It will be over."

This roused Lucha, as of course he'd known it would. Olvida. Lucha had already sacrificed so much to destroy it. To save her sister, and her mother, and everyone else who'd suffered so much. How could she abandon her cause now?

But something else returned with her sense of urgency. A memory.

"You told me to leave them behind."

For once, he was silent.

"In the thicket, when the compañeras came. You told me to run. That the rest were disposable but *I* had to live. You knew she was the reason I wanted to destroy Olvida most. You used it against me. But it was all a trick. I've been alone the whole time."

"Nonsense," he said. "You don't understand the half of what's at stake. Believe me when I say I would put your sister in a metal palace with a thousand armed guards for all eternity to ensure you kept your promise to me."

It was Lucha's turn to be silent. If this was true . . .

"It doesn't matter," she said. "I'm bound. Blind. And Lis is gone. They have the compañeras. Darts and weapons." *They have Paz,* she wanted to say. But she couldn't be sure, and it hurt too much to wonder. "Even if I escape I won't find my sister before they kill me."

"You *will,*" he insisted. "With my help, you will. But it has to be now, girl. Now or all is lost. You will never accomplish what you set out to do. That hovel of yours will keep pumping out toxins for generations."

"What does it matter to you?" Lucha asked. "What are you so afraid of?"

"I fear nothing." But he did. The urgency in his tone betrayed him.

"Then free me yourself," she said. In her vision he had wielded immense power—but she had never seen him do it in life. "Cut my bonds and kill my captors. Steal me away for whatever purpose you contrived in that cell."

Silence, again.

"You can't, can you?" It was so clear to her now. He couldn't free her. She was alone, and if Lis could be saved, if Olvida could be destroyed, it would be up to Lucha.

"I can give you whatever you want." His voice was velvet again. "Riches, immortality. Anyone who threatens you, dead. Anyone you love, safe forever. Anything, girl. Just fight for me now."

This was the truth of it, at last. *He* needed *her.* But he had never had anything to offer in return. Nothing but lies. Lucha had found her power with his help, but she could do without it. She *had* done without it.

In the background, far off but growing closer, there was a new sound. Something like a rushing river.

"There's no time for this. For any of this. You're in danger, all of you. Break free before it's too late."

"The only power you ever had over me," Lucha said, growing drowsy again, "was my belief that I couldn't do this without you. But I know better now. You can't save me. You probably can't destroy Olvida either. Lucky for me, I know how to be alone."

She had hit a nerve. His eyes told her so, when they darted everywhere but her face. He was boyish, in that moment. Almost handsome. What had he looked like, before he had become a nightmare?

"Lucha, please." It was the first time he'd ever said her name. She found that here, in this nothingness, she could admit she loved the way it sounded.

Fight, it meant. Her father had chosen it. For a girl who would never back down.

"Please."

Not a river, Lucha decided. A waterfall. The kind that dashed boats and skulls alike on the rocks below it.

"What will happen to me?" she asked. Guidance again. She had believed she needed him for so long it was hard to break the habit.

"You're asking the wrong question." His breath was a bracing fall breeze across her face.

"What will happen to you?"

"I will be gone and I will take your power with me. Rip it from your chest. You will be nothing again. Just a weak girl who watches helplessly as everyone she loves suffers and dies."

I won't, came that stubborn voice in her head. The one that had guided her through every storm until now.

"And when you die, alone, having saved no one good and destroyed nothing evil, I will find you and I will make sure you suffer. It won't be long, Lucha, until we're reunited. But by then it will be too late."

The roaring was unbearable in her ears now, and Lucha knew her choice. She would let the water take her. Take them both. If she lived, she would keep her promise to destroy Olvida. She would find Lis, and get her to safety. If she died . . .

If she died, Lis was strong. She could save herself.

"Goodbye," she whispered, and he must have heard the finality in her tone. There was no more cajoling. No more velvet-wrapped promises, doomed to be broken. In the end he traced her cheek with a ghostly finger—a final claiming. A reminder that he would be waiting.

Together, they listened as the sound reached its most unbearable decibel, and then.

All went silent.

All went dark.

The snuffing of the last candle in the dead of night.

He was gone.

The din left a ringing in her ears when it stopped, but it was nothing compared to the absence of him. Lucha didn't need her sight to confirm it. She could feel it in the hollow of her chest. She could feel it in every part of her. She recoiled around the place he had sealed their agreement, pain rushing to fill the emptiness.

This promise, he had kept. Lucha was utterly alone.

19

Lucha didn't know how much time had passed when her captors stopped their forward progress.

Her hands were still bound, and her eyes covered. Something in her mouth made it impossible to cry out. Her body was numb and sore from the ride, and she struggled to stay on her feet when rough hands guided her down. Even still, it was nothing compared to the yawning, aching absence in her chest.

Lucha told herself it was only the power she missed. That she'd grown accustomed to feeling the forest within her. But she hadn't left her mother without some understanding of how you could miss what was killing you.

Salvador had used her, and lied to her. He had made her believe in him, and then used that belief to hurt her.

And still, she looked for him. Still, she ached.

The blindfold was removed unceremoniously then, and after days of darkness Lucha's eyes watered and stung even in the low light of wherever she'd come to be. The gag came out next. She coughed, at first, but her eyes were clearing. The green shifted and danced before them, promising clarity.

Lucha's first instinct was to reach for her power. To skewer these two fuzzy, person-shaped outlines where they stood . . .

She gasped, instead, when she came up empty. It wasn't pain. Not exactly. More like an intense nausea. The kind that cramped in a hungry stomach.

I will take your power with me. Rip it from your chest.

"Where is my sister?" she forced out.

The woman beside her was the first to shed her hazy outline. Coppery-red hair, her pale face spotted with freckles much lighter than Lucha's. "All will be explained within," she said in a pleasant but incurious voice.

"Within where?"

As if in response, the woman cut Lucha's wrists free.

It's your funeral, Lucha thought, and reached down for her knife. The woman's was faster, deadly point at Lucha's throat before she could grasp the hilt.

"I wouldn't, if I were you. Not if you want to see your companions again."

At this, a memory surfaced. Something deeper than her anger.

I told you I needed another day.

Lucha's head spun. The ambush had come out of nowhere. How had their captors known where to find them?

I told you I needed another day.

"Where am I?" Lucha asked, struggling to orient herself.

"You have the honor of standing within the sanctuary of the forest goddess Almudena," said the redhead.

The shock of this sent everything else spinning out of

Lucha's mind. She scanned the faces of the women beside her, looking for proof of deception. She found nothing but pride. Devotion.

Could it be real, then? Lucha examined her surroundings, desperate for proof that the last and greatest of the stories she'd clung to as a child was true.

They stood in an open field, surrounded by large, unfathomably ancient trees. Trees she'd never known the names of, with trunks that put even the montezumas back home to shame.

The light filtered down, golden and soft, as it had in the clearing where she'd first seen the compañeras. At their feet, vivid green moss was scattered with tiny white flowers . . .

Some thousand yards up a well-manicured dirt path was a stone building larger than any she'd ever seen. Its carved wooden doors, twice her height, stood open to the sunlight. Beyond, there were gardens, stone dwellings, and a slope of terraces moving higher and higher.

There was no denying it now. "The *sanctuary*," she said, awestruck even as her heart sank. If this was the sanctuary of the forest goddess . . . if these were her devotees . . . could there be any doubt that Paz had been the one to set this in motion?

"How did you find us?" she asked, with more urgency this time. "What do you want with me?"

"All will be explained within," said the redhead again. And then, to her companion: "They're waiting for us."

The other woman stared for a moment with piercing blue eyes, then let go of her sword hilt, muttering something in a harsh, severe tone that sounded familiar. This was the woman Paz had argued with, Lucha was sure of it. If anyone knew the truth of her allegiance . . .

"As long as you swear my sister is safe, I'll go quietly." *Until I learn the truth,* Lucha added silently. As clear as the signs seemed, the trust between Lucha and Paz had been hard-won. The things they'd shared could not be so easily brushed aside.

Lucha's heart lurched at the memory of their kiss. She did not *want* to brush them aside.

Not until she heard the truth from Paz herself.

"My sister," Lucha said again. "She's here?"

"All will be revealed."

There was nothing left to do but follow.

The building had been impressive from afar, but up close it was a marvel. Timeworn and elegant, it both commanded and accentuated the scenery. Lucha had never seen anything like it, nor like the panes of colored glass that broke up the stone. Their mosaic patterns told stories that must have been older than the sanctuary itself.

Even being marched through its open doors by her armed captors, aching and alone and afraid, Lucha couldn't deny that she was moved by this place. By the simple fact of its existence, and what it meant for the horrors she had survived.

"La Catedral de Asilo," said the redhead as the interior came into view.

In all her life, Lucha had never seen a structure larger than the metal buildings in the north ward compound. Squat, low to the ground, they'd been built for utility. By contrast, this place seemed to exist for beauty alone. Its every line demanded grace from the person viewing it.

Standing here, head tilted back, Lucha received its message clearly: there was divinity in her, and in all things.

"We'll sit here, for now." The redhead directed Lucha to a long pew standing empty to their left—one of at least twenty filling the rectangular room. Some had an occupant or two, and as they sat, more filed in, looking upward, talking softly among themselves.

In a small group at the other end of the room, women in green robes like those her captors wore were singing. Near them was a stone dais with a podium. It was empty, now, but the redhead glanced at it from time to time, giving it significance in Lucha's eyes as well.

The instincts she'd developed after a lifetime in the Scar said she should escape, by any means necessary. Draw her knife. Hold one of the women hostage. Force the other to let her go. But how far could she really make it without her power?

Without Salvador guiding her?

Better to wait, then, Lucha decided. To gain all the information she could. To get her bearings. To leave on her own terms.

And if she discovered the truth of Paz's intentions along the way, so be it.

"Good afternoon."

Everyone quieted. There were at least thirty in the pews now, and they all turned their eyes to the podium. The speaker's robe was so dark green it was nearly black—far darker than the robes of the others in the room. Lucha filed that away for future consideration.

"Listen," hissed the blue-eyed woman to Lucha.

"I am Obispo Río, and I welcome you to Asilo—the sanctuary of the forest mother Almudena. Strong may we grow."

"*Strong may we grow*," echoed the other people in robes. Another glance around the room confirmed Lucha's earlier suspicion—there were varying shades, but this Río's was the darkest by far.

"Whatever has brought you here, whatever horrors or joys, lack or excess your past has held, you are welcome. We thank you for making this pilgrimage, and for offering your devotion to Almudena. We hope you will find meaning in her service."

So these were the goddess's pilgrims, Lucha thought, looking around at the faces of the plainly clothed people in the pews. People from all over Elegido who believed in the stories enough to travel this dangerous road. To see for themselves.

"At Asilo, each of us begins our journey as a seed. A seed that will be fertilized by knowledge and devotion. As you grow, greater responsibilities, privilege, and access will be afforded to you. Much like every tree, each person grows at their own pace."

Exhausted, battered, and aching, Lucha felt herself warm to these words. A new life. A place to rest. The sins of your past washed away . . .

"On the table behind me, you will find robes. Down this

hallway"—Río gestured through a stone archway to her left—"you will find suitable privacy for changing." The gathered pilgrims began to stand. She had them back in their seats with a single glance.

Power, Lucha thought. It radiated from her. None in the room were immune.

"Each of us has a reason for seeking the sanctuary—one we may or may not choose to share. Regardless, we begin today on equal footing. No riches, titles, or deeds elevate us above our brothers and sisters in devotion. Only through that devotion may we distinguish ourselves in the goddess's eyes, or in one another's." She paused, as if allowing her words to sink in.

Eyes open, Lucha reminded herself. She was here to find Lis. To learn whatever truth she could. And to escape. Even without Salvador, her aim was the same. She had to make it to the lightning-struck tree. To see if she had the strength to destroy Olvida without him.

"All of us have a beautiful opportunity in this room, at this moment," Río said now. "To begin anew."

All around the room, Lucha saw people weeping openly. Dropping to their knees. Clasping each other by the hands. Had Lucha arrived under her own steam, her companions not missing, would she have felt the same way?

"We ask that you treat the devotees with the respect their rank demands—as indicated by the shade of the robes they wear"—*Bull's-eye*, Lucha thought—"and your fellow pilgrims with the grace and patience you hope to find within our walls.

As you don your robes, please leave all personal effects—any reminders of your previous lives—in your changing rooms. We find the transition to service occurs most peacefully when we can break with the past, moving together into the light."

Break with the past, Lucha thought, goose bumps erupting across her skin. It was the same offer Paz had made her the night before their capture. Had she known what was coming? Set it in motion? Was that why she'd seemed so regretful and desperate?

Despite Lucha's promise to wait and hear the truth from Paz, her suspicions mounted higher the longer she spent in this place. A place where Paz would have been right at home . . .

"Rise, pilgrims," Río said, and Lucha rose as the singing began. A swelling, victorious melody that stirred her almost against her will. The new recruits moved forward to take their robes. Lucha had nearly forgotten her captors until they stood at her sides, escorting her with suspicious expressions.

So much for breaking with the past, Lucha thought.

When she reached the table, one last garment remained: a white linen robe. Just her size. She lifted the soft fabric reluctantly.

"My sister," she said. "Is she here? We were captured together. I need to know she's safe."

"Dress and bathe," said the redhead smoothly, as her blue-eyed companion opened her mouth to speak. "Then you will commune with Obispo Río, and all will be explained."

"It better be," Lucha muttered, then walked alone into the narrow stone hallway.

No doors, she noted as she searched for an unoccupied dressing alcove. Each was hung instead with a pale green curtain. Just like in the south ward of Robado, it seemed privacy was the province of the privileged. As was their right to deny it to those lower in status than themselves. Were all those in power grown from the same seeds, no matter the shape of their promises?

Inside, the alcove was larger than Lucha had expected. It had a private bath—filled to the brim with fragrant, steaming water. It made the space humid and warm. Lucha stripped down, discarding her traveling clothes.

The only window in the room was much too small to climb out of, but as Lucha let the warm bath ease her aching muscles she listened to the forest through it. Birds chattering. The wind in the trees. Beautiful, but impersonal. The empty place in her chest ached in response.

But was all truly lost?

Closing her eyes, Lucha moved slowly. Reaching inside herself to the place where her connection to the wood had lived. She remembered the warmth that accompanied it. The sense that she was but a single link in an infinite chain.

Outside the window there was a branch, reaching for the other side of the frame. She lowered the defenses—second nature, now—that kept out the chaos of the gift.

Are you there? she asked it.

What answered was not warmth. Not light. Just a bottomless nothingness that yawned below. It was the antithesis of everything her connection to the forest had been. Its inverse.

Its opposite. Instead of heightening her senses, supporting her intuition, it threatened to devour her every feeling. Every joy. Every moment of rage. Everything that made her who she was.

Lucha forgot the branch. The water. The robe and the sanctuary and even her sister. All she could do was cling to the edge. To remember.

I am not nothing, she told herself again and again. *I am Lucha Moya.*

Whether Salvador had taken her gift, or twisted it into something monstrous, it didn't matter. This was the result. To attempt to use her power now would awaken this slavering, insatiable void. She couldn't withstand it. She would have to rebuild without the gift she had once sworn never to use.

The gift that had become a part of her.

When at last the freezing fingers of the emptiness released their grip on her insides, Lucha forced herself from the bath. Naked on the floor, she cried silently until there were no tears left.

20

It took Lucha some time to gather herself, but she did. She would not be discovered cowering or crying in this place. They feared her, for now—enough to send guards with her everywhere she went. It was not a currency she could afford to give up.

Dressed in the white robe, Lucha strapped her bone knife to her thigh once more, tearing the towel into strips to hold it. When the robe settled, it was well hidden. Perhaps she no longer had the power of the forest, but she still had the know-how of a south ward dreg.

It had been enough, in the beginning. It would need to be again.

At the end of the hall, a doorway led to a small courtyard, encircled by a low stone wall. Here, among hanging vines and ancient trees, the rest of the pilgrims were gathered around Obispo Río. On their faces Lucha recognized the same awe she had felt in the compañeras' clearing. The realization that life was more than suffering. That magic existed outside the terror of monsters.

She wished she could share in it, but too much had befallen her. There was no going back. Her guards proved the point by flanking her the moment she stepped through the door.

"Welcome, all," Río began as Lucha joined the others. The uniform white of the robes created a striking effect against the wall of green. "You are now ready to begin your journey down the path of devotion. I began my own, many years ago. Dressed in white as you are now. Looked upon by these very same sentinels as I pledged my life to the forest mother."

Lucha looked down at her own robe, white as a dove's wing, and felt like an imposter.

"Along this wall," Río continued, "you'll find the altar of the initiates. Here, new servants pledge themselves to a life of devotion with a simple oath. Should your wick catch fire, the forest mother will accept you into her sanctuary. Should it fail to light, you will know your path lies in another direction."

Looking again at the wall encircling the courtyard, Lucha noticed stools at intervals, candles in glass jars at each place. All around her, the pilgrims shifted nervously, and she knew they were all picturing the same thing: a candlewick that would not catch. The new life they'd sacrificed everything for, over before it could even begin.

How many of the rest of them had arrived bound and gagged? Lucha wondered, her own anxiety kindling to life. How many of them had willingly entered a bargain with a monster? If anyone here was destined to sit across from an unlit candle, it was her.

If she was removed from the sanctuary, she would never

find her sister. She would be alone, powerless, in the forest. How long until she met her untimely end? Until Salvador made good on his promise to follow her into the depths of whatever hell her soul was bound for?

"This moment may feel intimidating," Río said now as the pilgrims took their places at the altar. "But know that Almudena forgives. She accepts. As long as you are prepared to move forward with a purified and open heart, you will not be denied."

"And if we don't make the oath?" The words were out of Lucha's mouth before she could consider them fully. Río's eyes snapped onto her face, some of her kindly-but-stern façade falling away.

"You are free to decline the oath, of course. But anyone who does not progress must leave the sanctuary, never to return."

Shudders. Whispers. Twenty pairs of eyes lighting on Lucha, then skittering away, as if they feared her dangerous question was contagious.

She thought of pushing her luck further. Refusing the oath outright and demanding to be set free. But the redhead and her scowling partner were still within arm's reach, and somewhere within these walls, Lis needed her. Somewhere the truth of her capture, of Paz's involvement, was hidden. Lucha didn't think they'd throw her out—not after all they'd done to get her here—but she couldn't take the chance.

So she would take the oath, instead.

"Once everyone is ready, we will begin the ritual." Río raised an eyebrow at Lucha—the only pilgrim who had yet to take a seat.

The wind tossed the trees overhead when Lucha approached the last remaining stool. Her guards were still with her. The emptiness echoed with every step.

"Pilgrims," Río was saying. "Please recite these words as you strike your flame and light your candle's wick."

Lucha took her match. Her hand did not tremble.

"*I swear to serve Almudena above all other gods, all other powers, until my dying day . . .*"

Unbeknownst to the others, Lucha was saying a quiet oath of her own: "Ever since I left home, all I've wanted is to destroy Olvida. To keep my sister safe. I've done things I never imagined I'd do. Things I'm sure you wouldn't approve of. But that's why. Because I want a better world. One where she doesn't have to be afraid. One where no one does."

"*. . . To treat my fellow devotees with respect and consideration. To honor the fellowship the goddess has granted me . . .*"

"If you're the kind of deity worth swearing an oath to," Lucha continued under her breath, "you'll accept this one: I will align with you, when our causes are in accord. I'll respect you and the faith of your devotees while I'm inside your sanctuary."

"*. . . To remain in the light, no matter the temptation of the shadows.*"

"If you cannot accept my oath," Lucha whispered, "let my

wick remain dark. Let my flame die in the wind through your courtyard. But let me leave this place unharmed."

"Now strike your match." Río's voice echoed through the courtyard.

Lucha struck.

"In your own words, you may now pledge to honor your goddess, this fellowship, and your faith."

"It's up to you," Lucha said to the silent trees. Around her the rest offered flowery tributes. "Take it or leave it."

Around the yard, the pilgrims lowered matches to wicks. Some dissolved into tears as they caught. Some let out exultant cries.

Lucha lowered her own match. For a moment, it seemed the wick would not light. Eyes turned toward her once more as the flame raced down her matchstick toward her fingers.

The eyes of every person in the courtyard were on Lucha when her candle lit at last. It created a flame so tall it cleared the glass that held it, making its acceptance of Lucha's pledge visible for all to see.

A shower of sparks rained down on the lap of her robe. The tiny burns marked her. For a moment, Lucha felt the emptiness within her recede, filled with something golden and shining. A shade of the way she'd felt with the forest's power coursing through her . . .

It didn't last long.

"Congratulations to you all." A hint of tension strained Río's voice. Every eye was still on Lucha and her towering flame. "The devotees will show you to your dwellings. To-night, we will honor you with food and song in the meeting hall. For now, rest. You have earned your place."

Lucha stood with the others. Her captors closed in quickly—but there was undisguised shock on both their faces.

"You, however," said Río, "can come with me."

There seemed to be little choice in the matter. Lucha read-ied herself to follow the older woman, but just then a gust of wind kicked up. It ruffled her white robe. Her bone knife clat-tered to the ground. Lucha did not blush, nor did she stoop to retrieve it. She kept her eyes steady on Río's, awaiting her reaction.

Río's face was impassive as she bent down, passing the weapon to one of her acolytes as though it were something tainted. "Dispose of it," she said, and then, to Lucha: "Even the goddess does not give without sacrifice."

Río's office was modest—but a tapestry behind her desk caught Lucha's eye. The intricacy of its weave was astonish-ing, though that wasn't what drew her attention. The image showed a woman locked in heated battle with a man. On her face was an expression of fierce righteousness, on his an inhu-man sneer.

Some of the details are wrong, Lucha thought, but other-wise she might have been back in the ghostly grove shown to her by the hare's vision. Salvador's cheekbones were sharper in life, his eyes more human. The woman had been lovelier by far than she was shown to be here; they hadn't captured her luminescence.

Or her tears, Lucha thought, remembering the way she'd wept as she defeated her son.

"You like my tapestry?" Río had followed Lucha's gaze to the wall. "It's been there a long time."

"How long?" Lucha asked, before she could stop herself.

"About five hundred years."

Five hundred years, Lucha thought. How long had it taken him to escape the prison his mother had trapped him in? How much longer to find Lucha? They were questions she couldn't ask. Not without confessing too much.

"So," Lucha said, tearing her eyes away. "I assume you're going to tell me my capture and imprisonment were just a misunderstanding and you'd prefer I didn't spread word of your tactics to the other pilgrims."

Río sat behind her desk, taking her time about answering. When she fixed Lucha with her no-nonsense stare, she said: "If you think I've invited you to my office because I owe you some kind of explanation, you've misjudged me."

The woman wore her gray hair cropped short. Her skin was paler even than Lucha's after decades in this holy shade. Her eyes were lined in a way that suggested a lot of wise squinting was done in this room.

"So why have you invited me?" Lucha asked, sitting in the chair opposite her.

"I said I didn't *owe* you an explanation," Río said, rubbing her temples. "I didn't say you weren't going to get one. You're here, Miss Moya, because you've put us in a real bind."

"How did I manage that?" Lucha asked, curious despite herself.

"You arrived at the sanctuary alive."

A blank buzzing filled Lucha's mind. She hadn't expected honesty. "My sincerest apologies for my . . . continued existence," she finally managed.

Río didn't crack a smile. "Lucha, I'm assuming that, as a girl from the Scar, you don't know much about the lore of Almudena."

More than you'd expect, she thought grimly.

"Not as much as you, I'm sure," she replied.

"We have an ancient library filled with tomes that don't scratch the surface," Río said. "But in the interest of time, allow me to boil it down to its most relevant points."

Lucha nodded, increasingly aware of her status as an unarmed prisoner. Her guards were flanking the door. Her knife was gone. There was a ravenous abyss waiting to swallow her if she attempted to manipulate the forest around her.

On top of all that, this wise old priestess had just admitted to wanting her dead.

"The forest is the source of all life in this world, and the forest mother, Almudena, protects that life."

"I'm with you so far," Lucha said. She remembered being a conduit for that life. She didn't need to rely on faith to imagine this was true.

"A thousand years ago, however—which isn't a long time

in the life of the universe—Almudena found herself lonely as the sole divine being in the world. And so she created a son, who she hoped would learn the ways of the forest. To share her power and her burden."

It was all Lucha could do not to gasp aloud at the revelation. It had been Almudena in the forest. In her vision. *She* was the mother who had wept as she destroyed Salvador. Río continued, oblivious to the effect of her words. This was just a story to her. To Lucha, it was so much more.

"As I say, she hoped he would take up the mantle of protector. But he was as unlike his holy mother as it was possible to be. Stubborn, power-hungry, destructive. He resented his creator for tempering his worst impulses, but he was not strong enough to oppose her."

Lucha's eyes returned to the tapestry. She remembered his words in the grove: *My power does not grow things. It does not nurture, or nourish, or feed.*

"As he grew older, so did his power expand and deepen. Eventually, it rivaled that of his mother's. It was then that he began to enact his hideous plan."

"Men and power," Lucha managed. "Not a historically winning combination."

"As true in this case as any other. The son still feared his mother's power. He dared not oppose her directly, not yet. So instead he sought an engine of self-perpetuating destruction. One she could not stop once it was in motion."

Lucha was on the edge of her seat now, hanging on this old woman's every word.

"There is an herb in the forest, Lucha, that the ancient devotees of Almudena used to commune with her." Río held up a single dried leaf. "Perhaps you recognize it."

Lucha shuddered. It was Pensa, of course. Silvery blue even in the room's muted light.

"Almudena's son found it in abundance at the edge of her forest, as far from her prying eyes as he could get. He did not believe in the art of cultivation, but this he could grow. Because in its growth lay the destruction of so many . . ."

It was as if the room had melted away. Rio's voice was distant. Lucha could no longer make out the words she was speaking. It didn't matter anyway. Nothing mattered but this simple truth—which had been kept from her for so long.

Salvador had created Olvida. The scene in the forest Lucha had witnessed. The destruction his mother alluded to. *He* had warped her sacred tool of communion. *He* had given Olvida to the kings. Infected the world with its forgetting and its greed.

Lucha was no longer in a room in a fabled sanctuary. She was back in a lightless cell with metal floors. She was desperate and starving and seething with anger. He had sensed it in her—all of it. He had used her.

She choked on the knowledge. Gasped around it.

He would never have helped her destroy it. His own creation. His rebellion against the goddess who had given him life. He had only been preying on Lucha's worst fears. Mobilizing her toward some end of his own.

But what? If he had never wanted to destroy Olvida, what had he wanted from her?

"Miss Moya, are you all right?" Río had noticed her drowning at last.

The cell disappeared. The aching did too. Lucha was back in her seat at this desk, abruptly more determined than ever to hear the end of the story. The secret to revenge against the monster who had let her hope for nothing.

"I'm fine," she said curtly. "Please, continue."

"We can finish our conversation later, once you've—"

"I *said* I'm fine," Lucha snapped. "I want to hear the rest."

Río looked at her for a long moment, but Lucha kept her face as inscrutable as she could. It didn't matter what this woman offered her; she wouldn't trust it. She would never again trust a person who had something to gain.

Finally, Río cleared her throat. "Almudena tried over hundreds of years to temper her son's nature. To teach him that the source of her power was life. Balance. But with his act of defiance, he set himself against her for the last time."

"So they fought," Lucha said, remembering again: her tears, his disdain.

"The fight was legendary, and the details are largely unknown. What we do know is that after all those centuries of trying to connect with him, Almudena was forced to reconcile her mistake and destroy all evidence of its making. Unfortunately, the engine her son had set in motion was in the hands of mortals by then. It could not be stopped."

"So she killed him?" Lucha asked, not willing to confess she knew the answer already.

"On that account, her mercy is said to have stayed her

hand. She loved her son, and chose to imprison him instead, in a crystal of amber she buried at the heart of the world. And for a time, it seemed to have worked. His destructive influence was gone, the balance was restored."

"He's immortal," Lucha said, more to herself than her lecturer. "To imprison him would be worse than killing him. An eternity of confinement . . ." She saw him in that moment. His hissing rage when he spoke of chains. The burning in his eyes when she'd tried to bind him.

"She was merciful," Río said. "Because he was her beloved son."

"She left him to be tortured for hundreds of years and then abandoned her people to his whims," Lucha said. Her anger bubbled over. "What did she expect to happen?"

When Río spoke again, her voice was louder. Sharper. "She did not depart our world for many years following their conflict. She loved her subjects, and despaired of leaving them without protection. But the forest had lost its luster for her. It would forever be the place where she had been forced to destroy the thing she loved most."

Lucha's head spun. "But why didn't she make sure he was gone before she left? She created him, and this whole mess, and then—"

"We do not speak ill of the mother in this house," Río said, steel in her eyes for a moment. "I will not warn you again."

Mutinously, Lucha sat, waiting for the end of the story.

"Knowing she would soon depart, Almudena created this sanctuary, and our order. By granting her gift modestly among her most devoted followers, she could ensure there was no threat, while exerting her influence on the outcome of humankind. Here, they trained to use their power to maintain the balance. When she was no longer needed, she departed at last, free to grieve her son in the celestial kingdoms above."

Outside the office's window, the afternoon had begun to age. Golden sunlight slanted through the trees. Inside Lucha, a battleground smoldered. She had wanted to destroy Olvida. Had wanted to free her sister, and everyone else confined to a life of forgetting.

But it was no longer only a matter of doing what was right.

Lucha wanted revenge against the monster who had manipulated her. She wanted to destroy the only thing he had ever created.

"The order of Almudena maintained the balance for centuries, but without the might of our goddess's divine power, the gift she had granted began to wane through the generations, and eventually to die out altogether. Into that vacuum, a new force has grown."

"Let me guess," Lucha said flatly. "The son wasn't as neutralized as she hoped."

"His body is entombed still in the prison she made him," Río said, sending Lucha's head spinning again. "He cannot free himself. Not truly. But his power is strong, and from beneath the ground he has managed to project himself forth, insubstantially, at least."

Lucha remembered Salvador's fear of captivity once more. The viciousness with which he rejected any attempt at confining him. She had thought it was a reaction to a trauma suffered long ago, but the truth was so much worse. He was confined still. At this very moment, and every moment Lucha had known him.

"His goal, we believe, has been singular in all the century he has roamed forth in consciousness," Río said, her words echoing Lucha's thoughts. "To find someone with his mother's gift. To take that person to the place where he is bound. To be free at last."

Río's eyebrows were raised. Her expression made her meaning clear, but Lucha's head was spinning again.

This was what he had wanted when he promised her destruction. When he bound himself to her. When he convinced, and guided, and shepherded her. Later, when he burned her.

"The lightning-struck tree," Lucha said, the emptiness yawning again. "That's where he's imprisoned. *That's* where he was taking me."

But if a feeble projection of Salvador had been enough to cause this much misery, what could he do if he were truly free?

21

When Lucha could make herself look, Río's face held a mix of emotions: Triumph, that much was clear. But something like pity also.

"We have tools, for tracking him," she said. "Ancient things, from Almudena's time. With them we sensed his presence drawing near. We expected a fight."

"So, you brought me here to kill me." Lucha looked up at the tapestry again. Weren't there times she would have done worse to be rid of him?

"To make sure you didn't free him," Río corrected. "As is our sacred duty."

"What's one little innocent life in a holy war, right?" Lucha asked. But was she really an innocent? After everything she had done?

Río didn't press the point.

"I thought you said his body was still trapped," Lucha pressed on. If she had to fight for her life here, she wanted to understand. "How can you kill a projection of consciousness?"

At this, Río had the good grace to look somewhat ashamed.

"You must understand. He cannot possess a mortal unless they have the goddess's gift. No one with that power has been born for a hundred years. We believed this moment would never come."

"Hold on," Lucha said, putting up a hand, her head spinning again. "I wasn't *born* with any gift. I never had any power at all until . . ." She stopped herself there. Better to keep the details to herself as they sat calmly discussing her inevitable murder.

Río seemed to have heard her unspoken words regardless. "It would have been impossible for him to forge a connection without it. You may never have noticed it, diluted as it has become. But it is there. It has always been there."

Lucha felt suddenly nauseous. Born with the gift? The first in a hundred years? None of this made any sense. She was just a girl from the Scar. Half an orphan. She had wanted Olvida gone, and her sister safe. To briefly act as a conduit for the forest's power had not seemed too great a price.

But this?

She put her head in her hands, breathing deeply. Out of nowhere, she remembered Paz, falling to her knees. Calling Lucha *savior*. The irony had never felt more poisonous. Had she really believed it? Lucha wondered. Or had it all been part of the act?

"So," she said in a shaky voice when she could sit up again. "You kill me. Deprive him of his liberator. But what then? You didn't expect *me* to develop the gift. What if there are more like me?"

Río's silence answered for her.

239

Lucha laughed, a little manic. "You'd kill them, wouldn't you? One by one. So much for being the protectors of all life."

"You misunderstand," Río snapped. "In order for the son to use a mortal as a vessel, that mortal must enter *willingly* into a bargain with him. Invite him over the threshold, so to speak."

Lucha remembered, as if the metal walls of her cell had sprung up around her. The hunger gnawing. Eternity stretching forth. The feeling of hopelessness as she'd lowered her defenses, and the pain. The pain.

"For all your ancient scrolls and tools, you don't understand him at all," she said, the taste of the grave in her throat.

Río raised an eyebrow.

"We don't all have the luxury of righteousness. I know it seems simple, up here in your sanctuary with your scrolls and your chosen status, but real life is more complicated." Lucha got to her feet. Her guards stepped closer. "You don't understand his power to manipulate. To convince you *he's* the only way out. To delve into your mind and bring forth your greatest desires . . . your greatest fears. I was never evil, Río, I was powerless. If you want to kill me for that, to kill everyone who doesn't have another choice . . . you're no better than he is."

But as she spoke, she saw. Not just her own life, but the lives she'd judged. Her mother. The olvidados from the Scar. Salvador's drug had made them the same promises the man himself had made Lucha. Tempted them with the same choice. To align with what you knew could ruin you just to make it through another day.

Lucha didn't have to agree with the choices her mother

had made, nor did she have to forgive her for them. But after all she'd been through, if she truly believed the words she'd just spoken to Río, she had to admit she understood.

Bowled over by the revelation, by everything that had befallen her since she'd been captured, Lucha sat back down heavily. The guards retreated to the door. Lucha felt Río's eyes on her for a long time, but she did not meet them. The silence stretched on.

At last, Río said: "I'm not going to kill you."

"Why not?"

"Because the forest mother allowed your candle to be lit. She has some use for you." A long pause. "And we may have something to learn from you as well."

"Aren't you worried he'll find some way to use me here?" It seemed inconceivable that they could trust her, just like that. Lucha sensed that some larger plot was being worked.

Río shook her head. "No part of him may enter this place. We are protected from the signature of his energy."

The waterfall, Lucha remembered. It had been the only time she'd ever seen him show real fear. The pain as he was torn from her had been unbearable—right at the place where he had joined them together. "You thought your boundary would kill me, too." Had that been the moment the void was born within her?

Río didn't answer, only got to her feet.

"We believe he can sense you still, even though he is forbidden from entering this place. We believe he will wait. And while he waits, as you must understand, we cannot permit you to leave the boundary." There was an air of crisp finality to her voice. Another item marked off a long to-do list. "For now, you are welcome to reside with us. To train as an acolyte. Juana"—the blue-eyed woman scowled—"and Francisca"—the redheaded woman waved—"will show you to your lodgings."

"Wait!" Lucha said, scrambling out of her chair. "You were supposed to tell me where my sister is! And the girl we were traveling with, Paz. Was she part of the plot to capture us? I need answers!"

"Your companions are safe," Río said without meeting her eyes. "That's all I can say for now."

Panic rose in Lucha's throat, but even through its haze she understood. They believed Salvador would continue to manipulate her if she left the grounds. That he could convince her once again to free him.

Keeping Lucha apart from Lis was their insurance. They believed she wouldn't leave without her sister. If Paz was innocent, they would use her for the same purpose. And if Paz had betrayed them . . . that would only be more motivation for Lucha to leave.

It had been neatly done, she had to admit.

"We will share more as we gain a greater understanding of the situation and its risks. Until then, get some rest."

Seething, Lucha watched her go.

Río so clearly believed she was acting for the greater good, but was she really any different from Alán, back in Robado? From Salvador himself? To achieve their own ends, all of them had been willing to manipulate Lucha's desire to keep her sister safe.

"This really isn't necessary anymore," Lucha said to the women on either side of her as they led her through the courtyard. "Her methods are much more effective than yours."

If they heard her at all, there was no evidence of it.

They left the courtyard, taking a winding path through the trees. Frosted-glass lanterns had come to life, burning brightly against the encroaching evening.

It was beautiful, Lucha thought as they followed the path past stone cottages with small gardens. All around them, ancient trees stood sentinel. The world dripped with green. With life. Small altars to the mother appeared along the path, offerings and tokens before them.

They passed other pilgrims, and devotees in robes of varying hues. They peeked out of windows, they spoke to each other in small groups. It was a community. A home in a way Robado never had been. In a way Lucha had always longed for.

Her fury toward Río softened at its edges. If Lucha had been entrusted with a place like this—wouldn't she do all she could to protect it, too?

They left her at last in front of a cottage much like the others. The white-painted door stood open to the evening. There was a lamp burning outside, and three garden beds, already tilled. Inside the window, another cheerful lamp burned.

"We hope you'll join us for the welcome meal," Juana said as they left. Her expression betrayed her distrust. They'd be watching her, Lucha knew, but at least for the moment she was alone with her conflicting thoughts.

The inside of the cottage was ancient. Patches of moss

formed swirling patterns on the stone walls. But the floor had a bright rug, and a scrubbed wood table sat beside a washbasin. On the other side of the room was a bed with a straw mattress and a wool blanket.

It was comfortable. A small window overlooked the garden. A candle in a brass holder burned on the table. A tray sat there, with a pitcher of water and a glass.

For a moment, thinking of where she'd come from, Lucha could imagine what it might be like to be a pilgrim in truth. To be overjoyed for this new beginning.

And what if she let herself be? she thought, pulling out a scrubbed wooden chair and pouring herself a glass of water. She could gain a deeper understanding of her power. Pledge that power to Río in the fight against Salvador. Against Olvida, in time.

If they trusted her, perhaps they'd let her see Lis again. Ask her questions of Paz. Put her distrust to rest at last. They could all be neighbors, tending their gardens and leaving offerings to the mother along the road. Lucha saw it so clearly, like the picture Paz had once painted of their future, before everything had fallen apart.

The image kindled a comfortable warmth in her chest. They could stop fighting. Stop surviving. They could *live* . . .

It wasn't difficult to find her way to the celebration—everyone seemed to be heading in the same direction.

The meeting hall loomed into view before long, a large,

low building covered all over with twinkling, glowing lanterns. The wood was real—not the pulp-pressed panels of buildings in Robado, but richly colored slats that showed the grain of the trees they had once belonged to. Every knot and gnarl.

The courtyard outside was elevated, and the view was spectacular: the trees, the cottages, even the massive Catedral de Asilo in the distance with its stained-glass windows blazing.

Inside, the air was warm and humid, the myriad conversations overlapping until they became a pleasant hum of impersonal chatter. Lucha approached a long table piled with dishes and took a plate.

Young potatoes, roasted with peppers and corn. Wild forest greens tossed with some fragrant oil. Tiny cakes of cornmeal stuffed with spiced vegetables. Lucha served herself a little of everything, acutely aware of how long it had been since she'd had a real meal.

One that didn't make her hallucinate, anyway.

No one stared—at least not openly—and the gazes she met were friendly. Smiling. Lucha wanted to believe this place was worth the lengths Río had gone to, to protect it from Salvador. From her.

But after the loneliness of Robado, the isolation of her cell in Encadenar, days traipsing through the forest with only two companions, Lucha soon found herself overwhelmed by the bustle of such a crowd.

Outside, she found a stone bench with a nice vantage point and ate her meal with gusto.

It wasn't long before someone joined her—an acolyte who

scarcely looked older than Lucha, despite the high status indicated by her robe. "I can always spot another wallflower," she said with a smile that crinkled her hazel eyes at the corners.

"Guilty," Lucha said, swallowing a large mouthful of potato just in time.

"How are you settling in?"

"It's hard to believe this place is even real," Lucha said. "I guess I'm just trying to take it all in. Find where I fit."

The acolyte nodded sympathetically. "I've been here my whole life, and sometimes I still feel that way."

"Your whole life? Did you come with your parents?" Lucha asked.

The acolyte smiled. "My birth mother dropped me off at the boundary to be raised by the sanctuary. The forest mother never turns away a child."

Abruptly, there wasn't enough air in the clearing. In the whole forest. Lucha had kept her mother so carefully compartmentalized in her mind since she left Robado. Focused on the goal ahead. On Lis. On her plan to eliminate the thing that had destroyed her family.

But her realization in Río's office had cracked the wall she kept up. The understanding of her mother, feeling cornered as Lucha once had, choosing the only way out she'd been offered. Just as Salvador and the kings who did his bidding intended.

She found herself remembering something Paz had said on their first night in the Bosque: *I suppose they'll always be with us, whether we can leave them or not.*

"I'm sorry," Lucha said to her companion, blinking back

tears. "Just thinking of my own mother. Some people aren't cut out for the job, are they?"

"My mother made the brave choice," the acolyte said. "I have a home and a family here I never would have had on my own. I thank her in my devotions every day for doing what was best for me."

"What about the ones whose mothers waited too long to give up?" Lucha asked. She remembered the lullabies. The dancing. The stories. The long silences, the dark windows, and the screaming.

Would Lucha truly be better off had she never known her?

"You're here, aren't you?" the other girl asked. "Almudena finds a way."

Lucha turned this over in silence for a long time. Eventually, her new friend drifted off to find a livelier conversation partner, but Lucha stayed stuck to her bench, thinking of Lydia. Of the last time she'd seen her. Of the cord she'd cut between them to survive.

Where was she now? Lucha wondered. What fate had befallen her back in Robado?

And had the acolyte been right about Almudena bringing Lucha here? She looked around at this beautiful place. The strong women who ran it. The motherless children who had found homes here. Found peace.

Suddenly, Lucha felt bone-tired. Weary to her soul. She got heavily to her feet, ready to make her way back to her little bed and sleep like the dead. Perhaps it would all make more sense in the morning.

But as she passed a knot of light green robes in focused conversation, she couldn't help but overhear their words. Words that reminded her she was not a pilgrim, and never would be.

"She's detoxing in Ring Five."

"They say it's *the* drug! The one *he* created. Can you imagine?"

"What will they do with her?"

"I don't know, but if they're keeping her in the inner sanctum they obviously don't want her leaving . . . or anyone knowing she's here."

Lucha silently begged them to say more, but they seemed to have exhausted their information, and the talk drifted to other matters.

She clung to the scraps they had given her—so much more than Río had disclosed. This new information chased musings of mothers and abandonment out of her mind as she latched onto her goal like a lifeline.

No matter how tempting this place was, no matter what whimsical fantasies it inspired, it could never be her home.

She could not let herself be a prisoner when she had a job to do.

22

Lucha awoke in the straw bed, rested. The determination she'd found at the party carried through to this bright, cheerful morning. It was as if she'd spent the night awake planning, when in truth she had slept without dreaming.

She could not let herself be lured by this place. By its beauty or its community or its history. Salvador had used her. Twisted her hatred for the drug he had created, and manipulated her with it. But the aim she had started with had not changed. She would see all the Olvida burn. Would see the kings dethroned.

Even if she had to destroy Salvador to reach it.

Especially then.

Lucha had let Salvador prey upon her emotions, and it had nearly cost her everything. She would not let Río twist her love for her sister, or her desire for a safe place to call home. All she could do now was find out whether Río was a worthy ally or an enemy.

And there was only one place to begin.

Lucha dressed in one of several white robes folded in a

chest of drawers, washed her face and hands in the basin, and stepped out into the morning sun with a plan.

She needed to learn more about Salvador, to find out whether Paz was prisoner or accomplice here, and to find and free Lis. The quickest way to achieve any of these goals without arousing suspicion was to go straight to the source of power.

"Where does Obispo Río breakfast?" she asked the first green-robed figure she passed on the path.

"In the hall, with the acolytes," the startled young man responded.

"Thank you," Lucha said, and turned back toward the scene of last night's celebration.

The single, laden table from the night before had been replaced with at least twenty smaller ones. Knots of conversing groups sat with steaming bowls of what appeared to be some kind of porridge, but Lucha wasn't hungry.

Río was seated with her guards beneath the largest window, sipping from a clay cup with a handle. Lucha wondered suddenly if she always traveled with bodyguards, or if this was a reaction to the presence of suspected evil in their midst.

"Good morning, Obispo," she said when she reached the table.

Río's eyes on hers were inscrutable as ever. "Good morning, Miss Moya. Please, join us."

Lucha took the empty chair.

"I trust you rested well."

"Very well, thank you," Lucha replied. "I feel more clear-headed than ever."

"The air within the sanctuary is said to promote mental acuity," Río replied. "I'm pleased to hear it wasn't lost on you."

"I've been thinking about your offer to train me as an acolyte," Lucha said, losing her patience for small talk. "And I think we both know there are better uses for my particular skill set."

Francisca's and Juana's eyes flitted to Río's, but the obispo kept hers locked on Lucha's.

"Is that right?"

"You kidnapped me," Lucha said bluntly. "You're holding my sister hostage. I have no doubt that you're prepared to react with drastic measures should I attempt to leave the sanctuary grounds. Do you disagree with my assessment?"

Río surveyed her as she sipped her steaming drink. "I fear you have rather the wrong impression of our intentions," she said at last. "Your residence here, as well as your sister's, is for your own good as well as the greater good."

Into Lucha's skeptical silence, she continued: "You know as well as I do what will happen the moment you step outside these grounds. Are you prepared to stop it?"

For a moment, ghostly flames seared the scarred place in Lucha's chest. *He* would be desperate, after her rejection of him. He would waste no more time with convincing. It would be compulsion now. Torture, until she acquiesced or died.

Could one ever be prepared for something like that?

"My point precisely," Lucha said, shaking off her fears like flies. "We have the same goal, Obispo. His destruction. I want freedom for myself and all the victims of his drug. You want your people removed from the threat of his influence. Why not work together?"

Juana scoffed.

Lucha ignored her.

Río seemed to ponder her words. "What exactly do you propose?" she asked after a beat.

"Honesty, to begin with," Lucha said without hesitating. "I know there are things you haven't told me. Things you're holding back because you're afraid I'm still in league with him. Let me assure you, once and for all, that I had no knowledge of his plot. He was a means to an end, and his promises were lies. I have nothing more to gain from his fellowship."

"You expect to waltz in here and be handed the secrets of our order?" hissed Juana, evidently unable to hold her tongue a moment longer. "A girl from the Scar with the stench of *him* still lingering on you. Why should we trust you?"

Lucha met her eyes coolly. "Because it sounds very much like I'm your only chance to get rid of him."

"Or doom all of humanity trying!"

"Enough." Río's voice was soft, but it rang with authority. Juana was cowed at once.

"Honesty goes both ways, Miss Moya. Until we can ascertain the true nature of your power, of your connection with him, we cannot afford to take chances. Of course, we could study these things over time, with or without your participation. But with cooperation it will be much easier."

Lucha thought of all the secrets she'd kept—since storming into Pecado, and before. The things she'd done. The idea of sharing them with sanctimonious strangers was less than enjoyable. But she wanted Salvador gone. She wanted Olvida destroyed and its victims free at last. Wasn't this a smaller price to pay than the torture Salvador had subjected her to?

"Let's get on with it, then," she said at last. "I'm an open book. I'll warn you, though, it isn't a pleasant story."

"I didn't expect it to be."

"And once you've heard it, you'll answer some questions of mine?"

Juana leaned forward again. "Obispo, I must object. We know nothing of this girl's history. Nothing of her intentions. We cannot trust a story tainted by his influence, not without—"

This time, Río held out a hand for silence. "I had something other than talking in mind."

Río and her guards led Lucha beyond the hall. Here, the path took a decidedly upward slant. It was narrower, and the forest more dense. They'd been walking about twenty minutes when they reached the first gate.

"You need more security than the boundary?" Lucha asked, testing their agreement.

"Each ring of the sanctuary houses acolytes at different levels," Río explained. Lucha watched closely as she removed an ornate ring from her finger and pressed it into a mechanism at the gate's center.

A *sapphire*, she noted as Río replaced the ring and the

gate opened itself before them. She wore three others. Lucha hadn't noticed them before.

As the four of them stepped through the gate together, Lucha heard the rushing sound from the boundary—quieter here, but she shivered as she walked through it nonetheless, the emptiness flaring to life within her.

She clutched her chest, wincing. This barrier clearly identified magical aptitude, and any encounter with it stirred the void within Lucha. Juana's eyes missed nothing.

Honesty, Lucha told herself, then said: "The place I was separated from *him* feels . . . hollow. Empty. The enchantment in your boundary intensifies the feeling. It's not altogether pleasant."

Río raised her eyebrows but did not comment.

"How many rings are there?" Lucha asked when she had recovered.

"Five," Río replied, confirming her suspicion. "The gates are said to have been enchanted by Almudena herself. They help us keep order among the devoted, as well as providing a safeguard against intruders with ill intentions."

They walked through the second ring as she spoke. The cottages were stone here as well, but the gardens were larger— each one a riot of carefully tended growth.

"The new pilgrims reside on the outer ring," Río continued. "Some remain there for their lifetime of service, content. Others attain the rank of devotee, and progress inward, to this ring."

In the second ring, they wore pale green. Lucha's was the only white robe in sight. There had been an air of novice excitement in the pilgrims' ring, but here it was replaced with industriousness. Their small processional passed buildings too large to be dwellings, in time, and from them came the sounds of hammering.

"What are they working on?" Lucha asked.

"I'm sure they'd be delighted to show you, once you've joined their ranks," Río said.

It would never happen, Lucha knew. That fantasy had closed itself off to her the moment she rededicated herself to the destruction of Salvador. She kept that thought to herself for now. Honesty only went so far from captive to captor.

This time, the ring that opened the gate was set with a ruby, and the yawning of the void in Lucha's chest was stronger. She felt clammy and weak once she'd passed through, her hands shaking as she pushed her hair off her face.

"I'm fine," she said, before Juana could remark, but she scarcely noticed the landscape of the third ring. She was already bracing herself for the next gate. It opened with an emerald, and Lucha had to steady herself on a low wall on the other side.

Río waited patiently for Lucha to collect herself. When she had, they set off through the fourth ring. It looked much like the others—robes a shade darker, houses a little larger—save for one important feature: in this ring, shaggy yellow-eyed cubs trotted at the heels of the acolytes.

"Compañeras," Lucha said. She couldn't help but be charmed by the little things—even considering the role they'd played in her capture.

"It appears you're more aware of our customs than you let on," Río said. She bent down to scratch the ears of the next cub that passed. The emerald-robed acolyte escorting it bowed her head in reverence.

"My traveling companion was a pilgrim," Lucha said. The now-familiar heaviness that accompanied thoughts of Paz settled alongside the lingering pain the boundary had caused. "She had heard the tales."

Once I've done what Río expects, I'll ask all my questions, Lucha vowed. *I will not accept less than the truth. And if Paz sent them to capture us, I'll never forgive her.*

Dread pooled in her stomach as they approached the final gate. Lucha had hoped she was being led here—to the inner sanctum where her sister was held. But as the emptiness reached for her from this gate—ancient, and overgrown with ivy—her courage nearly faltered.

For Lis, she told herself, and gritted her teeth as Río removed a sparkling diamond from her left ring finger.

It was worse, by far, than the moment in the bath at the Catedral. Nearly as bad as the boundary itself. Lucha teetered on the edge of a vast nothingness that threatened to erase her senses. Her memories. There was no hope, said the emptiness. No victory promised. There was only power, and Lucha had lost all of hers.

She heard herself cry out as if from the bottom of a dark well. She could hear nothing else. See nothing of the inner sanctum. Lis could have pranced in a circle around her and she never would have known.

Sobs threatened to choke her throat. Someone was crying. Someone . . .

A hard smack rattled her skull, the print of it stinging on her cheek. A little of the emptiness ebbed. There was green. Gold. Sparkling lights.

Smack.

Lucha saw stars. But stars were not nothing. She squinted, and slowly a face came into focus. Dark hair. Blue eyes.

"No need to hit me again," she managed. She was on her back on some hard surface, and she struggled to right herself. "I'm all right."

Juana stepped back, and slowly the fifth ring came into focus. Every ring had been lovely, Lucha thought, but there was no comparison to this. She got to her feet, trying to disguise the trembling of her knees, the tenuous grasp of her consciousness on her own living body.

She focused on her surroundings. The light. The life. The beauty. There was plenty to behold here. A mosaic wall surrounded it all, with a design so intricate it was hard to believe it had been made by human hands.

The trees here were immense, pulsing with an ancient energy that intimidated Lucha even as it awed her. There were polished benches and planters made of shining gemstones, fountains and other water features that sparkled and flashed in the late-morning sun.

The few who gathered in this ring radiated an inner calm that made Lucha twice as aware of her trembling hands, her unsteadily thumping heart. They walked with calm purpose— trailed by the cats Lucha recognized. No longer kittens but fully grown, with piercing predators' eyes.

"Is this where Almudena lived?" Lucha asked, pushing herself to her feet. It was a fitting backdrop for a divine being, but Lucha was less interested in this than in any sign of her sister. She scanned the place as best she could while her guide spoke, but saw nothing to suggest Lis was here.

"In a manner of speaking, yes," Río was saying. "It now houses our priestesses and our rarest tomes of arcane knowledge, as well as acting as training ground for our holy warriors and their compañeras."

"Well, it's certainly well protected," Lucha said, wincing as a wave of vertigo hit. "What are you hiding in here, Obispo?"

Río gave her a swift, searching look. Could she tell Lucha knew Lis was in this ring? If she could, she didn't let on. "If you're ready to proceed," she said, "our destination lies this way."

One last obstacle, Lucha told herself. *And then freedom, allies or no.*

23

Lucha lagged behind her guides, the effects of the gate's boundary stubbornly persisting until their destination came into view: a two-story stone church, tall and slim. Its spire seemed to pierce the sky.

They approached from the west, but Río led them around to the front doors, pausing as if to allow a moment to admire the effect.

Lucha Moya was hardly the first person to fall to her knees at the sight of the inner sanctum's holiest temple, but as she did, she thought little of those who had come before her. She thought only that until this moment, knees biting into stone, she had not understood reverence—and now, all at once, she did.

A stained-glass work of art took up much of the chapel's north wall. Like the mosaic, it seemed too otherworldly to have been created by any methods mortals could devise. It depicted a woman with glowing brown skin, raven hair falling in waves to her waist. Her palms were open, golden light streaming from them.

Lucha had seen her, of course. The weeping woman from her vision. The goddess had an immortal beauty that dazzled—but that was not what made it impossible to look away from her. On Almudena's face was an expression of perfect serenity. An expression that said the girl on her knees was forgiven, but more than that—she was loved.

Lucha had never had much use for royalty, or gods. Those with power, she had always known, could not be trusted. But the woman before her now was not only a goddess. Not only a queen. Her eyes—looking straight into Lucha's now—said she was a mother first. A mother always.

Later, Lucha would blame the boundaries for weakening her resolve. For cracking her heart open. For making her susceptible to this trick of glass and light.

In the moment, however, she looked into the abyss within her at last. To a depth of pain that had not begun with Salvador. She saw doors that would not open. Eyes that would not focus on her. She saw the snarl on the face of the woman she had hated—but only because she had wanted so badly to be loved by her.

That yawning, endless void told Lucha she could never be good enough. Never work hard enough. Never love her mother enough to have that love returned to her. That she was worthless, flawed in some way that made her unworthy of it . . .

In front of her, the shining face of Almudena told her the truth at last: that Lucha was not to blame. That she was worthy. That her mother's choices had been made by a broken heart, but Lucha's could be whole if she chose it.

Tears streamed down her face. She did not bother to wipe them away.

Lucha thought Río had brought her here to inspire devotion. To show Lucha she could have a place here. Could heal here, and be whole. But upon Lucha, it had the opposite effect. She thought of the effect resources like this, *hope* like this, could have had on the people of Robado. On Lucha's mother.

What could Lydia have done if she had been allowed to heal?

Río wanted to protect her precious sanctuary, but all she had accomplished was to deprive the people who needed this most.

People with power used it to protect their right to be powerful, Lucha realized as her tears dried on her face. But that was not its purpose.

Lucha got to her feet, tore her eyes from the beloved face. But something of what she'd seen stayed with her—like a ray of perpetual sun warming her heart.

"Moving, isn't it?" Río asked.

"More than you know," Lucha replied.

"The ceremony will take place inside."

Lucha followed. She felt she was ready for whatever came next.

"It's an old ritual," Río continued, "from the days when the gift was still among us. It will tell us of your nature much more truly than words can."

"And if my nature isn't to your liking?" Lucha asked. "Do I have your word I'll remain safe?"

"If we see anything concerning, we will discuss it afterward," Rio replied.

"*Your word*, Obispo," Lucha insisted, ignoring Juana when she stepped forward.

"You have it," said Río after a long pause. "Provided you remain within the boundary."

Lucha did not give her own word. There was no need. She would be leaving this place with or without their permission. They passed through a blue-painted door in silence, entering what appeared to be a small library. Ancient, leather-bound tomes were shelved on every wall. Among them were scrolls, some looking close to dust.

What Alán would have given to see this, Lucha thought, remembering his collection, the jealousy with which he'd guarded it. It seemed a lifetime ago.

Río sat on one side of a square tea table in the center of the room, gesturing for Lucha to sit opposite. There were no chairs, and the table was low. Lucha crossed her legs, feeling the soreness in them.

"Francisca, if you would," said the obispo.

Lucha watched as the red-haired woman opened a wooden cabinet in the wall, busying herself over something Lucha could not see. When she was finished, she placed a steaming teapot and two small cups before them, backing away to guard the door.

"What is it?" Lucha asked, immediately suspicious.

Río's gaze was cool on hers. "Tea," she said, "made from the leaves of the Pensa plant."

Lucha recoiled. "No," she said forcefully, pushing away from the table. "I won't."

"What you must understand," said Río calmly, as if she had expected this, "is that Pensa, unaltered, was a gift from the goddess to her devoted. It allows us to see as she sees. The truth, unfettered by our limited perspectives. The truth that will set us free."

Was this why Almudena had sent the hare? Lucha wondered, remembering the reverence on Paz's face with a painful twinge. There was no doubt the vision had served her—Salvador and his divine mother, the truth of their final conflict—but at what cost?

"The Pensa was grown here," Río continued, oblivious. "In our own gardens. It is untainted and pure, I give you my word. You will suffer no ill effects—unless you fear the truth."

Of course Lucha feared the truth. But there was no other way. So when Río drank from her cup, Lucha did the same.

Perhaps *this* was what her mother had been seeking in the throes of Olvida, Lucha thought, before the wave overtook her. Perhaps she'd only wanted to feel close to something divine . . .

The effects of the drug were no less disorienting because Lucha expected them.

One moment, she was seated across from Río at the table, the next she was back in the devastated grove. The place, marked by the lightning-struck tree, where Almudena had buried her son.

From a little way on, she heard the sound of a woman's voice chanting. Lucha followed the sound until she beheld her. Almudena, unmistakably, standing before the jagged, broken giant with her arms extended. Her palms faced inward to cup a ball of light that rivaled the sun for brightness.

Was this part of the ritual that had contained Salvador? Lucha wondered as she watched. Had this vision begun where the last one ended?

But the trees surrounding the dead grove were taller, she realized as the details of the scene settled and sharpened. The air was warm. This was another season. Another year. Sometime after she'd imprisoned her son, and before she'd left this world forever.

For the moment, Lucha only watched, unable to understand the ancient language of the song. The scarred place in her heart glowed once more with the warmth she had felt in the sanctuary.

But soon enough, the ritual happening in front of her began to clarify. The ball of light Almudena held had not been conjured from nowhere—the natural luminescence the goddess had shone with even in her darkest hour was fading as her orb grew brighter.

She was feeding it her own divine life, and Lucha couldn't bear to watch.

"Stop!" She stepped forward, knowing she could not be heard, but unable to restrain herself.

Almudena did not stop. She continued to feed the ball of light until her skin was sallow, her expression pained. Only when her hands began to shake did she seem to release the connection at last.

I am not a root, Lucha remembered. The forest, drawing life from her.

The orb was pulsing with light, and Lucha couldn't tear her eyes from it. The play of colors on its surface was so subtle, so lovely. An early-summer morning made liquid. She watched as the goddess guided it forward, toward a knot in the tree's jagged lower trunk.

For a moment, Lucha thought Almudena meant to restore this tree to its former glory. Certainly it was transformed by its connection with the orb, vines bursting from its lifeless surface, flowers blooming along their lengths.

It would spread, Lucha thought. Bring life back to this desolate place. But the blooms withered mere moments after they appeared. The vines lay as listless and pale as their surroundings. Almudena did not seem surprised, only exhausted. There was an air of finality about her, Lucha thought, as she took a vivid red blossom from her crown and placed it in the knot.

This flower did not wither.

Satisfied, Almudena turned her back on the scene. Lucha readied herself to follow, sure there was more to see—but the goddess approached her instead.

"Will you walk with me?" she asked, her gaze locking onto Lucha's. "There is much to discuss, and we have less time than we need."

Lucha whirled around, expecting to see another figure. For a wild moment she thought it might be Salvador, risen from his amber grave. But there was no one there. Only Lucha's own shadow, stretching across the pallid grass.

Slowly, she turned back to face the goddess. "Can you see me?" she asked. Her voice trembled on the words. Her heart was in her throat.

"I can," said Almudena. "Now, please, let us walk."

24

This is a *dream,* Lucha told herself as she followed the forest mother through the graveyard grove. *A hallucination. It isn't real.*

"A vision," Almudena said, answering her thoughts. "But no less real for that, I assure you."

"Why me?" Lucha asked the burning question first.

"Why not you?"

There was no point in concealing the truth. The goddess could hear her every thought. "Because I made a bargain with Salvador," she said. "Because allying with him was not too high a price for what I wanted . . ."

They walked for some time in silence, Lucha lost in her thoughts, the goddess listening. "Thank you," she said at last. "It has been some time since I heard his given name spoken. Of course, by now you know what it means."

"Savior," Lucha said.

"Yes," Almudena replied. "It was my wish for him. I believed if he was born here, if he knew no other place, he would feel an empathy for our people that I never could."

Lucha thought privately that Almudena could hardly have been more wrong about her son.

Another silence, and then: "You believe the trust you placed in him makes you unfit for the task at hand." It was not a question. "But you have not considered the obvious: that in making him, *I* trusted. That in not stopping him sooner, I trusted. That in not *killing* him, I trusted. Would you judge me as harshly as you judge yourself?"

"The obispo . . . ," Lucha said, attempting to explain. "Her acolytes. They act as if I'm contaminated. Unfit to walk the sanctuary's paths. I'm here as part of a test. If I fail . . ."

"If you fail because of your connection with my son, we share their censure."

"They would never condemn you. They worship you."

Almudena tilted her head thoughtfully, and Lucha was reminded of the compañeras. Sharp-eyed. Dangerous. "They find it easier, now that I am a story. There is divine will, and then there is its interpretation by those who seek to serve. They cannot be mistaken for each other."

Lucha pondered this. All the ways pure will could be manipulated in the wrong hands. Pensa had been created by it, and Olvida derived from that. One had taken Lucha's mother. The other allowed her to speak with the mother of all.

She thought of Los Ricos, the way they'd further perverted the drug. The profits they made. The way they used its influence to oppress and control, to marginalize and withhold.

And Río . . . Río, who had been entrusted with divine will,

and had used it to divide. To protect one elite group and condemn so many others.

"Just so," Almudena said to Lucha's swirling thoughts and memories. "It is not power that is corrupt, but mortals who corrupt it."

"Can they help it?" Lucha asked. It seemed important. Perhaps the most important question she had ever asked.

"I was hoping we could find out, together."

They had reached the edge of the devastated grove. The border was stark: Here, death. There, life. One only needed to step across the line.

"What would you have me do?" Lucha asked. "I could command the power, once. The obispo says I was gifted, but I never knew. *He* . . . took it with him when I rejected him at the boundary." She shuddered. Remembered the ravenous void within instead of describing.

The look on Almudena's face said she understood.

"The power was not his to take," she said. Anger in her voice for the first time. "But even that can be restored. There is power here. For the one who decides to do what I could not. I could not kill him, but neither could I leave my people unprotected."

The orb, Lucha thought, remembering the way it had drained the goddess. The single, perfect flower that marked its place. Here, in the grove where he was buried. The place where he would have led Lucha, had she not been abducted on the way.

A weapon, for anyone willing to come here and wield it.

"I cannot interfere with the paths of mortals," the goddess said now, a little wistful. "I can only inform. Your choices must be your own to make."

They continued walking until the skeletal trees were behind them. Lucha lost track of time. Of everything but the warmth of the divine being beside her. She did not know if this was only in her head, only that she would remember it as long as she lived.

Almudena stopped when they reached a curtain of emerald vines. Lucha stood beside her.

"When I pull back these vines, you will see one possible future," she said. "If you do not desire it, you are free to choose another. Do you understand?"

"I do," Lucha said, trembling. She did not want to see the future. She was afraid she would not want it. She was more afraid she would.

Almudena did not ask if she was ready, only pulled back the curtain and stood silently as Lucha beheld her fate.

She was dressed in a dark pine robe, a crown of red flowers like the goddess's own upon her brow. Her skin shone, and she laughed as she sat upon what could only be described as a throne. Beside her, Lis played with a green-eyed cub. The shadows were gone from beneath her eyes.

All around them, pilgrims and devotees knelt. Their eyes glistened with tears.

Lucha felt her own eyes fill as she looked upon the scene. She looked happy. More than that, she looked like she belonged.

Everyone around her loved her. Worshipped her. But as the scene drew back, she gasped.

The boundary was in place around the sanctuary. Strong as ever. Within it, all was light. Abundance. Outside, there were flames. Twisted, bleached-white trees like the ones in Salvador's grove. Sombralados. Bones. Endless mountains of bones.

"Obispo Río is seeing her own vision now," came Almudena's voice from beside Lucha. "In it, she will see your power. Your connection to the divine. She will see that you *are* the savior who was promised, despite her misgivings."

"I am?" Lucha breathed.

"You will be if you choose to be," Almudena said. "There is no fate, child. Not for mortals. Where there is will, there can never be destiny. But you have the gift. And you have the knowledge. Now you must choose."

The inner sanctum was back, but this time the scene looked different. Lucha's smile was frozen on her face. Around her ankles there were chains. Delicate and silver, beautiful in their own right. But chains nonetheless.

"She'll never let me leave," Lucha said, realization dawning. "Not if it means risking the only gifted mortal born in a hundred years. She'll make a mascot of me, and he will never be destroyed. Olvida will never be destroyed."

"Remember," Almudena said, "there are no chosen. There is only will. If you decide to put aside your task, another will take it up in time."

"How much time?" Lucha asked.

Almudena only spread her hands.

Lucha understood. Someone else *would* come along. Someone else with the gift. Whether it took a year or a hundred or a thousand. Lucha could give up this burden. Be loved. Be safe. A beautiful bird in a gilded cage. Almudena would forgive her . . .

The world would suffer, for a time. But it would not be her doing. And Lucha's suffering would be over at last.

Almudena closed the vine curtain then, but the scene lingered in Lucha's memory.

"Will you show me what happens if I make another choice?" she asked, knowing the answer.

Almudena shook her head. "You have the information you need to choose. The rest is already within you, and our time together is nearly at an end."

The tea, Lucha remembered, like she was looking into some past life. The dark room. The obispo, across from her, learning the truth of Lucha's nature. Readying the chains.

Río would be determined, Lucha knew. To keep the savior of humanity under her control. It would be a fight, if Lucha chose another path. Relinquished the shining future she had seen.

But hadn't she fought enough? Hadn't she sacrificed enough? Lis was safe. Salvador could not reach her. Didn't she deserve to rest?

"There is no deserving," Almudena said as the landscape began to fade around them.

"Only choice," Lucha finished. "Will I ever see you again?"

"We shall see what the future holds," the goddess said with a smile. She stepped forward even as she faded, her cool arms encircling Lucha's shoulders, removing the burden of a mother who had not known how to love her. Replacing it with the love of one who would.

"Always," Almudena said with tears in her eyes. And then she was gone.

By the time Lucha returned to herself, the choice had already been made.

It would not be enough to know that in some distant future Salvador would pay for what he had done to the world. To Lucha herself. Any peace promised to her by Almudena's vision, by Río's protection, would be impossible as long as he still lived. Perhaps Lucha *had* earned peace, but it was not the only thing she had earned.

And the right she most wanted to claim was this one: to look into Salvador's eyes as his reign of manipulation and destruction was ended.

Life was made of choices. Destiny was a myth. But there, in the hallowed halls of Almudena's most private sanctuary, Lucha Moya chose the only future she could live with.

It was time.

Obispo Río was still deep in her trance. Her closed eyelids fluttered. On her face there was a radiant smile.

There would be time, now, before the obispo came back to herself—but there were the guards to consider. Francisca and Juana were posted by the door. Only, when Lucha looked closer, she saw that their backs were turned to her.

She got to her feet as silently as she could, creeping up behind them. It was there she saw what had made distrustful Juana abandon her post: In the hallway—where before there had been nothing but blank stone—water dripped from the ceiling. It turned the pale gray of the wall dark in a very specific pattern.

The image of the goddess. A sign to her devoted.

Río stirred behind her. There was no time to waste. While the guards were still consumed with their miracle, Lucha crept behind them, down the hallway and back through the blue door.

Closing it, she moved a heavy wooden pew, blocking them in. It would not hold for long. Within minutes, the whole of the sanctuary would know her for a fugitive.

And then: shouting, from the library. Right on cue. Someone—Juana, Lucha would have bet anything—threw their weight into the blocked exit. The temple doors were open wide to the sunshine outside, but how far could Lucha possibly run? Unescorted, in a white pilgrim's robe in the most protected part of the sanctuary?

She'd be lucky if she wasn't captured immediately. And if by some divine intervention she wasn't, the gates would weaken her. She would not be able to outrun them, or to fight.

But she had spent a lifetime hiding. That, she could do.

With silent footsteps that had crept past many a soldado

in their time, Lucha crossed to an unassuming door, easing it closed behind her.

It was a cloak closet. Small, impossibly dark. But they believed she had fled. Whatever Río's vision had shown her of Lucha's power, it was not enough to temper her distrust. Her belief that Lucha would return to Salvador.

Outside, a crashing sound indicated that Juana had pushed the bench aside at last. Footsteps entered the room. Three sets, Lucha noted. That meant Río was awake. In fact, the obispo's voice drifted past the closed door now, confirming Lucha's suspicions.

"We have to find her before she crosses the boundary." Her voice shook with anger—or was it fear? "Her importance cannot be overstated. If he is allowed to regain his hold on her . . . all will be lost."

"We will question everyone in the inner sanctum," Juana assured her. "If she has left the fifth ring, we will know in minutes. We *will* find her."

"Don't bother," Río said. "We need to think a step ahead. The boundaries will be useless against her. They may weaken her, slow her, but they will not stop her. If we don't make the most of this time, she could be across the boundary in less than an hour."

"To the fourth ring, then?" Francisca, this time.

"Yes," Río replied. "And quickly."

More footsteps, running now. The slamming of a heavy door. And then they were gone, along with any other path

Lucha might have taken. If they discovered her after this, there would be no alliance. No golden throne. Somewhere, behind a curtain of blessed vines, another future had taken shape.

She hoped it showed Salvador, destroyed at last. The Olvida warehouses burning. But this time she'd have to find out for herself.

With steady hands and dry eyes, Lucha pulled one of the deep green cloaks on, covering as much of her telltale white robe as she could. Thus disguised, she emerged silently into the empty room.

With slow, measured steps, Lucha made her way across the inner sanctum.

Her eyes were peeled for an infirmary, or any building that looked like it might be hiding her sister. She had not come this far to abandon Lis now. And despite her questions, her suspicions, she still hoped to find Paz with her. A prisoner herself. The details of their capture as much a mystery to her as they were to Lucha.

Lucha passed two small libraries, a dining hall, a low fenced area that seemed to house compañera mothers and their cubs. With her hood raised, her white robe covered, no one gave her a second glance. The search was undoubtedly beginning in the fourth ring. In trying to stay a step ahead, Río had missed the mark.

If she'd truly understood Lucha, she would have known there was only one place to look.

Lucha spotted it at last. A small white building, a green cross in a circle painted above the door. If Lis was still detoxing from the hare, or the sedative in the dart, she would be here.

But before Lucha could find a way to sneak inside unnoticed, she stopped short at the sound of a familiar laugh drifting out an open window.

Heart in her throat, she crept up to it and peered inside. Her hood obscured her face, but no one was looking at her. Inside, Lis sat up in bed. Her cheeks were pink, and her eyes sparkled. There was a tiny yellow-eyed kitten in her lap. She wore the pale green robes of a second-ring devotee, and around her three healers teased the kitten, laughing along.

The longing to barge in, to take Lis with her wherever she went, was so strong it nearly sent Lucha crashing through the window. But the road ahead was dangerous, and Lis looked happy. Safe. Tears gathering in her eyes, Lucha realized she hadn't come here to rescue her sister . . .

She had come to say goodbye.

And now that she was here, she couldn't even do that.

Lis would demand to accompany her, or else beg her to stay behind. Lis would not care for her personal safety if it meant sending Lucha off into danger alone. She was no longer the spoiled little sister Lucha had imagined her to be for so many years. Perhaps she had never been.

She was strong, and brave, and selfless, and she would be all right.

With her heart tearing in two, Lucha took one last look at her sister. A look she hoped would not have to last the rest of her life. She would be back, if she could. Once the work was done. But there were no guarantees.

Only choices.

And so Lucha turned away from the window—only to find an arrow pointed directly at her throat.

25

For a moment, Lucha didn't recognize the woman holding the bow.

Her hair was pulled back into a severe braid, her robe the deep green of the inner sanctum. Her expression was determined and fierce, but not afraid. This was not her first time holding a weapon. If she killed Lucha, here and now, that wouldn't be a first either.

And then, slowly, the rest came into focus. The shape of her beneath the robe. The light in those eyes, behind her narrowed gaze. The girl's expression wrenched in Lucha's chest, and she had her answer—the one she'd been waiting for since that first muffled conversation on the road—at last.

Lucha hadn't realized how potent her hope had been until the moment it was shattered. She felt the loss of it keenly, mingling with all the rest.

"I didn't want to believe it." Lucha stepped sideways away from the window. She spoke in a voice that would not carry. "Even when I overheard you after we were captured. Even when I realized where we were and who had taken us." These admissions cut on their way out. Somewhere inside her, the girl Lucha had been in Robado—the girl who trusted no one—was laughing.

"Let me explain."

"You told them where to find us," Lucha said, as if she had not heard her. "You've been leading them to us the whole time, haven't you?"

Her memory called up every moment they had shared, mocking her. After sixteen years in the Scar, *trust* had been her undoing.

"If you just come with me, I can help you understand." Paz's voice was patient. Steady.

Hope flared again, and Lucha stamped it out viciously. "I understand everything I need to. You had your agenda and I had mine. The only question left is what you'll do now—because I'm leaving this place, and I won't let you stand in my way."

"I can't let you leave."

"Then you'll have to try to stop me." It was time to run. Or to fight. Time to make her choice. The bow followed her as she crept toward the greenery at the pavilion's edge. A tether, connecting the arrow's point to Lucha's pounding heart. "Before I go," she said, the words torn from her against her will, "tell me: Was any of it real?"

There was more than a holy warrior's devotion in Paz's expression. A hurt of her own was blooming, and it kept her bowstring taut. "I could ask you the same thing."

Strangely, the hurt on her face was a relief. It meant Lucha had not been alone in it. It was enough to get her through what she had to say next—a gamble the girl she'd been in the Scar would never have taken.

"There's something I have to do," Lucha said. "A task given to me by Almudena."

"The goddess doesn't give tasks."

"A choice, then," Lucha said, too aware of every second passing. "She gave me a choice, and I've made it. I need to leave the sanctuary."

"And return to *him*?"

There it was again, Lucha thought. Pain, at the edge of her voice. "Yes," she said. "But not in the way you think."

"What's to stop me from taking you back to Río?" Paz asked. "They told me what you are. What you *really* are. I can't let you destroy the world, Lucha, no matter how much I cared for you."

"I don't want to destroy the world!" Lucha said in a tense whisper. "Look, it doesn't matter how you feel about me. It doesn't matter whether we can trust each other. It matters whether you believe in divine will or the bureaucracy that sprang up to carry it out. Only one of them is going to save us all."

"You're saying Obispo Río is corrupt?" Paz said, her tone withering. "And *you* are somehow the paragon of divine virtue? After everything you've done?"

"I'm saying Río has power, a position, and people to protect. It clouds her perspective. But mine, in this moment, is crystal clear. So are you going to help me rid the world of

El Sediento? Or does this end in a fight? Because I'm crossing the boundary, Paz. With or without you."

The moment of silence between them stretched endlessly. Paz pulled the arrow back farther still, the creaking of the wood and string ominous. Lucha waited as warring emotions passed across her beautiful face.

You could have stayed, said the Lucha on the throne. The shining mascot. *You could have had everything.*

And then, just as Lucha thought it would turn ugly, that Paz would loose her arrow at last, something happened: from the sky—though there were no flowering trees nearby— a perfect red blossom floated down on a gentle breeze and landed at Paz's feet.

Lucha watched, the tension palpable, as Paz's eyes filled with tears. She lowered her bow and bent down to pick up the gift. Lucha could have run while the other girl was distracted. But something made her stay. Something made her hope.

Paz looked up, and her expression was filled with wonder. The same expression from the night she'd fallen to her knees and called Lucha *salvadora* . . .

"I know a way," she said. "Follow me. And keep your hood up."

The atmosphere in the inner sanctum had changed. Everywhere there was urgency. Hurry. On every face was a look of fear.

"Keep your face covered," Paz said, leading Lucha back the way she'd come. Toward the church with its towering spire.

But they did not enter. On the south side of the building, there was a metal disk recessed into the ground. Paz looked around furtively before lifting it and gesturing into the darkness below.

A dark tunnel; a ladder. Lucha could not see where it would take her. She climbed down anyway, knowing it was her only hope. That if Paz betrayed her again, there would be no way out.

The ladder's rungs were slippery and cold under her hands. When Paz followed her, replacing the disk behind them, there was no light at all. Lucha found her way by feeling alone. One rung, then another, then another as they left the surface of the world behind.

Down they climbed. Was it ten minutes? An hour? Lucha had no way of knowing. By the time her feet touched solid ground every muscle in her body ached.

Paz reached the ground beside her. "Let's go," she said, turning west and taking off at a run.

"Wait," Lucha said, her voice echoing strangely in the dark. "Where are we going?"

"They know this place is here," Paz replied. "They won't expect *you* to know, so they won't check right away. But soon enough they'll be after us."

They were in some kind of underground cavern. A very dim light came from somewhere far off—enough to stop them from tripping, but not to see anything in detail. Soon, Lucha heard the sound of running water.

Her blood ran cold. Another boundary? She was already exhausted. Relief washed over her when they reached a narrow underground river.

"I hope you can swim," Paz said, stripping off her robe, tying it around her head, and walking into the water.

Lucha followed suit, letting the cloak sink to the bottom. The water was shockingly cold, but together she and Paz let the current carry them into velvety darkness.

The water moved swiftly, and soon the distant light grew brighter. Lucha could see rock ceilings a hundred feet above them. She couldn't help but admire the ingenuity of these priestesses—or was it the goddess who had created this escape route?

As they floated through the cavern, the ceilings dropped, the space shrinking into a narrower and narrower tunnel, which ended all too abruptly. They were falling before Lucha could get her bearings, and she screamed, air and water rushing around her, her heart in her throat as she fell and fell.

A *waterfall*, she thought dizzily. And then she hit the pond below.

The impact felt more like stone than liquid. Lucha gasped, struggled to rise.

"Quiet," Paz said when her head broke the surface at last. "Do you want everyone in the sanctuary to know we're here?"

Lucha didn't bother to answer. Paz, at least, had known

the waterfall was coming. Would it have been so hard to warn Lucha? She hauled herself, teeth chattering, insults unspoken, onto the bank.

"Get dressed," Paz said. "We're just beyond the Catedral now. It isn't far to the boundary. I assume you know where you're going after that?"

Lucha pictured the grove from her visions. The bones. Towering above them all, the lightning-struck tree where Salvador was entombed. Lucha shuddered. She didn't know how to get there. But if Río had been right, Salvador would be waiting. He knew the way.

"In a manner of speaking," Lucha said after a long pause. A familiar awareness flared to life as Paz climbed out of the pool, clad only in weapons and undergarments—a knife at her thigh. The bow on her back. Their kiss in the sombralados' glade seemed a lifetime ago in Lucha's mind, but her body remembered.

She shook herself. There was no time to parse out the complexities of attraction and trust. Not when Río and her holy warriors would be close behind.

But if Paz was determined to accompany her, there were things she needed to know.

"Listen, Paz—"

"Not now." The other girl was wringing water from her braid. "We need to get out of the sanctuary first."

By then it would be too late, Lucha knew. But they could make it to the boundary at least. There would still be time for Paz to turn back.

They averted their eyes as they dressed—whether from awkwardness or politeness, Lucha didn't know. She only knew her cheeks burned. *She sold you to Río,* she told herself, tugging her own robe over her cold, clammy skin.

But she had chosen to follow Lucha today. Against the orders of the obispo . . .

"We need to go east," Paz said, every word clipped. "It's the quickest way to the boundary that doesn't cross a road."

"Lead on." Lucha did not have to solve the problem of their conflicting loyalties today. She had only to trust the will of the goddess who had offered her this role. There would be time to figure the rest out later—if they lived.

Together, Lucha and Paz stole through the trees. Their gaits matched, their bodies well accustomed to traveling together through the underbrush. Suddenly, Paz swore, pushing Lucha against a tree and pinning her there. There was little space between their bodies. Their noses grazed. Paz turned her head to the side. Lucha didn't know what to do with her hands—she'd never been so aware of them before.

"*The obispo said she'll be alone, making for the border,*" said a voice. Too close.

"*Do you think she is what they say she is? The savior?*"

"*If she is, why is she running away?*"

Their footsteps passed less than a yard from Lucha and Paz's hiding place. The tree was barely large enough to conceal them. As the acolytes moved, Paz shifted around the trunk, pulling Lucha with her, keeping them out of sight.

It was a good plan, Lucha thought. Though she could have done with less pressing of their hips against each other . . .

"Let's go," Paz whispered, stepping back the moment the footsteps had faded.

They traveled another two miles, perhaps less. This time Lucha heard people approaching in time to hide herself. More voices from the sanctuary drifted past—discussing whether El Sediento had gotten to Lucha yet. Whether an age of destruction would follow . . .

Lucha could not focus on the details of their conversation. Not here, where the boundary was audible. It sounded as it had on her trip into the sanctuary—blindfolded and bound. A rushing river. A waterfall.

They were close, and the emptiness in Lucha's chest knew it. Her hands were clammy and cold. Her stomach turned agitated somersaults.

There would be pain. That much she knew. *He* would punish her for her final act of disobedience. But he could not kill her. Not if he wanted to rise again.

It was all the assurance she would get for now.

"This whole place is crawling with acolytes," Paz said when a third set of footsteps had passed. "We're not going to be able to cross in broad daylight with so many people looking for you."

A reprieve, then. Lucha told herself she wasn't relieved, but her next breath came easier.

"What do you suggest?"

"We need to find somewhere to hide. Once it's dark, we can move more freely. We'll get across the boundary then."

Lucha nodded her agreement. They found a dried gulch a half mile away, filled with leaves and branches. If Paz wondered why Lucha didn't use her gift to create a shelter, she didn't mention it. Did she know the power had been lost in the crossing?

They settled in, Paz heaping leaves up to protect them from view on the other side. Once they were well camouflaged, an awkward silence settled, filling slowly with all the things they no longer knew about each other.

"Did you even have an uncle?" Lucha asked, when she could stand it no longer. "Was it *all* a lie? I know they don't hand those robes out just because people look cold, so you must have been here long enough to earn it. Or did they give you one for bringing me in?"

Paz's eyes flashed in the afternoon sunlight. "I can't believe you, of all people, are lecturing me about honesty."

"I never *lied* to you," Lucha said. "I left things out, yes. Big things. But I didn't invent a story that wasn't true. You never knew me. I *thought* I knew you. There's a difference."

"Some difference," Paz scoffed. "You knew who I was. What I believed in. You knew how I would feel if I found out what you did."

"But you knew the whole time, didn't you?" Lucha asked, getting heated now. "Why else were you in Robado? Why else would you have agreed to bring us back here? They sent you to look for me! Don't deny it."

"I had no *idea* what I was looking for!" Paz said, fury in every line of her face. "Healing the afflicted is part of our ascension process. A cover story is standard practice. An uncle dead from Olvida was a sufficient explanation for the rest of them. But you . . ."

"So no uncle, then," Lucha said, trying not to show how much it hurt. "My *mother* is real, in case you were going to accuse me of that next."

The haunted look in Paz's eyes was clear enough even in the dim light of their shelter.

"I was sent to Robado three years ago to heal the sick," she said. "To bring relief to those addicted to *his* drug. I was hardly the first to be assigned that task. There have probably been ten more of us in Robado in your lifetime. I didn't know you existed. None of us did."

"So I'm supposed to believe our meeting was a coincidence? Why stitch up my face, then? Why help me with my mother?"

"Because I thought you were . . . fierce! Brave! Beautiful! I wanted to know you! Is that so hard to believe?"

There was a rustling nearby. Lucha used it as an excuse to be silent. To think. Of course it was hard to believe. No one had ever wanted to know her. Only to use her.

"You spent your whole life in that hellish place," Paz continued when it had been silent for some minutes. Her tone had gentled. "I understand you're naturally suspicious. But at first I swear that's all it was."

"At first?" Lucha asked. She couldn't examine all the rest.

Not knowing how it had ended up. What did it matter now if Paz had thought her fierce and beautiful a lifetime ago?

"When they took you to Encadenar . . . ," Paz began haltingly. "I heard the stories. The dead guards in Los Ricos' club. The way you called out for *him*. I was probably the only person in Robado who knew El Sediento wasn't just a story. That he was Almudena's son. I was terrified."

"So you waited for us outside Encadenar," Lucha said. "Did you have your orders yet? To bring me in?"

Paz hesitated. Her eyes flicked to Lucha's, to her lap, back again. "I was forbidden to send messages to the sanctuary from Robado. It's too dangerous with Los Ricos on high alert. If they found out about the sanctuary, it would be the end for us." It wasn't the whole story. Paz's guilty expression said that clearly enough.

"Why wait for me, then?" Lucha asked. "Why agree to accompany us through the woods?"

Another pause. Longer this time. The afternoon was aging. Soon it would be time to go. *At least I'll know,* Lucha thought, *before it's too late.*

"I wasn't going to," Paz began. "But before an initiate leaves on their mission, there's a ceremony. We drink Pensa tea, and our vision shows us where we're needed. I saw Almudena in mine. It's very rare to speak with her directly. After she told me about Robado, about the drug there and all the people in need, she said something to me." Paz drew a deep breath. " '*You'll know when it's time to come home.*' "

The words sent Lucha back there. To the ground outside

the Lost House where, grieving and hurting, she had shouted at Paz.

"You said something to me after your mother attacked you," Paz said, her words aligning with Lucha's memories. "You said, '*Why don't you just go home to your goddess and leave us alone.*'" Paz took a shuddering breath. "I knew then that it was her will for me to help you. That it might have been the very reason I was sent to Robado in the first place. So I came with you."

"For the goddess."

"Yes." Paz hesitated. "But, Lucha . . . the way I felt about you . . . the closeness between us . . . I—"

"They knew where to find us," Lucha interrupted. She couldn't stand to hear the rest. Not yet. "And when I was bound I heard you talking to them. You said you needed another day. Our *closeness* didn't matter when you were selling me out to them."

Paz was silent for a long moment. The longest yet. "I began communicating with them when we entered the forest. When we were out of Los Ricos' reach."

"How?"

"Messages by dove. I told them what I suspected. That if you were in league with him it wasn't your choice. I told them we needed to help you."

Lucha remembered now. The bird flying overhead when Paz had wandered into the forest. The feather on her sleeve in the clearing. All the time she'd been sending them information . . .

"I had no idea what they were planning to do with you.

When they showed up with darts and compañeras I was as surprised as anyone. I didn't learn the truth of your allegiance with him until I had returned to the sanctuary, and by then it was already too late."

They had reached it at last. Lucha's own deception. Her head spun with the layers and subtleties of it. Paz had lied, yes, but hadn't Lucha lied too? Who had broken the faith first? Who had cracked it deeper?

"Why didn't you tell me who you were?" Paz asked now. "Did you only need a nurse for Lis? Did you really think so little of me?"

And Lucha was going to tell her everything. Come clean about Salvador's manipulations and the agreement she'd brokered with him. The distrust she'd felt in the beginning, and the feelings that had grown in its place. She owed Paz honesty after all she had just confessed, no matter what it meant for their future.

But before she could speak, a shout rang through the gully, far too close. "Tracks! Leading down into the creek bed! Call the others!"

Paz and Lucha exchanged horrified looks. They'd been found.

"I have to go," Lucha said in a fierce whisper. "I have to run. Paz, I can't let them catch me."

"I'm going with you," Paz said without pause. She drew a knife from a sheath on her thigh and handed it to Lucha. The silver of its blade was pale as the moon, and there was a flower carved into its hilt.

The same flower that had drifted down at Paz's feet before they made their escape.

A sign from the goddess. Paz would have seen it as proof that Almudena wanted them to do this together. But what did Lucha believe?

"You can't," she said, though it made her heart ache to say it. "The sanctuary is where you belong. I'll run, and you tell them you saw me but point them in the wrong direction. When I come back I'll"—her voice broke—"I'll tell you everything. You deserve to know it all."

But Paz was shaking her head. "If it comes to a fight, you'll need me," she said.

"And you'll fight your own people?" Lucha asked as the seconds passed too quickly. "Put arrows in the hearts of your own sisters? You think I could ever forgive myself if I asked that of you?"

Paz didn't answer. Finally, Lucha met her gaze. Her heart quickened.

Footsteps were coming their way.

"I'll go with you," Paz said. Her voice was low and husky. A song drifting out a greenhouse window at night. "Because my goddess desires it."

Lucha looked down again at the flower in the dagger's hilt. This was an argument she wouldn't win—and she'd never been so relieved to lose.

"I'll need to lie to him, Paz, better than I've ever lied. You'll have to trust me."

"I will trust in her. It'll be enough."

"After, I'll tell you everything," Lucha promised again. "You can decide about me for yourself."

Paz nodded, her eyes liquid in the light from the setting sun.

There was no more reason to dally. Nothing more to be said. There was only the line between living and death, and Lucha poised. Ready to find out which side she belonged on once and for all. Paz stood beside her, shoulder to shoulder.

The footsteps filled the gully. The acolytes searched for them feverishly. The moment they broke cover, it could be deadly for any one of them.

Paz took Lucha's hand. "It's time," she said. And together they darted out of their quiet little world and fled for the boundary as fast as they could.

26

It didn't take long for the acolytes to spot them. The chase began. Running, Paz drew her bow. Held it at the ready.

If she fights, she fights for Almudena, Lucha told herself, but her traitorous hope flared to life again.

Shouting, from behind. Then, chilling Lucha's bones, the sound of low growls. The compañeras had joined the chase. Growling behind them, rushing before. The boundary was close. Would the acolytes dare cross it, knowing what awaited them there?

The rushing grew louder. Lucha thought Paz fired an arrow. Thought she heard someone fall. But the emptiness was there, swallowing everything, beckoning and repelling at once. Lucha did not turn back. Could not. The boundary reached inside her chest like prying fingers, pulling her open at the fault lines.

She didn't resist this time. She let the emptiness overtake her. The pain. Let them melt down her resolve and forge it into a weapon that would not fail her when the time came.

Everything else faded. Paz's presence beside her. Their pursuers. The trees themselves.

She knew she had crossed over when the wave crested. When the pain receded on the tide, leaving her stripped of her pretenses and nearly feral in its wake.

He was waiting, of course. Leaning against the base of a tree. Lucha wanted to recoil at the sight of him. But as the trees had once bent toward her, so did she bend toward him. Some ties could not be severed.

Into the emptiness, into the place where all that was Lucha had once lived, seeped something much more sinister than her own consciousness. Something captive and seething and furious.

"You've brought a friend." The first words he'd spoken, though they bloomed like thoughts in her own mind. *A friend*, she thought deliriously. *But who?* Her mind felt cleaved in two, details slipping down into the chasm between what was him and what was her.

"Lucha?" a voice asked. "Is it still you?"

Such a question, Lucha thought. It had seemed so clear, before she crossed. In this new mind she saw these divisions she had lived by as a human invention. There was no trunk without roots. No leaves without branches. No forest without each of its seemingly separate parts.

The voice said her name again, stirring some fragmented memory within her . . .

"Kill her," Salvador said in her mind as Lucha struggled.

It was a jarring note. One that brought her borders into sharper focus. He was a visitor here. She was in control.

"Kill her?" Lucha repeated. She could not do as he commanded.

If only she knew why . . .

"Kill who?" the girl asked, hand darting toward her knife.

At the threat, weapons awakened around her. Above and below. Hanging in the air. Not the bright, clear assistance she'd been offered by the forest, but something else. Something of *his*. The power did not whisper now, but clattered like bones.

The knife the girl wielded would be useless, of course. A plaything. The look in her eyes was a much more effective deterrent.

Paz, Lucha remembered. A thought of her very own. She remembered fingers in her hair, and along her cheekbone. This girl's voice, painting a beach at sunset. A searing kiss within a thicket. Flowers blooming through bones.

Promises, and lies.

"The sanctuary's acolytes are patrolling," Lucha heard herself say. She would deny his request. Carefully. "A body will draw suspicion."

"*Bury it.*"

"They have the beasts with them." The thrill of defiance—and the terror—spread through every part of Lucha's mind that still belonged to her. "Besides, the girl has studied in the sanctuary. Reached the highest level of ascension before priesthood. She may prove useful."

"Fine. But bind her. And hurry." He was impatient. She could sense the new eagerness in his thoughts. It made him distractable. The old Salvador would never have let her question him this way.

"Lucha, what's happening?" Paz's eyes were wide. Fearful, but discerning. Above her head hung a new vine. His urge within her said to feed it, use the gift to bind the girl. But the memory of the emptiness was still there.

Lucha took the vine in her hands instead. Wrapped it around Paz's wrists.

Salvador's eyes burned into her. She met them. They flickered green, like hers, then back to black. In the dying light her fingers grew long and pale, then retreated. She felt the weight of his rings. There, then gone.

"*Lucha,*" Paz said, struggling against her bonds. "Look at me."

She looked, and what she saw was beautiful. The dark, warm brown of living soil. Inside Paz's eyes, life stirred. Primal. Vital. Such a contrast to the destruction seeking purchase in Lucha's mind.

"*Don't let him take you.*"

Salvador laughed. The sound spilled from Lucha's lips.

"Soon enough, you'll wish she'd killed you. I promise you that."

Had Lucha spoken these words? Had Paz heard them? Her eyes were still pleading, and Lucha remembered more. A flower falling at her feet. A bow drawn to protect her.

I'll go with you . . . Soft as a song . . .

"Remember who you are. Remember that you have a choice."

Salvador raised his arms. Manic delight flooded Lucha's mind. Her stomach spasmed with laughter she could not hear over grinding wingbeats.

Two sombralados—larger still than the ones she had destroyed in the clearing—landed before them.

Salvador had never looked more corporeal than he did at this moment. The wind tossed the dark strands of his hair. There were two spots of color high in his pale cheeks. His eyes burned in a way Lucha could feel in her own face. He was joyful, and Lucha's heart leapt with his—

Until pain speared Lucha through, sending her gasping to her knees.

The shadows she'd felt writhing in her chest were pointed now, and barbed. They fought to be free of her. Lucha screamed. Paz called her name. In a moment, Salvador was above her, looking down.

"What did they tell you in that place?" he asked. A feral snarl.

The pain burned away every place a lie could have hidden.

"Everything," she gasped. "Your mother. The fight. Your amber cage in the grove. What you would have asked of me. I know. *I know.*"

"And they sent you to do away with me?"

The pain intensified. His eyes were livid coals in their sockets.

"No," Lucha sobbed. "I . . . escaped. I came to find you on my own." The truth. And now he knew it.

"Why?"

Even through the agony, Lucha could see it. Her robe. Her throne. The adoration of the acolytes. The beauty of the chains around her ankles, holding her fast.

"Because they never would have let me be free."

For an eternal moment, Lucha thought he would increase the heat again. Kill her where she stood and damn the rest. She knew there were no claws tearing her from the inside out. That the pain was in her mind, and so was he. But how long before a tortured heart gave in? Hers had seconds left, every beat told her so.

And then, as suddenly as it had come, the pain was gone. There were tears on Lucha's face, blessedly cool. Somewhere, someone was sobbing. Or were the sobs her own?

Her body ached. She got to her feet slowly, gingerly. But this time, when she looked at his face, she knew who she was. How had she ever mistaken this pain for connection? This desperate dependence for power?

And when would he learn that hurting her only made her stronger?

"You know what you must do?" he asked her now, unaware of the change his pain had wrought.

Lucha saw everything so clearly in the aftermath of agony. The twisted grove. The amber prison.

"I know what I must do," she said.

"And you're willing to? Despite the danger? Despite what it will mean?"

She called up her vision: Almudena, holding back the

curtain of vines, displaying her future. "I'd rather be dead than in chains," she said, and the smile that lit his face was inhuman in its glee.

But locked inside Lucha's heart was the truth he had not heard: She didn't plan to be either.

"Lucha." Paz staggered toward her. Lucha had never seen her so undone. "What did he do to you? Are you all right?"

"Never better," Lucha said. She met Paz's eyes with an expression she hoped would say what she couldn't. That she was herself. That she needed to conceal that fact at all costs. That it was time to lie, as she'd warned her she would. "It's time to go."

She grabbed Paz by the vines tying her wrists and led her to the closest sombralado. In a moment, Paz was mounted, her eyes searching Lucha's for something she could not display. Lucha mounted the other beast. She felt the eager hammering of her heart—or was it his?

"Are you ready to make history, Lucha Moya?" Salvador asked.

"I am," Lucha replied. Truthful to the last.

"*Volar*," he said in Lucha's voice, and their mounts launched them skyward.

From the back of a creature of nightmare, Lucha surveyed the forest she hoped to save. From a distance, it all looked so peaceful. Swirls of color and texture no mapmaker could have captured even if they'd bothered to try.

She thought of those dark blots of ink as the grinding of the sombralado's bones marked the seconds. The minutes. As they drew Lucha toward the fight she had chosen.

Río would have said she was putting the world at risk. That they didn't know enough to act. But Lucha knew more than enough. She knew what this monster had created. What he had destroyed.

She would be the one to bring him down—for the girl she'd been, the mother she'd lost, the sister she loved. Most of all for the girl she had grown to be. A girl who deserved the satisfaction of the final blow.

All the stories came down to this, didn't they? A daughter and a son. The end of the world, or the beginning.

She saw it first, from far off. The grove from her vision. It was white as death among the green—a warning. Lucha felt his eagerness to land. Her hands shook where she gripped the crow's bones.

When her feet touched the ground at last, she could sense it in the air. The rot. The decay. But also the way it pulled at Salvador like the swiftest current. This was where he had last stood on the earth a free man.

He stared intently at the place where the trees turned white. The sun shone through him like a ghost's translucent flesh. The power it took to project himself was in use elsewhere. Lucha could feel it, heavy in her own chest.

"Bind the girl to a tree," he said. Almost an afterthought. "If you do as I instruct, she will not be harmed."

Insurance, again. But she knew Salvador could not harm Paz. Not without Lucha's hands. And she would not hurt this girl again. Never again. She bound her to the tree loosely, trusting in Salvador's distraction.

"*It's still me,*" she said as she checked the knots. A whisper so quiet it was barely a sound.

Paz's face relaxed.

"*I'll be back.*" Leaving Paz behind her, Lucha joined Salvador at the border.

"You must tell me how to do it," she said. "I have a feeling we only get one chance."

"One chance indeed." He turned to face her. "Close your eyes, Lucha."

She did it without fear. She'd already survived the worst he could do to her.

"Stay with me," he said, though he did not take a step. Then, suddenly, Lucha understood. His power drew her consciousness into the grove, plunging into the infertile soil and down . . .

The earth here was a haunted room, long vacant. Nothing would grow. There was not a root, or a worm, or a seed to be found. But there was a presence. Something so malevolent Lucha's mind recoiled from it instinctively.

Still, she followed. Followed until soil became stone. Rigid and unyielding. It was there, wedged tightly, that she sensed it. Amber. And within that—

Lucha gasped, returning to her body all at once. Salvador

was beside her. Paz just out of sight. Lucha's chest ached where the emptiness had been so recently, and she understood.

"We'll have to part." It wasn't a question.

"They've told you, I'm sure, that this is only a projection of my consciousness. To withstand the ascension I'll need to reunite mind and body. You'll be on your own."

Lucha nodded. The weight of all she was heading for seemed heavier now. Each breath was a labor.

You can still turn back, said a voice within her. *You have a choice.*

"You will enter the grove," he said. "And use your power to withdraw the amber prison. Free me from it. After that you will have all I have promised you and more . . ."

For a moment, Lucha was back on the floor of her cell. Starving. Afraid. He was faintly luminous in the corner, his voice low and hypnotic as he showed her the warehouses burning. The kings ruined. She had believed him. And *that* was why she had no other choice.

The agreement they'd struck would be carried out. She would free him. Olvida would be destroyed. She would make sure of it herself. And he would die for what he had done to her family. For what he had done to her.

For a long moment, there was silence.

"I knew you would do," he said at last. His voice was different. Softer. "You had some form of the gift, and that was all I needed. Without it, people tended to . . . disintegrate on some basic level. Frustrating, at best."

Lucha tried not to listen. Tried not to picture someone disintegrating on a basic level. But he hadn't finished.

"And someone both gifted *and* willing? I thought I'd rot down there an eternity without finding it. Before, the gifted were venerated. Marked by my mother's blessing. Those witless zealots inoculated them against me before I ever had a chance. But you . . ."

Lucha saw it now, as he must have. The lone path to freedom in a desolate wasteland. She remembered how he'd panicked at the thought of imprisonment. The fervor in his voice when he'd promised to free her . . .

And yet the drug he'd created had imprisoned so many in their own minds and bodies.

"The gift had been gone a hundred years. No one was looking for you in that mud pit. But I never stopped looking. And see how I've been rewarded? Not only with a vessel. But with someone who *understands* . . ."

A nameless emotion passed across his face.

"You came back when you needn't have," he said. A book snapping shut. "You could have hidden from me behind those walls the rest of your natural life. I expected you to. But you came back. And for that, you will be rewarded beyond imagining."

It was as if he'd parted a vine curtain before her. Another future: Lucha, pale and red-eyed, a long trailing cape. Ruling over the bones alongside him.

"I only ever wanted one thing," Lucha said. Careful, even

now. "Your first promise to me. The destruction of the chains you placed around Robado."

"Then go, Lucha Moya of the Scar. Go and claim your destiny."

But there was no destiny, Lucha thought. There was only what you chose.

27

Lucha Moya stepped into the wasted grove, barely noticing the bones, the trees leached of all their color. Salvador's malevolent power pulsed throughout the place. But it was something else that drew Lucha onward—until at last she stood before the lightning-struck tree.

There, in the knot, was Almudena's bloodred flower.

When she'd drunk the Pensa tea, she'd seen the goddess create an orb of her own life force. Heard her describe the power she'd left for her champion to claim. The power to defeat Salvador.

But until Lucha stood before it in her living, breathing body, she had not truly believed it would be here. It had been an act of faith, to come. And that faith had been rewarded.

As if it sensed her presence, the knot in the tree began to glow golden. Lucha leaned closer. Would the orb rise up for her to take hold of? Would the tree open to reveal it?

So far, there was nothing. Only light.

She cleared her throat. A dry twig snapping in the quiet.

"My name is Lucha Moya," she said. As if she were a hero

in a story, not a girl from the Scar. "I was shown this path by Almudena, and I am here to—"

But what she had come to do was irrelevant. The stump had recognized her at last. Only it did not release the orb. Instead, a thorned vine of pure, dark gold rose from it like a snake and pierced Lucha's heart clean through.

28

If this is the way I die, Lucha thought, *so be it.*

The pain of the thorn was bright. Purposeful. Nothing like the burning sensation of Salvador's punishment, or the bottomless nothingness of the void he'd left behind.

But death did not come. The thorn did not pull free, leaving her to bleed out on this cursed ground. Instead, it lifted Lucha up until it was her only connection to the earth. Light traveled down it. Some nectar headed straight for her heart.

Lucha was afraid. She was no saint. No martyr from the stories. Only a girl who had expected a blessing and received a fatal wound in its place. Struggling to breathe around the torment, she watched the light come closer.

She thought of the white hare in the clearing. A gift for the goddess's chosen.

She thought of Almudena, who could have warned her.

Was this how Lucha would be of service? Had the choice always been Río's mascot or Almudena's sacrifice?

When the light reached her breast, she was very nearly

beyond caring. The pain took everything, leaving an almost-peaceful nothingness in its wake. And then, images came to life within it. A trickle that became a flood.

Memories, Lucha realized, as they took over. She forgot the thorn, and the grove, and her choice. Even her pain. She was awash in memories. Borne away on their tide ...

Some were her own. These, she recognized easily enough. She was a baby, and a man with warm brown skin smiled down on her. She was barely toddling, gripping a table's edge, determined to stand on her own. She was awake in the dark, shaking beneath her covers. She walked into the forest with swift, purposeful strides, and the paths opened wide to her ...

But there were other memories. Memories she had never made.

She stood at a river's edge, watching it rise and fall as the seasons changed.

She watched through a window as a child grew from a baby to a lanky young man.

She saw a comet tracing the sky, and knew it would not return for thirty years. She saw its return as well, following the same path.

In these visions, she was not herself. The lens she viewed them through was infinitely more nuanced—like an extra color on a spectrum she'd always known. They had the weight and heft of history.

But there was something else. An undercurrent that

bound them together. It took Lucha a moment to recognize it, but when she did, it was undeniable.

Loneliness, she realized. Utter, devastating isolation.

She was witnessing the making of Salvador as she knew him. Salvador after he had been confined to the ground and abandoned by the mother who created him. But why?

Lifetimes passed in search of a kindred soul, finding nothing familiar. Anger crept in, took root, and grew. Lucha found herself in a dark room. A cracked mirror hung on a wall. She did not want to look, but her feet moved of their own accord.

The face she glimpsed was gaunt. Pale. Nearly translucent. Soon it would fade altogether.

It was his face, of course. Salvador's. Her fist darted out like the strike of a snake, shattering the glass, not knowing which of them had wanted it gone.

She walked with him, *as* him, feet leaving no imprint on the ground. She felt the horrible burden of his exile as if years were truly passing. Decades. Centuries. But as the time passed, she noticed something beneath the rest. The thing that repelled him each time he considered ending it on his own terms.

It was fear. Fear that teetered on the edge of madness. Fear of the unknown beyond death for a being who was never supposed to experience a natural end. And that fear gave way to determination. A promise to himself, that when the opportunity came he would seize it. He would rise again and make his mother pay for every moment of torture he had endured.

Lucha stayed with him until he saw *her*, a blade of a girl stalking through Robado's mushroom grove. The girl she'd been before her imprisonment. Before their bargain. The imprint she left behind tasted of anger, too. Of a fear that burned as his did. Of the same hope for freedom.

She felt his tortured glee as he recognized himself in her. As he saw the way forward at last, when for so long there had been nothing but emptiness . . .

When finally the memories ceased, the resulting quiet lasted an age. Lucha's exhausted mind reeled. She struggled back to herself. The visions were gone, but they'd been tattooed on her heart in searing ink. She knew she would never be free of this history, this burden, for as long as she lived.

And still the thorn pierced her chest. Still she hung suspended in the air, waiting to learn what her future would hold.

Let me rest, Lucha thought. She could not speak. *Please, let me rest.*

The voice that replied was not a voice. It was a force. The beginning of all things, and the end. The ocean. The land. The sky. The fires burning at the heart of the world. It did not speak in words, but Lucha understood.

There would be no rest. The vine in her chest was white-hot again. That clean, bright pain that told her she had made her choice. That she had sought this power, and now she would find out what it cost.

Lucha's veins brimmed with burning brightness. Her skin was paper-thin, and then it was gone. She was exposed. Veins, bones, the fragile encasement of her mortal life laid bare to be judged.

No human body could have withstood the power coursing into her heart. And as she surrendered to it, Lucha returned to the wisdom she had learned too late.

She would not live.

But she would not die.

A transformation was always something of both.

29

When at last the golden vine released the girl, she was no longer only a girl.

She walked barefoot across the ghostly grove, and beneath her feet, life returned. Grass turned lush and green where she touched it, and the living spread. It awakened its neighbors. It banished the mourning silence that had held them still so long.

The trees, when her fingers brushed them, stretched tall and burst into full leaf, then bloom. A celebration. With her new eyes, she could see the subtle beauty in every blade. Every blossom. Her mortal gaze could never have beheld it.

She laughed, a joyful sound, and puffy seeds floated on the breeze it made. Where they landed, flowers unfolded, reaching out to greet her as if she were the morning sun.

There was no need to hold space between this power and herself. It *was* her, and she was it. A symbiosis that had always been and would always be.

The girl was alone, until she wasn't. Footsteps entered the grove. Halting and tentative, but not afraid. Reverent, perhaps.

"*Salvadora . . .*" A second girl stepped into the pool of green and light, falling to her knees, and Lucha Moya remembered.

"Paz." The voice was new. A babbling brook and a cool evening breeze and the ringing of a thousand chimes. "There is no need to kneel."

If the grove was magnificent with divine eyes, there was no word in any language for Paz. Lucha had seen her beauty. Had read this or that on her face throughout the time they had known each other. But there was so much more that had been hidden from her.

Determination, of course, in every line of her. The posture, corrected over time. A slumped-shouldered girl becoming a straight-backed warrior. There were scars, too, beyond the physical. Their origins were mapped as plainly as the marks themselves. Lucha could have discovered any truth about this girl. Relived any moment of her history.

Instead, she turned away. She would not use this power to pry. To gain information that would not be freely given. There would be time to learn the truth. Time after . . .

Suddenly, as if a door had opened in her mind, the rest came in. The task before her. The son awaiting her outside this place. Paz had been tied to a tree—how had she escaped? These new questions, new memories, made homes in the infinite corridor of her mind.

She had lived only her sixteen years, but the scale of her life now skewed heavily toward her future, which had no natural end. There was a distance that made each concern less immediate. Still, something of her distress must have shown on her face, because Paz stepped anxiously forward.

"How might I serve you, Salvadora?"

"You can start by calling me Lucha," she said. "You know I'm no savior."

"The thorn pierced your heart," Paz began, halting. "There was such light . . . and then . . . and *now* . . ." She gestured at Lucha's form as if it were strange to her. As if she had never held it in her arms. Kissed it. Pointed an arrow at its heart.

"And so we must change how we see each other again," Lucha said. "We ought to be used to it by now."

"This is different." That stubborn line between her eyebrows. Lucha's heart delighted at it. Something of the girl she'd known among all this piety.

"I won't pretend to be an expert on what's happened here," Lucha said. "But I know what I feel. I'm still me, Paz. I'm still Lucha. Will you pretend you don't know me?"

Paz raised her eyes from her clasped fingers. They were squinted slightly, as if she were staring into the sun.

"I know you, and I don't," she said. "I suppose that's the way it's always been."

"Will you tell me what happened out there? While I was . . ." *Dying? Transforming?* What was the word for what had happened to her?

Paz understood. She spoke in hushed tones. "I couldn't see anything. I thought I could sense him, but I couldn't see. And then . . ." She paused, biting her lip. "I heard someone scream."

It had been Lucha who screamed. She remembered it all. The pain, the clean heat of it, and the memories. Of course Almudena would not equip a warrior to defeat her son without helping them to understand him.

Lucha would never forget his isolation. His rejection of the end, and his fear of it. It did not change what needed to be done. Salvador had made his choice. Lucha had made hers. It was the closest thing to destiny they would get.

"Go on," she said to Paz, who had fallen quiet.

"The vines holding me to the tree unraveled," Paz said. "I thought you had died. The light went out. It was . . . so cold." She shivered once, then continued. "But after that the whole place began to glow. Brighter than the sun. I covered my eyes. I felt it when he left the grove. When I was alone."

Lucha understood, if Paz did not. Salvador had heard the screaming, seen the light. He had returned to his prison to await the freedom she had promised him.

But he would not stay there for long.

This golden moment, the sunlight falling across Paz's face, glistening in her hair, Lucha committed it all to memory. Even with this power, there could be no guarantee of the future.

"Do the stories tell you what must happen next?" Lucha asked gently.

Paz shook her head.

"Almudena's son is trapped below us in the amber cage his mother created."

"*Here?*" Paz asked. Her eyes darted around the newly green grove.

317

"Yes," Lucha said. "My task—the *choice* I've made—is to release him."

Paz gasped. Her fingers twitched toward her knife.

"Release him, and then destroy him. In the name of Almudena and all those who would suffer in a world under his control."

"Why can't we just leave him in the ground?" Paz asked. Her face was horror-stricken.

"As long as he can project his consciousness, he's a threat. He can use anyone with the gift for his twisted purpose, so long as they agree to help him. And he can be quite . . . persuasive when it suits him. The next person he manipulates could free him for good."

"This is too great a risk," Paz argued. "There haven't been gifted in Elegido for a hundred years."

"Until me."

A long silence stretched. Something thorny sprouted from the peace between them.

"I promised you I would explain how I came to be connected with him," Lucha said. "And I will. But we are running out of time."

"He manipulated you," Paz guessed. "Made you some promise he never intended to fulfill to bind you into agreement with him. He brought you to this place to free him. And now you're going to do exactly what he wanted you to."

"That's only true if you don't believe I can destroy him."

Faith battled with reason on Paz's face. Her trust in

Almudena. The doubts she'd carried about Lucha since the beginning. Finally, she drew her bow.

"Then I will pledge myself to you in the fight against the shadows," she said. "I will stand beside you, protect you should you require it, and—"

"And if I seem likely to fail, or to turn to his cause," Lucha interrupted, "you will kill him in my stead, and destroy the monstrosity he has created."

"What if you defend him?" Paz asked.

"Then you will do what needs to be done."

Something steely flashed in Paz's eyes. This time, she took only one knee.

"Rise, Paz León of the Shadow Grove," Lucha said. "We have a battle to fight."

30

Amid the riot of color Lucha had brought back to this dying place, a single patch remained stubbornly pale. Right at the base of the lightning-struck tree.

She could no longer feel him in her chest—the place he'd once inhabited had gone when she changed. But the urgency stirred in every leaf, pulsed beneath her feet, and Lucha understood its wordless demand.

She had lived his long isolation with him. He was desperate for freedom. It would not be an easy fight. But this next part was simple as breathing.

Lucha closed her eyes, hearing Paz's bowstring tighten as she stood guard. The wind whipped around them, marking this occasion. When she found his prison this time, sensed his power, she did not scurry back to the surface in fear. She met it as an equal.

She grabbed hold of the amber cell. Up through the rock. The dead soil. Lucha kept her eyes closed as she guided him toward the light. Behind her, Paz gasped, and Lucha felt the reason beneath her feet: The decay was spreading again. Welcoming its master back after five hundred years.

When the prism cleared the surface, the ground beneath it closed as if he had never been buried there. But Lucha knew the earth did not forget.

She opened her eyes at last, taking in the magnificence and the cruelty Almudena had wrought. The crystal was enormous. Nearly as tall as the jagged sentinel watching over it. Ten feet thick in places, it was physically impenetrable, and sealed with powerful wards.

Around the top and the bottom, symbols were carved. Evidence of her intentions.

She had underestimated him. Lucha would not.

Deep within the gem, at its very center, Salvador appeared peacefully asleep. Trapped in time by a mother who could not kill him, but could not let him live. He had withdrawn the consciousness that haunted this forest for centuries. Body and soul were one.

It was time.

Paz stepped up beside Lucha. Shoulder to shoulder. The wind snapped between them. The end of Paz's braid tickled Lucha's cheek.

"Are you ready?" Lucha asked.

"No," Paz replied. "But we'd better get on with it anyway."

There was only one way to destroy amber. Lucha called on the power of the sun, raising her hands, shaping the shafts of golden light into a single, piercing beam.

The surface of the crystal began to melt. To bubble and boil as the heat penetrated. Steam rose in spirals as the enamel began to run in golden rivers down its sides.

When Salvador rose at last, there was nothing of his centuries-long sleep evident in his posture. He stepped from the cooling pool of amber like a king greeting his subjects. No longer the pale, indistinct shade who had haunted Lucha's steps—he was every bit the shadow-wreathed prince who had challenged his mother on this very spot lifetimes ago.

He lost that day, Lucha reminded herself as Salvador stretched his fingers. Rolled his shoulders. Tipped his head back to the sky and let out a bone-chilling sound—like the call of a crow that had spotted a corpse.

Paz was close enough that Lucha could feel the tension in her bowstring. She loosed the arrow before Lucha could tell her it was pointless. It flew directly at Salvador's heart, while his head was still tilted back, marveling.

In the instant before it would have struck him, a wall of shadows materialized. It swallowed the arrow—point, shaft, and fletching—like it had never been there at all.

The shadows dispelled, and Salvador turned to face them. A sinister, sparkling intelligence danced in his eyes.

"Not quite yet, I'm afraid," he said, before turning to Lucha. "*You* made a detour."

"I made a choice," Lucha replied.

"Ah, choices," Salvador said, pacing around the colorless grove. There was joy in every movement of his limbs. "My mother's favorite medicine. I knew she'd get to you in that stuffy henhouse of hers. I just thought you were ambitious enough to resist."

In answer, Lucha gathered a spear of light and launched it at precisely the place where Paz's arrow had aimed. She marveled in the might of this new power. The responsiveness. She was no longer a human vessel struggling not to come apart. Lucha was a force of her own.

Salvador stepped aside neatly to dodge it. It singed a hole in the dead grass.

"In time I will show you how useless these tricks of yours are," he said. "But you seem so determined to make your *choice*, girl. And even my mother would agree: will isn't truly free unless you know all your options."

"I know my options," Lucha said. "You promised me the destruction of Olvida in exchange for my assistance. You never told me you created it. You would never have destroyed it. Our agreement is void."

"Creation this, destruction that," Salvador drawled. He sounded bored as ever, but his eyes followed her every move. "It's all so dramatic. Of course I wasn't going to *tell* you I'd created the thing you hated most. We both know that wouldn't have ended well for either of us."

As he spoke, Lucha catalogued every weapon at her disposal.

"And perhaps I simplified things a *little* when I promised the destruction of Olvida," he said with a smirk. "But I didn't lie. The drug will be destroyed . . . along with all other life in this corrupt world. It's time to begin anew."

Even in her new form, Lucha was not immune to the shock of this confession. It had been a deception, not an outright lie. He had fed her the piece that would lure her here and concealed the whole monstrous truth.

He would raze the world. The ultimate act of revenge on a mother who had created it. Protected it . . .

"I showed you the worst of humanity," Salvador said. His voice was that low, hypnotic pulse again, boring in through her horror. "Abuse, power, corruption, and greed. I taught you to tap into your own strength . . . that gift of creation my mother never understood. I can destroy this place just fine on my own—" He closed his eyes for a brief moment, concentrating. The decay at his feet spread. "But who wants to live alone in a dead world?"

Paz made a guttural sound. Her disgust was clear in every rigid line of her body.

"So you level the entire planet," Lucha said calmly, as if they were discussing the weather. "And I rebuild it in your image. Is that the new bargain?"

"I wouldn't expect a mortal to understand the true nuance of it," he said. "Let me show you."

His shadows were upon her before she could object, stealing in like smoke. When they parted, Lucha saw a different world than she'd ever imagined. Not a pile of smoking bones. A world in balance. Harmony. Salvador lording over death and decay while Lucha created abundant, verdant life.

An ecosystem. Power held in perfect equilibrium.

But the shadows obscured this world as they had the last,

and showed her the alternative: her body, burning and broken on the ground, and Salvador rising from her ashes to blot out all that grew. All that breathed. Here were the bones. The smoking ground. The rot and the lye and the dying.

The choice was clear: Join him, and create a new world. Or fight him, and die with this one.

For the first time since she'd risen from her transformation, Lucha felt the bright purpose within her falter. Had it been hubris that had brought her here? Hubris that made her believe she was better than those who had sought power before her?

Was this balance truly the way to end it without bloodshed?

Perhaps it was what Almudena had wanted all along. The reason she'd flooded Lucha with the memories of a captive, tortured man. Helped her understand him. Perhaps she had left this power to create his equal. Someone who could temper, and—

Cold steel at her throat shook Lucha from her musings.

The shadows cleared once more. Salvador still stood opposite her, a look of unmistakable delight on his face. But if Salvador wasn't holding the knife . . .

"You won't use her this way," Paz said fiercely. The blade was steady at Lucha's throat. She could have stopped Paz in a hundred different ways, but she knew this was what she deserved. What she had asked for. "I would rather see her dead than a vessel for your twisted purpose. And you would follow in short order, I promise you that."

"It's all right, Paz," Lucha said gently. "I'm all right now." The steel left her throat, but Paz stayed close by. A promise and a threat.

"Such drama," Salvador said. Something of his old drawl was back in his voice. A reminder of all they had been through together. "But I'm growing tired of these games." He looked at Lucha now, his eyes boring into her, laying bare every fear she'd ever had. Every insecurity. "I made you from nothing," he said, in a voice that came from the grove itself. "I turned you from a sad salt leech into a goddess. Join me, and find out what else I can do for you."

Lucha could sense it on the changing wind. A stage being set.

"You didn't *make her* into anything," Paz said, venom in her voice. "She was chosen by the goddess. Blessed by her gift. This is her destiny."

Salvador's mouth turned up in an amused smirk. "Chosen, was she? As if the potential for great power doesn't lurk in half you sniveling mortals. She wasn't chosen. Not destined, or fated, or foretold. She was a mud brat who wanted to live and she did what she had to do. She *followed* who she had to follow. And look at her now."

It was a less-forgiving description than Almudena had given Lucha, but it was the truth. The gift hadn't chosen Lucha. She had felt it. She had shaped it. She could have left it all behind, and someone else would have come along. She could walk away now.

But she wouldn't. Not because she'd *been* chosen, but because she *had* chosen.

"The way I came into my power is not the relevant issue," she said. "The strongest blade must be forged by fire. The issue now is that I have chosen this path. I have accepted your mother's blessing."

As if to prove her point, green began to spread once more from the place where Lucha stood. Grass grew knee-high, and from within it yellow blossoms burst into bloom.

"Her power is mine by right," Salvador said, eyes narrowed. "By birth."

"Yes, but *I'm* her savior, aren't I?" Lucha said. The ground beneath him writhed, tiny vines wrapping themselves around his legs.

"I'm her SON!" Salvador screamed. The vines fell to the ground, dead. The grass wilted. "She would have left it all to me. All of it. If only—"

"If only you hadn't created Olvida," Lucha said. "If only you hadn't been determined to destroy everything she loved."

His face fell. A momentary slip. Lucha saw hundreds of years in that single second. A boy, aching for love. A mother, disappointed by his every effort . . . His features were smooth and unreadable again almost instantly.

But Lucha knew well enough by now that the surface didn't tell the whole story.

"You are a cheap mortal vessel, and I am a prince of the divine." He circled her faster now, and she matched his steps.

"But you need to *see* the difference, to be humbled. I understand. Let me show you what you've done by refusing me."

Lucha could sense Paz close by. Her knife. Her bow. True to her promise. Reminding Lucha of all there was to lose by giving in. As if she needed another reminder than the man before her. The monster who had destroyed her world.

Before them, the whites of Salvador's eyes went completely black.

The battle was beginning.

31

The ground at their feet began to tremble. An earthquake of Salvador's making. Lucha closed her eyes—she would not wait for whatever trick he planned to use against her. She had plans of her own.

Closing her eyes, she searched the forest for a weapon that would do this battle justice. The forest clamored, each sliver of wood and fungal spore eager for the honor. From them, Lucha selected a vivid green vine, thick as her own arm. Four-inch thorns protruded from its surface, dripping deadly venom.

Beside her, Paz had her bow. Her knives. Most terrifying of all, a look that said she would not stop until they had won. "He won't hold back," Paz said. "I suggest you don't either."

Lucha nodded, and then she stepped forward, brandishing her weapon.

Salvador's eyes were still focused inward. Inky black and unseeing. The quaking of the ground intensified. Lucha grounded herself in her power and cracked the vine out like a whip, encircling his throat. She felt it, along the length of the tendril, every place the thorns had pierced his skin.

She cinched it tight mercilessly, willing it to bind. To crush his airway. To choke the life from him . . .

As he struggled to free himself, Lucha heard the whizzing of arrows past her cheek. Paz, firing again and again.

Salvador roared in protest, the black fading from his eyes. The ground ceased its shaking as he threw his hands back. Lucha felt the stem creak, threaten to break, but it held. It held until his pale face began to redden.

It was only when he looked Lucha in the eye that she realized he wasn't protesting. He was laughing.

Salvador wrapped his long, pale fingers around the whip. From the place where he made contact, the vivid green turned white. In seconds it was nothing more than a sagging necklace—grotesque around his crisp black cloak.

The ground resumed its shaking.

"My mother's chosen champion and a little flower stem," he said. "Perhaps I overestimated what you would accomplish with such power. I hoped for an opponent, a worthy match. But it seems you need a few more lessons."

The insult chafed. Lucha's memories, more vivid than ever in this expansive mind, showed her the sharpening of her wooden darts in Encadenar. Her body, pinned to the ground by the force around her as Salvador stood by, teaching her separation.

I am not a root. I am not a leaf.

"The power one wields is limited by one's imagination," Salvador said. "Let me show you."

And before Lucha could protest, could seize another

weapon, the source of the shaking ground became clear at last. From behind Salvador—its arms raised in a grotesque mimicry of his posture—rose a creature that made Lucha's assault look like child's play.

From beneath the ground, he'd drawn thousands of bones. Bound them together with shadow tendons and gristle and cartilage. The humanoid creature straightened up at last—twenty feet taller than the largest human Lucha had ever seen. Its red eyes rolled around to fix on her. Rage burned within them.

Lucha readied herself to draw it beneath the ground. The forest's whispers were now a roar, promising to make swift work of it on her behalf.

"It's only a distraction," Paz said, urgent in her ear. "We destroy it, and he raises a thousand more. Let me keep it out of your hair. You focus on what matters. You take him down."

Lucha nodded once. "Be safe," she said, and Paz was gone, darting through the bushes, her bow at the ready. Salvador didn't even spare her a glance, but his creature turned at once, tracking the threat.

"You're no longer bound to a single element, girl," Salvador said. "The power of creation is at your disposal. Show me what you'll make with it. Show me how you'll stop me . . ."

Lucha bristled at the way he spoke to her. As if she were some disappointing child at lessons. She was no protégée of this monster. She was a girl with a goddess's power, and she was not afraid to use it.

From her center, Lucha sent a gathering call out through

the forest. Whispering through the chattering leaves, pulsing through the mycelium below. In an instant, the ground around them was seething with new growth. Thorny vines rose like vipers from the grass. Vivid flowers with poison pistils protruding from them like tongues. Above them, branches creaked and groaned ominously, swiping and snapping against the wind.

Stories would call the evidence of this rapid growth proof of the savior's ascension. Pilgrims would one day walk this path to stand where Lucha Moya had embraced her power at last. But none of them would be able to imagine the majesty with which she reclaimed her vines, wreathing them in the light of the heavens.

He wanted to reanimate bones with shadows? Fine. Lucha would meet him with life.

From the ground, two long, deadly slivers of sharpened bone leapt into his hands. He wielded them like swords, the whites of his eyes going dark again. Where his boots touched the ground, white death ate greedily through the life Lucha had summoned. Creeping and rotting and killing every living thing it touched.

But it did not stop there. Like a disease, it spread, turning everything deadly pale before Lucha could gather herself to stop it. She knew in that moment that Paz had been right. These were only distractions, and Lucha would have to choose.

To heal the forest as he destroyed it, leaving herself vulnerable to his attack.

Or to ignore his distractions. To end this, as she had come here to do.

As if in answer to her question, a roar of agony split the air. Above them, Salvador's bone monstrosity clawed at its glowing eyes. Paz had found its one point of weakness, and Lucha's heart surged with pride. In a moment the creature had fallen to its knees. In another, it had disappeared from view in a cacophony of rattling collapse.

If Lucha expected Salvador to make another attempt at convincing her, she was mistaken. He struck immediately, with a ferocity that said this would end with compulsion or death. Nothing less final.

Lucha had carried a knife at her hip since she'd been old enough to wield it. She had been known as a cazadora. A hunter. But she had never known until this moment what it was to truly fight.

Her instincts did not falter—but his own were equally deadly. Her whip cracked along his cheek, burning his flesh till it bubbled. In response, he cut it off at the handle, forcing her to regrow it. To spend costly moments and fuel calling the light down once more.

Recovered, Lucha snatched one of his bones, wrapping it in vine and sending it clattering to the ground. He used her distraction to deliver a blow to the ankle that left a nasty, festering slash, sending her stumbling back on her heels.

Vine to wrist. Blade to rib. Light against shadow, as it had always been.

The world shrank to this barren stage and the blows they

traded. Lucha had not seen Paz since the downing of the bone creature. She could not let herself wonder where the other girl had gone. Back and forth she and Salvador parried, lunged, stabbed, and sliced until even Lucha's new strength began to falter. Outside, silhouettes prowled. Creatures living and dead, drawn to this display of force like moths to their final flame.

Salvador did not tire. Indeed, he appeared energized by the sparks that flashed between them—his first dance in five hundred years. "Don't you see?" he asked—another vicious swipe at her throat barely missing. "The power we could wield? Together, we would be like nothing this pathetic world has ever seen."

Lucha could not reply. She felt her human weariness, more profound than ever in contrast with the divine gift she'd been given. She could no longer feel the forest around her. Could no longer hear more than whispers . . .

You've given all you have, they said. *Rest, child. Rest.*

But there could be no rest. And there would be no surrender.

From outside the circle, a guttural growl shook Lucha to her core. Some other monstrosity? she wondered, delirious. She could not hope to combat one more threat in her current state.

But Salvador's face showed fear. A flicker, visible only to Lucha's divine senses. Whatever was prowling out there, he had not called it. And that meant . . .

Before she could make sense of his reaction, a cat larger than any Lucha had ever seen broke the sanctity of their fighting ground. It skidded to a halt between the two of them, teeth bared at Salvador, eyes flashing gold in the light Lucha had summoned.

A compañera, Lucha thought, her heart in her throat. And it was not alone. A storm of footfalls, hoofbeats, and all manner of shrieks, caws, grunts, growls, and roars crashed onto their battlefield, wreaking havoc as Lucha breathed deeply, recovering her strength.

Salvador backed away to the edge of his bleached arena. The cat closed the distance with a pounce and a yowl that raised the hair on Lucha's arms. She could press this advantage. All was not lost . . .

"Look out!" called a familiar voice from beyond the crush of bodies.

Lucha glanced around, spotting two things simultaneously: first, that Paz had returned, looking much worse for wear. A gash across one cheek bled freely down her face. One arm she held awkwardly, the other brandished a dagger.

And second, Salvador's step back had not been a retreat. She saw too late that his eyes had gone black again, his palms spread wide. The ground began to rumble once more, spooking the animals who were not accustomed to battle.

Across the backs of a herd of fleeing does, Paz's eyes met Lucha's, horror-struck.

Among the living, fighting creatures rose monsters of

shadow gristle and decay. They reassembled into grotesque facsimiles of the features they'd worn in life. Rodents, birds, felines, and canids.

When the ground went still again, Salvador's army was vast. Each creature was swathed in shadow, and they obeyed his will, no instincts of their own. These creatures would not flee.

"What are you waiting for?" Paz called, and Lucha turned to Salvador, still recovering from this display of power.

Lucha struck out with her light-infused vines. She sent seeds to root down in Salvador's skin and bloom up through it. The vivid blossoms scattered his blood across the soil. Pale as milk. It burned wherever it touched the ground.

But he was not distracted for long.

As Paz called out in some ancient language, the wildlife of the Bosque took on the deathly creatures, and Salvador and Lucha circled each other once more.

Lucha no longer thought of her weariness. She dodged every swipe, every stab. The limits of her power were close at hand, but she had this one last chance, and she took it, lashing out with both vines, pushing him back, then grounding herself and turning her eyes to the sky.

The beams of light she drew now rivaled the sun for brightness. They suffused the war-torn grove with a divine glow. Wherever they touched Salvador's shadow creatures, the monsters disintegrated on the spot. But the creatures were not Lucha's target.

Before Salvador had a chance to do more than goggle at

them, Lucha drew her hands back and flung them straight through his chest.

His eyes went wide. Drawn to the light, the greenery began to take him. To bind him. And then, from outside their fighting ground came a cry of pain.

Paz. Lucha lost all focus. The mortal in her overrode the divine as she scanned the tree line for the girl who had fought beside her.

Salvador was on his knees, but the light was gone. The vines fell dead from his limbs.

When Paz cried out again, the sound was nearer. Lucha didn't hesitate.

She found her in a thicket of brambles, her face pale with pain, her arm held gingerly against her chest. But it was her leg that caused concern. A deep gouge bled freely beneath her robe. The wound was shot through with shadow . . .

"What are you doing here?" Paz asked, commanding even in her agony. "Don't you have a war to win?"

"Not without you," Lucha said fiercely, tearing the other girl's robe aside to look at her wound properly. "What happened?"

"One of his beasts," Paz said through gritted teeth. She had grown paler still in the moments since Lucha found her. Fear fluttered like wingbeats between them. "But I'll be fine. I'm a healer, remember? You're the only one who can defeat him."

From the clearing she had left, Lucha heard Salvador cough, then struggle to his feet.

"I don't know if I can," Lucha said. She felt the enormity of her words as she spoke them. She saw the light dying. The vivid green giving way to deathly pallor.

"You *can*," Paz said. "You made this choice. You earned the right to defeat him."

These words stirred something in Lucha. The old, human anger—reckless and desperate—that had driven her to this place. It sparked within her, decidedly unholy.

Paz was fading, though she tried to hide it. This, Lucha could fix. With the strength she had left, she laid her hands alongside the wound, closing her eyes, calling on Paz's body to expel the poison. To knit the skin closed.

As the pain left her, Paz's face relaxed. A moment of peace stole into the thicket. The eye of the storm, again.

But in the clearing Salvador called for Lucha, and her heart froze with dread.

"Even Almudena couldn't defeat him," she said, the spark flickering. Dying.

Paz's eyes were too serious on Lucha's. "Almudena wasn't you."

The shock of this made Lucha pause.

"You have all the tools you need. Not only hers, but *yours*," Paz said. Back on her feet, she moved gingerly, but her face was determined. "I'll hold off the monsters. You finish this."

Lucha nodded, already feeling the pull back into the glade. Back to the battle she had chosen.

"And, Lucha?" Paz asked, something unfathomable in her eyes.

"Yes?"

"Come back to me," the other girl said. Then she pressed a kiss to Lucha's lips and darted off into the trees, already drawing her bow.

Lucha touched her fingers to the place where Paz's mouth had just been. The words she'd spoken became wheels that turned in Lucha's mind. As she got to her feet, she thought of Almudena. Of all the things she had learned from her.

But it was the human in her that had brought her this far, not the divine. Her anger. Her desperation. It had been personal, this grudge she held. She had wanted to watch Salvador die. She had wanted to be the one who delivered his justice.

Not because she'd been destined to balance some godly scales tipped centuries before.

Because she *hated* him, and everything he had done.

She was not Almudena. She never would be. But Almudena had not defeated her son. It was time Lucha proved that she could.

32

Salvador awaited Lucha in the clearing. He seemed no weaker after all the light Lucha could throw at him—which only confirmed the theory now rooting in her mind.

She trailed her power behind her like a cloak. Not only the power of Almudena's gift, but of all the scraps she'd stolen before she ever received it. Lucha was a girl from the Scar. Raised on mud and misery. Denied hope in every place she might have sought it.

Since the moment Salvador rose from his tomb, Lucha had let him define her by what he lacked. Believed she must be a holy warrior of life and green and light to oppose him. But the truth was, she carried more than life within her.

Lucha Moya had tasted death. Had fed it. Had been a hunter and a vessel for a prince of shadow. But she had also chosen transformation. Life. The gift of the forest goddess now burned bright in her veins. Who understood balance better than she?

There could be no light without shadow.

No life without death.

And so Lucha faced Salvador one last time. Not as his mother reborn, but as a girl who was the sum of her choices. A girl who was no longer afraid to wield the power she had earned.

Salvador spread his arms wide, shadowy swords at the ready. But Lucha did not reach for her vines. For the light. Instead, she remembered the centuries she had walked in the memories of this broken man. A man trapped in a tomb. A man petrified of the very destruction he wielded.

Almudena had not given Lucha these memories so that she could temper him—but so that she could discover his true nature. A master of death, who dreaded the end above all.

So Lucha closed her eyes once more. When the torrent of shadows shot forth, she could see the shock in his eyes. The panic. He had commanded these forces for so long, sought to control them. But subjugation born of fear could never last.

The thing you oppressed always turned on you, in the end.

He had taught her that.

"What are you doing?" he cried as the shadows consumed him. Not only the ones Lucha aimed in his direction, but more. Shadows that crawled out from within him. Free of his attempts to twist them to his purpose at long last.

They stripped away everything. The ornaments he had defined himself by—the rings, the cloak, even the hair falling into his eyes. The luminous, divine flesh came next, exposing bone beneath it as he screamed.

But Lucha didn't stop. Couldn't stop. All she could

remember was the way he had hurt her. The way he had manipulated her. The way he had held her sister hostage to bargain for the one precious thing Lucha had ever been allowed.

Hope.

Why should this monster have a place in the cycle of life? she wondered as the shadows kept coming. In his bones they clung to one another. Wound around his ribs. Peered out of the sockets of his eyes.

This is who he truly is, Lucha thought as the sky darkened above them. He deserved this fate and worse. So much worse.

His jawbones creaked as they opened, and from within his skeletal maw poured the sound of laughter. The rumbling returned. Lucha redoubled her efforts, sending more and more darkness to consume him. But there was nothing left to consume.

For the first time since she'd taken Almudena's gift, Lucha felt the void within her yawning, threatening to swallow everything. Horror overcame her as Salvador's skeleton stood, enveloped in the shadows that had destroyed him.

That had *revived* him.

"You thought death would be the end of its master?" he asked, his empty eyes horrible as he stepped toward her, skeletal hands outstretched. *"You fool . . ."*

She was not Almudena, Lucha thought as all the light left the world. She had chosen wrong, and there was no way out . . . not now . . .

But into her despair came a sound. Familiar. Distant. A

song she had heard for the first time in a night greenhouse a lifetime ago. Paz's throaty voice. The round curves of her words. They filled Lucha with warmth. They reminded her of life.

Other voices joined the first. Human and animal. Root and stem and leaf. No longer only whispers. The sounds of the forest joined in chorus until the song was palpable in the clearing, and Lucha got to her feet.

Decay and rot emanated from Salvador's bones as he swept through the scar they'd made. He was death personified. But Lucha knew death was not the end. Not the beginning. Only the point in the cycle that connected the two.

And as she had so many times before, Lucha called on the mushrooms. Lacy mycelium strands beneath the ground that took Salvador by the bones of his ankles and began to do what they did best: feed.

Lucha guided them with her regrets. Her fear that she had lost too much of herself. That she had doomed them all at the moment she could have saved them. Every last bit of divine power she'd been granted fed these spores as they multiplied and divided. Grew and consumed at a rate never before seen in this forest or any other.

It would take everything she had. But it would be over.

"*Even your power has limits,*" came Salvador's rasping voice from within them. "*Soon you'll have to stop, and then . . .*"

His words were swallowed by the flesh of the fungus. Replacing that which he had lost. Breaking down his centuries of fear and agony and creating rich compost from which new life would grow.

A transformation.

Lucha felt the light in her dimming, but she did not stop. Would not stop until all that had been Salvador, El Sediento, Almudena's rogue son, was no more. She had come to this place with a goddess's power—but it would be her mortal self that endured, if anything did.

If this was not her end, too.

From the compost the mushrooms made, new life began to take root. A seed that shot deep into this formerly dead place, growing higher and taller, drawing Salvador's life force into massive, bloodred branches that sprouted bright white leaves.

But the gilded heart inside Lucha, transformed by the goddess's gift, was failing.

"Goodbye, Salvador," she said. Letting him go. Letting the pain go. The last of the gold drained from her as she did, and the emptiness was as clean as the pain had been.

He was gone, and so was Almudena's gift. The mortals would be left to build their own world. *I only wish*, Lucha thought as the unknown rushed to meet her, *I could be here to see it.*

And with that thought, her ears still ringing with Paz's song, Lucha's heart squeezed out one last, glorious beat. Then her eyes closed, and all was peaceful at last.

33

Sunlight streamed through a stained-glass window. Somewhere nearby, someone sang.

Lucha came back to herself slowly, as if from the end of a long tunnel.

"Are you awake? Lucha, open your eyes!"

Pressure, against her fingers. Agony everywhere else. Lucha's body felt broken and empty, but some seed within her persisted. Enough life to open her eyes.

If she could have smiled, she would have. It was as she had hoped. The goddess's power was gone, but the mortal girl lived on.

"Lis," she croaked. The skin on her lips was scaled, her throat a desert. Every blink was pushing a boulder up a hill. Even the air felt too heavy against her skin.

"You're alive! Thank every god . . ." Tears choked this voice, falling into Lucha's hair as her sister bent over her.

"It worked?" Lucha managed, seeing it all again. The shadows. The skeletal face of Salvador. The fungus consuming him. The tree that had grown from his centuries of decay . . .

"You could have died!" Lis cried. "They said you might not wake. Your heart stopped, but I told them." She sniffed. "I told them you'd never leave me."

There was water next, from a clay cup. A few sips later Lucha tried speaking again and found it much easier.

"I had to get back," she said with what she hoped was a smile. "We have a flower cart to paint."

Another laugh that ended in a sob. Another squeeze of her fingers. "Let's just focus on getting you well first," Lis said. "And then we'll talk about the flowers."

Lis looked so strong, Lucha thought, remembering the half-conscious waif she'd carried from Encadenar. She couldn't take credit, though. She knew that now. Her sister had always been strong.

"What happened?" she asked, exhaustion settling in. "After . . ."

"I can get the obispo," Lis replied. Lucha sensed the deference in the way she spoke this title. The admiration. "She said a lot of things I didn't understand. The savior returned, the son defeated? I've learned a little, since I arrived, and they seemed pleased, Lucha. Very pleased. They called you a hero."

Hero, Lucha thought with a wince. The word rattled like a chain.

"Paz has been here every day," Lis was saying now. "She went to rest, but I should get her. Tell her you're okay."

Paz. The thought of her was too big, too bright to settle among all this pain. In Lucha's immortal, divine mind it had seemed so simple. But now? Her consciousness slipped down into the warm darkness, protecting her from the answer a little longer.

When she opened her eyes a second time, Lucha knew she was truly awake. Lis was gone, and Río—sans bodyguards—was sitting beside her bed.

"Did I pass the test?" Lucha asked.

Río allowed a small smile. She leaned forward to help Lucha as she struggled to sit. Handed her the clay cup of water once she was settled.

The room was bright, with white-painted walls. Sunlight streamed in through high windows. It was the same room where Lis had played with a silver cub. Where Lucha had said a silent goodbye—not knowing, not *dreaming*, what the future would hold.

"Is he gone?" she asked Río. There was no future until she knew this answer.

The obispo's expression turned thoughtful. For a long moment she gazed out the window at the leaves stirring in the wind. "The effort it took nearly destroyed you," she said instead of answering.

Lucha nodded, knowing the truth. That if she hadn't lost control—hadn't turned herself over to the shadows—she might still have Almudena's power. But the place in her chest where it had lived was vacant. Not the brimming brightness of the gift. Not the cold void where Salvador had left her once.

Only a chest. Only a mortal, beating heart.

"Miss León told us the details of what happened after your escape," Río said. "From what we can gather based on our texts—and some guesswork, of course—the power you absorbed from the goddess was extinguished in the fight against her son. It very easily could have killed you. But even after your transformation, it seems there was just enough human left in you to live on."

Lucha nodded, struck by the irony, even though she had hoped for this very result. It had taken a goddess's power to defeat Salvador, but a mortal's to survive. *Balance*, she thought, growing tired again already. But there was more she needed to know.

"Twice, when I took Pensa," she began, "I saw Almudena. She showed me where to find the power. How to defeat *him*. She said it was my choice, all of it, but how . . ." Lucha trailed off. She did not know how to ask what she truly wanted to ask.

"You want to know whether you were a pawn or a champion," Río said.

Lucha nodded. It was close enough.

"There have always been those in tune with the fluctuations of power in this world," the obispo began. "Many of them seek power for themselves. Some for righteous reasons, some for less. But the world strives toward balance. Power and responsibility. For those aware of this balance, they must always exist together."

"So you're saying because I was born with some latent gift I was always going to try to save the world?"

Another smile. Barely there. "Before you arrived, I would have called it destiny. Now . . ." She spread her hands out before her. "You have called a great many things into question, Lucha Moya. Ask me again in a hundred years."

They sat together for a long time in silence. The only other question Lucha had was slow to come. Tied up in Pensa and visions, kisses and sunsets, signs and devotion. As the moments passed, Lucha released it. It wasn't for Río to answer, in any case. There was only one person who could.

And given what came next—what *had* to come next—she wasn't sure the answer mattered anymore.

"Before I left the sanctuary," she said, looking forward with some effort, "you told me I was your ward until more information could be gathered. You forbade me to leave this place . . ."

"An edict you disobeyed rather promptly."

"Does it still stand?" Lucha asked. "Am I your prisoner? Or am I free to go?"

The startled expression on Río's face wasn't a surprise to Lucha. Nor were the words that came next: "We had hoped, given your role in our mythology, that you might choose to remain."

Lucha could still see it so clearly. The future Almudena had shown her. Robed in green, chained in silver. But she had already given up her role as the goddess's champion. That in itself made this moment easier.

"I understand the purpose of power," she said. "And the role of responsibility. But I believe the scale tips both ways. Power without responsibility makes a monster, I know that now. But responsibility without power makes a mascot, and I can't think of anything I'd like less to be."

Lucha could tell that Río bristled at this description. That it was in her nature as someone *with* power to object. To attempt to control. But after a moment her face softened.

"Given what we can measure, there is no longer a threat from Almudena's son. Therefore, you are free to travel as you like."

Relief washed over Lucha in waves.

"Although, as a friend, I'd like to extend our welcome. The sanctuary of Almudena is forever open to you, Salvadora."

"Please," she said. "Call me Lucha."

Río inclined her head. A gesture of respect, and perhaps a little regret. "Where will you go?" she asked, not ungently.

"Where I choose," said Lucha simply. But she saw so much more than choices ahead. The monster who had promised her burning warehouses and dethroned kings was dead, but she was not. There was work to be done.

Río did not press the issue, and soon after, she took her leave, getting to her feet and turning toward the door. Before she could make her exit, however, Lucha called out to stop her.

"My sister," she said, already feeling the loss. This new absence in her chest she'd have to be strong enough to bear. "I think she'd like to stay with you."

This earned a proper smile. "She's a remarkable girl," Río said. "And she'll be well cared for here. Fulfilled. We understand what she's been through. We will help her heal, and she will help others."

The implication was there. That Lucha's wounds could be healed here too.

"Thank you," Lucha said. "For everything."

With one last bow of her head, Río retreated.

Three days passed before Lucha was strong enough to travel.

When Paz came to visit, she feigned sleep. She wasn't prepared to say the thing she had to say, but the days went by too quickly. The time she'd chosen for her departure drew closer, then arrived, and it was too late.

Perhaps it's for the best, Lucha thought as she made her slow way to the boundary. Her sister alone accompanied her, and they leaned on each other as they marched toward farewell.

"For now, at least," Lucha said when they reached the sanctuary's edge. "Don't think I won't return to make sure they're feeding you."

"Plus, I hear they're planning a glorious stained-glass window to immortalize your battle with the prince of evil," Lis teased. "You won't want to miss that."

A light seemed to shine from within Lis. The peace of belonging. Lucha tried to feel purely glad for her sister, but old jealousies died hard. How she wished this was her place. That she could remain here in service to others. A shining silver cub at her heels. That she could share this life with her sister—and perhaps a cottage with the girl she had grown to care for so much that her heart ached to leave.

"You don't have to go," Lis said, echoing Lucha's thoughts. "I think you could learn to love it here, as I have."

"You may be right," Lucha conceded. "But it would be different, for me. This is your place, and you've earned it. Be happy, at last."

They embraced. There were tears on Lis's cheeks when they broke apart.

"And you really won't tell me what you're going to do?" she asked. "How am *I* supposed to check on *you?*"

Lucha shook her head, thoughts already wandering down the path ahead. "This is something I need to do on my own," she said. "But I'll be back the moment I can."

They laughed, tears still falling. "I hope you'll make some time for joy out there," Lis said. "You deserve it. You saved me, Lucha. You saved all of us."

Lucha knew she meant it kindly, but with the task looming ahead of her it was hard to think of joy. Perhaps later. When the job was done.

Behind them, a gentle throat-clearing announced an intruder.

Lis leaned in once more and said: "Be safe. And don't forget about the Gilded Princess you planned to marry, hm? The pious one with the magic garden?" With that, she inclined her head to Paz and disappeared up the path.

Lucha could hardly make herself meet the gaze now trained on her. She already knew what she would find in it—and how difficult it would be to turn away once she had.

"You were going to leave without saying goodbye." Paz's curls danced free of their braid. The sunlight illuminated the brown of her skin so that she seemed to glow.

"I thought it would be easier that way." Lucha's voice was already too full. Her heart took refuge in her ravaged throat. She remembered how simple it had seemed, through the eyes of the savior. How little the minutiae of human will had mattered.

But it mattered now. It mattered more than anything. Even the soft play of sunlight against this beautiful girl's cheeks. Even more than the question in her eyes.

"I said I would tell you everything," Lucha said. "But I don't think I realized then how little I knew."

Paz nodded. "I need you to understand, before you go," she said. As if she'd memorized the words. Spoken the spell of them into a mirror a thousand times. "I am a follower of Almudena. It's been my life's calling since before I knew the meaning of devotion. I followed her to you. I followed her into that battle, and I followed her home. But the way I *feel* about you . . ."

Her voice broke here, and so did Lucha. Just enough to hurt. Not enough to change anything.

"The way I feel about you is my choice. *You* are my choice. And I would go with you anywhere, if you'd have me."

Lucha saw the emotion in Paz's face. The way it gathered like morning dew at the corners of her eyelids. There was true affection in that gaze. Desire. Perhaps even love. But there was something else, too. Something of the pledge Paz had made to Lucha on the battlefield, when the fate of the world was in their hands.

Reverence.

Was it for Lucha? Or for the salvadora of Almudena? She could not tell. Perhaps time was the only thing that could unravel all those threads from one another.

And until Lucha had fulfilled her purpose, she could not afford to take that time. Could not afford any distraction.

"Ever since the moment Salvador bound himself to me, I've believed I was doing the right thing," Lucha said. She tried to keep her voice steady. "I believed I was acting for the good of others. But it wasn't just me. And it wasn't just you. We were both being led by something greater than ourselves. Something with an agenda beyond our happiness."

Paz waited, her expression inscrutable.

"I'm not a savior anymore, Paz. But I'm not the broken girl I was when I met you, either. I don't know who I am. But while I'm doing what I have to do next . . . I need to know *all* my choices are my own. I have to leave this behind." She gestured vaguely, in a way she hoped could encompass the sanctuary, Salvador, Río, Lis, and Paz herself in one.

"I understand," Paz said. The words were heavy. Stones breaking the surface of a still pond and sinking . . .

Lucha wanted to promise her something. Anything. But she found herself turning away instead—toward the future she had chosen. The task still undone.

"I'll wait for you!" Paz called, and Lucha could not help it.

She turned back. "Whether you do what you mean to do or not. Whether you return to me or not. I'll wait. That's what *I* choose."

Lucha nodded. Her throat was full of tears and regrets and wild, protesting heartbeats. Paz covered her mouth to stifle a sob. Perhaps whatever still bloomed between them would withstand the seasons.

All they could do was hope.

And so, as she faced the road ahead, Lucha made herself the promise she could not make to Paz. That she would choose, for the girl whose will had been compromised. That she would become whole, for the girl who had been broken. That she would become free, for the girl who had been chained. That would be her offering to the future she wanted. The woman she hoped to become.

It was with that pledge in her heart, and a love behind her, waiting, that Lucha Moya turned her sights toward home.

Acknowledgments

My most sincere and heartfelt thanks go out to:

The incredible team at Make Me a World for shepherding this story as it transformed from a chaotic and feral thing to the (relatively) housebroken book you are holding in your hands. Christopher Myers, Michelle Frey, Arely Guzmán, Lois Evans, and every other member of the MMAW team, I am so very grateful for your vision, support, and hard work on this project.

My agent, Jim McCarthy, who somehow manages never to balk (at least visibly) when I present the next layer of my strange inner world, and whose keen insight and unfailing enthusiasm have been instrumental on this path.

The most magical creative community anyone could ever hope to be part of—Lily Anderson, Michelle Ruíz Keil, and Nina Moreno, the three of you are the best surprise this often terrifying corner of the creative world has served up so far. I would be nowhere without your friendship and the inspiration I get just from orbiting your brilliance.

Additional thanks to Samantha Shannon, Marie Lu, and Roshani Chokshi for delighting my fangirl heart with their endorsements for this book. To Emily Henry, Isabel Quintero, Tess Sharpe, Valerie Tejada, Abdi Nazemian, Kacen Callender,

Emily Prado, and so many other authors who have shared advice, comfort, inspiration and commiseration over the years.

My readers, who I'm convinced are the best bunch of book people in the world. I'm so grateful to all of you for your letters, emails, fan art, and fiction. Your enthusiasm for each new announcement and release. Your patience as I figured out what I wanted to say next. You are the reason I'm still here, doing what I love. No words will ever be enough.

The tireless advocates for representation in children's literature, and comrades in the fight against censorship and book banning. Because of you, we still get to tell these stories, and the readers who need them can still find them.

The friends, family members, educators, and librarians of my adolescence and early adulthood, who supported this dream long before there was evidence of it on a bookstore shelf. There wasn't a lot of proof that a career like this was possible for someone like me, and your confidence has made all the difference.

The spirits, ancestors, and guides who give meaning to my words and to my time here in this world. I write to honor you, and to be the kind of person worthy of your grace.

To Alex, my partner in crime, my sounding board, my collaborator. You inspire me not just in work, but also in life. I'm so grateful I get to spend my days dreaming with you.

Last, but never least, my A—who is not so little now. There is no greater gift in this world than the one you give me every day just by being yourself. I love you more than trees. More than the moon. More than anything.

A Note from Christopher Myers

When writers imagine fantastic planets, when they vividly create societies where the rules are very different from the way things are in our own society, when they invent whole civilizations and histories as the setting for their adventures so that you can almost hear the new language that their characters speak or read the headlines on imaginary newspapers—that is called world building.

The term is especially popular with reviewers and editors of literature tinged with fantasy or magic. Good world building is part of why we love reading, why we use phrases like "escape into a book." The richness of the world that the author builds, the completeness, makes a reader feel that somewhere beneath the fantasy and magic, there is truth.

Great world building is the difference between imagining the warm blood of characters racing through their veins, their fears and laughter thick as the dirt under their fingernails, their hopes racing across the sky like thunderclouds, and those same characters as paper dolls on cardboard stages, flat imitations of what it means to be human.

Of course, world building isn't limited to fantasy. Realistic works of fiction try to build their worlds too, try to make us feel the underlying truth of their settings, to delineate internal and external geographies that match their authors' points of view.

In fact, world building is part of every kind of writing. And while poorly delineated or flattened worlds make for boring fiction reading, when world building fails in the writing that makes our news or our public policy, the results can be devastating and very real.

Every "bad neighborhood," every "underdeveloped economy," every "ghetto," every "wrong side of the tracks" has been written into being by newspapers and developers, loaning institutions and lawmakers. By people who don't live there. Instead of vibrant communities, with hopes and dreams and ideals, these neighborhoods, districts, cities, and even whole countries are rendered as cardboard cutouts.

Lucha and the Night Forest is a book that both builds an exquisitely realized world and asks important questions about world building itself. How does a place where "nothing grows" come to be that way? What does it mean to grow up in a place that has been written in such a way, under paper skies that read "despair." And how can one young person attempt to unwrite the world she has inherited?

Lucha and her family, both chosen and biological, all struggle with how their world has been built. And the forces that build our world are formidable and wide-ranging; they invade not only other people's imaginations of us and our neighborhoods but also our imagination of ourselves. But Lucha points the way—as powerful as those forces are, they cannot stop us from writing our futures, from building a world of our own.

Christopher Myers